COLLAP$E

COLLAP$E

FREDDIE P. PETERS

HENRY CROWNE PAYING THE PRICE BOOK 1

Collapse

First published 2018 by Freddie P. Peters

www.freddieppeters.com

Text copyright © Freddie P. Peters 2018

The right of Freddie P. Peters to be identified as the author of this work has been asserted by her in accordance with the Copyright, Designs and Patents Act 1988.

ISBN: 978-1-9999811-1-2

A CIP catalogue record for this book is available from the British Library.

Cover design by Lucy Llewellyn at Head & Heart
Typesetting by Aimee Dewar at Head & Heart

To Lucie

Henry, mon ami,

This letter took me a while. I realised I had not put pen to paper for such a long time. I do not mean emails or texts. I mean actual writing, the act of my hand on paper, the slight hesitation that precedes putting down what cannot be erased. Mais enfin la voici.

A sketch of it came on the day I left you behind. The heavy doors closing on you brought a chill to my heart. So it felt right, maybe even necessary. And I have come to realise that a good letter must divulge something intimate about its writer, so I will start with my own news. I have decided to reconnect with my previous life, the one I thought I had left forever behind. Don't be alarmed and think I am recanting after talking so much about giving up the rat race. I have found an unexpected use for my old talent, my new-found bohemian style joined up with the impeccable training of this legal mind – well, you have seen the result!

Of course, you may already have gathered that I received a little nudge. It came in the shape of our mutual friend Mr P. I want, no ... I need to plunge into the City once more, but this time on my own terms. A final test, maybe? Time will tell. To be completely honest, the gentleman in question attracts my interest terribly. There you are. How about this for a confession – ha!

I think I should finish swiftly, and now that my letter lies in front of me I hope it will be the first of many. Please reply, for I know that coming to terms with the act of terror you lived through and the deceit you endured will bring you resolve. But for today I simply say – I understand. The rest is up to you.

A très vite
Nancy

Chapter One

A stretch, a barely disguised yawn … Henry Crowne was nonchalantly sitting in front of his four plasma screens on GL's trading floor. He propped himself up in a sudden move, once more focusing on the vast room spread in front of him. He loved the position of his desk, not his office, no … his desk. From here he could see rows of machines and men, plugged into world markets, ready to take action as the markets moved, action that was wiping out, in seconds, billions of dollars.

Today however the atmosphere on the floor was subdued. Henry started rocking slowly on his leather chair again. He was not a trader but a structurer. He knew himself to be good, in fact remarkably good, yet the takeover had unnerved him. His reputation and that of his team were spectacular. He had flair, nevertheless competition at HXBK was fierce. He knew his rival only too well, hard working, hand of steel. Anthony Albert was a force to be reckoned with. The two men had been unspoken enemies ever since they first met. Everything served to make them opposites, not only their attitude towards people and work but also their very cores.

The phone ringing brought him back to reality with a jolt. He looked at it with suspicion. Should he answer? His black phone was hanging at the side of his desk. He preferred it the old-fashioned way and was one of the few people on the floor not yet wearing a headset. One of his team picked up for him; a phone never rang more than twice at GL.

"Ted for you, line two."

"OK, thanks. Hey Ted, what's up?" asked Henry, pleased to hear one of his best mates at GL.

"I need to speak to you outside the floor. Can you get to your office right now?"

The voice on the other end of the phone sounded shaken, hardly recognisable, very much unlike Ted whose sense of humour had defused many an argument they'd had.

Henry stood up, towering over his desk.

"Sure, I will call you back on your mobile," said Henry already moving towards his office. The distance he had to walk was minimal. Time was money. Henry closed the door and dialled Ted's number.

"Ted, what on earth is happening? Has the committee come to any decision about the team, I thought—"

"Listen," said Ted cutting him short, "nothing to do with your team Henry, Anthony Albert is dead."

The enormity of the news and its implications hit Henry in slow motion. It unfolded gradually, a mixture of relief, shock and disbelief. The phone stayed silent.

"Henry, are you there?"

"Impossible, I just can't believe … what happened? I spoke to him only yesterday."

"Look. I don't want to talk about this over the phone. I am at Canary Wharf. I want you here as soon as possible. Can you make it now?"

"Sure, sure. On my way."

He stood at his desk for a few minutes, fighting the strong emotions raging inside him. The sombre news was confusing him, so much had been at stake and so much done because of Albert and now … now, the old enemy was dead, a twist of fate, brutal and unbelievable even by City standards.

"Guess who is going to head the combined team now?" muttered Henry as an enormous weight was lifted from his shoulders.

Henry was still standing at his desk, his CV spread across it so that he could give it the final touch before submitting it to the integration committee. It wasn't as though the committee members were unaware of who he was and what he had achieved, but it was the rule.

His last year at Dublin University; a first in mathematics; his interview at BZW, the then investment banking arm of Barclays. Mathematicians earn nothing but it's the bankers that make the money, he remembered saying to Liam, his old university pal as he celebrated his departure for London. And the first innovative structured transaction he completed there. He touched the CV lightly and a smile rose on his face.

"Yes, the combined team."

His own words shocked him. This relief, this near elation, was based on someone's death. The rapidity at which his mind had assessed the situation, decided it was a 'good thing', without regard for Albert, unsettled him. But Henry knew how to rein in his feelings.

Come on, come on, he was a manipulative little shit – still. Henry had always prided himself on being a considerate man.

His PA tapped at the glass partition, she needed to have a word.

"Are you OK? You look as if you've seen a ghost." Her strong Scottish accent grounded him into reality.

"Morag, that is not funny."

"Why? You really look pale. You're not losing your sense of humour. I couldn't bear it." Her intelligent smile beamed at him.

"Sorry, sorry – a lot on my mind. I need to go to Canary Wharf straight away. Cab, please."

"Done," said Morag.

He grabbed his jacket and mobile and strode towards the rear of the building where his black cab was waiting. The cabbie would wait fifteen minutes before calling the office to enquire about his passenger. Henry walked out of the building and took a sharp right. The small newsagents he had earmarked in case of emergency a few months ago sold burner phones. Henry picked one up and paid cash. He walked back towards the building checking his watch. It had taken him less than ten minutes.

Henry had hardly sat in the back of the cab before he was setting up the burner phone to dial a number.

"Liam, it's me. Are you still in the UK? … OK, back in Dublin then."

Henry listened to what was being said on the other side of the phone and frowned.

"This mobile is not traceable … I know, but a situation is developing and I might have to speak to the cops."

"I don't think it has anything to do with our business."

"Listen. LISTEN. It probably has no bearing on the transfers. I will contact you again only if I need to. OK. Bye."

Henry inhaled deeply and put the mobile back in his trouser pocket. He would get rid of it as soon as he could.

Henry started scrolling down his emails on his BlackBerry. The call with Liam had been securely stored in the impenetrable part of his mind. He was not expecting to see any details of the Albert incident yet but the habit of using his time to do business whilst on a cab ride gave him a sense of security. He noticed a mail from his art dealer and was tempted to call but he chose not to. A conversation about his latest acquisition would unfocus him. Henry however smiled at the challenge surrounding the purchase of the piece. Anthony Albert and he had found themselves invited to the same preview of a young up-and-coming talent.

"Sorry mate but I think we're there, right?"

The distant voice of the cab driver reminded Henry that he was on his way to meet Ted. Henry bent over to see the building on his left-hand side through the black cab window. He could now see the slick glass and steel offices of HXBK.

"Yep, we're there."

Whilst the cabbie was looking for a place to park, Henry took a meticulously rolled Hermés tie from his top pocket and quickly knotted it around his neck. A few years back GL had adopted a dress down code on its trading floor but Henry felt uncomfortable without his Savile Row suit. The only concession he made to what he regarded as a ridiculous policy from Silicon Valley was to wear

6

his shirt with rolled-up sleeves and without a tie. However, tie and matching cufflinks were always kept in his pocket, ready to be used on the first occasion. Henry stepped out of the cab, his shoulders squaring up to the imposing building.

HXBK's atrium was rumoured to be the largest in Canary Wharf and spread over two floors. The ground floor resembled an art gallery with its Andy Warhol that covered the far side of the entire wall – four immense panels of pop art.

Henry walked up to the reception desk where a well-spoken Japanese woman took his name. He climbed the escalator two steps at a time, passing on his left another valuable piece of art, this time an installation by Damien Hirst. The reception area lost its serenity when he reached the first floor. Two large metal gates had been installed in the wake of 9/11. He was met by a couple of security guards who approached him with the required stern expression.

"Please put your keys and mobile in there, sir."

The man was pointing at a small tray on the side.

"I know, I know … been here before," Henry grumbled.

The news of Albert's death had started to sink in. It remained incredible, an insane joke only the City could produce.

Ted was sitting down, stirring a cup of coffee when Henry opened the door to the meeting room. The pool of liquid in Ted's saucer indicated his nerves. He looked tired, his curly blond hair was a mess, shadows lodged deep beneath his baby blue eyes. Lack of sleep and extreme pressure were the lot of those appointed to serve the integration committee. Ted did not complain.

"Coffee … Henry?"

"Thanks, I'll pour. You tell me the story so far."

"I'll tell you what I know. Got a call this morning at around 8am, I was with Jason Gateway and Mathias Wunderlink. We were reviewing the consolidated presentation to be handed over to the integration committee. Anyway."

Ted took a mouthful of coffee, pulling a face at its bitterness.

"Apparently the plane carrying Albert crashed early this morning. He was flying on one of the bank's private jets. A rumour was circulating that you also were on board. They don't know what happened but I have been told that they may not be treating this as an accident."

Ted had spoken the last words quickly, swallowing yet another mouthful of his over-stirred coffee. Henry frowned and pulled his chair over, sitting uncomfortably close to Ted.

"No. This is ridiculous. Which bloody newspaper has been stirring it up this time? BANKER MURDERED IN HOSTILE TAKEOVER BID. I can see it from here." Henry gestured in the air as if to underline a title.

"This is not a takeover. This is a merger."

The company approved mantra had clearly sunk in with Ted.

"Anyway. Nobody knows yet, Henry … this has not been released to the press. The police are involved … hell I don't know. I am so bloody tired. This is going to be such a fucking nightmare."

"We are all tired Ted, but who would realistically want to murder the old fart? You, me? Half the City …"

"Don't say that," Ted protested. "This is not funny."

"OK … OK," said Henry, dropping his sarcasm.

"I still can't believe he is dead, let alone that there's foul play. I have a shedload of catching up to do here. Maybe I am just too bloody whacked to take it all in."

"I have been told the police will want to interview anyone who has been in recent contact with him," said Ted without looking at Henry.

Henry observed Ted closely for a few seconds. Was his friend holding back information? No, he wouldn't dare.

"Understood. Let me know when," replied Henry standing up. He left the room without waiting for Ted's response.

Henry walked out of HXBK's building and took a sharp left towards Canary Wharf's main concourse. He turned left again onto a large plaza and crossed towards the water's edge. He spotted a small bench on the waterfront, secluded enough. Henry sat down and placed his work mobile to his ear. He looked around. There was no one in sight. He stood up abruptly, still pretending to be involved in an animated call, took the burner mobile out of his pocket and let it slide into the water. Still no one around. Good.

Henry retraced his steps and terminated his fake call. He hailed a black cab. He so wished he had called Charlie for the return journey. This thought propelled him back to a trip he had taken three months earlier with his driver.

Charlie had rung the doorbell at 5.25am on the dot. Henry's private car had been booked for 5.30am. Charlie made it a point to arrive five minutes early, avoiding for his best client the where-is-my-wretched-car morning stress. Henry was ready and acknowledged his driver as soon as he rang the doorbell, a little punctuality game the two men enjoyed playing. Charlie had been Henry's chauffeur for the past five years and was always made available to him by his Limo service. Henry managed to smile at the memory.

"Morning Charlie, quick trip to Biggin Hill today. Boy, it's cold."

"Good morning Mr Crowne, indeed dreadful weather for late spring," Charlie had replied in his reassuringly manicured voice. Henry appreciated Charlie's eccentricity. He spoke an impeccable English unexpectedly combined with the bulk and allure of a CIA agent.

As he left his building Henry had looked up towards his dwelling. He had moved in a few months ago. The sumptuous old building still impressed him. He had noticed a light on in the duplex apartment opposite his. His neighbour, the enigmatic Nancy Wu, was already up. Their brief encounter had aroused his curiosity. But Charlie was standing at the door, patiently holding it open. It was time to leave.

Henry sat in the S-Class Mercedes and reached for the large cup of Assam tea waiting for him in the cup holder in the middle of the rear seats. One of Charlie's many personalised touches. He was about to switch over from Jazz FM to Radio 4 to catch the early morning news when Henry stopped him.

"A little jazz will do us good. I am not sure I want to hear more news about the global collapse of the financial markets right now."

"As you know Mr Crowne, jazz is always my music of choice."

"I have not asked for a while, Charlie ... how is the jazz club doing?"

"There may be a financial crisis but we are doing fiendishly well. Our latest Arun Ghosh Sextet show has been a roaring success."

"I'm not surprised. You guys know your stuff. I did listen to the Miles Davis CD you recommended. I might be getting the hang of it, I think," said Henry.

"A genius, all about timing of course."

"Timing is everything Charlie – everything."

"I am glad we share the same view, Mr Crowne."

"Talking about timing. How is your other business going?"

Charlie features tensed. From the very moment Charlie had become his driver Henry had guessed that he had done time. A childhood in Belfast had made Henry more familiar than he would ever admit with the Nick – or rather the Paddy. He had managed to gain Charlie's trust and convince him that his past did not worry him, somehow impressed by Charlie's determination to rebuild his life. Charlie would be on parole for a little while longer though.

"My parole officer is not a bad person, but I am looking forward to not having to meet him again."

"But all going fine, right?"

"It is. Thanks for asking. The jazz club and my driver's job make all the difference."

Henry nodded and Charlie turned the radio up. They fell into a comfortable silence.

Henry's mind drifted towards his trip to New York, trying to anticipate the reason why Douglas McCarthy, CEO of GL, had asked him to join him on his way to the US. DMac, as he had been nicknamed by the market, had spent over forty years in the financial sector. His reputation was as a ruthless man, whose success at the helm of investment banking had been impressive. He was a man of extremes, capable of arguing the most desperate of cases and winning support in the tightest of spots. Henry had been working as one of his few direct reports for nearly three years. He had an affinity with McCarthy that few enjoyed. Henry had developed the habit of speaking his mind and in return was consulted on matters relating to the overall running of the firm. He had won this privilege during the negotiation of a protracted but essential transaction with Morgan Stanley which had put GL on the front pages of the *FT* and the *Wall Street Journal* for weeks. Henry had been clever enough to let some of the more senior management bask in its glory, while taking a voluntary backseat.

Upon arrival Charlie had resumed his role of chauffeur, opening the Mercedes' door and confirming he would be there for the return journey. "Much appreciated," Henry had said, discreetly placing a £20 note in Charlie's hand. He was now eager to join DMac. The invitation had been unusually formal. He needed to know why.

Chapter Two

Nancy switched on the news as she was drinking her first cup of tea of the day, a strong Sichuan with a little milk. Breakfast TV bored her but she enjoyed the early morning programmes on the Bloomberg channel. She always found snippets of information that would not be repeated during the day, news that was usually very telling to the discerning mind. The Asian commentator was exploring the implications of the announced merger between GL and HXBK and questioning whether this merger between two of the giants of investment banking was not a merger but rather a reverse takeover. Nancy poured herself a second cup of tea and frowned, too much milk. Her mind wandered back to the programme, paying a little more attention. She had spotted her neighbour, Henry Crowne, leaving the block of flats early that morning as she was opening her curtains. She had surmised he was working on the trading floor of a large investment bank, hence the early hours, and recollected he was indeed working for GL. The commentator speculated for a while as to the reasons for the merger and Nancy got a little irritated.

"A bank the calibre of GL would only agree to merge for one reason, lack of capital, of course," she said aloud.

Nancy opened up her agenda and looked at the day's schedule. She had a meeting late morning with a young artist who was hoping for a grant to support her next show. The Bloomberg programme was going nowhere in its exploration of the GL-HXBK story. Nancy switched off the TV and turned her attention to the world of art. She had a few hours to review her notes and make herself ready to meet her young friend. She grabbed a large portfolio of prints that had been left with her and delicately lifted the sheet of light tissue paper protecting each of them. Nancy gave a wide smile, so much talent for someone so young. She forgot all about the news and slowly slid into a world of intensity that engulfed her.

* * *

The bombshell hit all Bloomberg terminals at 11.47 GMT. A short but speculative piece announcing the death of Anthony Albert AKA … AA the recovery man:

In the bitter battle for the reverse takeover of GL and HXBK, a dramatic development has rocked both stocks in this morning's London session. Anthony Albert, a major figure at HXBK, has been killed in a tragic plane crash. Police are treating the incident as suspicious after several eye witnesses reported what seemed to be an explosion shortly after the plane took off. HXBK and GL have been contacted but so far have not been available for comment.

Henry had been told to prepare his team for the news. They had just walked out of their meeting room when the news hit their screens. James Radlett, Henry's number two, said aloud what everyone else was thinking privately.

"Hey guys, look at Bloomberg. Mr Recovery Man is famous at last. I am sure the little prick would never have thought it would come to him that way."

"Not appropriate James," snapped Henry.

James shrugged whilst most of the team privately enjoyed the rebuff.

Henry was exposed, knowing he must be the last person to have had contact with Albert. Something was wrong, very badly wrong. With a long career on the trading floor Henry had developed the ability to sense danger, to feel and recognise the dark undercurrents of a disastrous situation. Now that the news had settled in, a sense

14

of disquiet had started to rise within him. Then again what could he possibly be scared about? His planning had, so far, been immaculate.

James went back to work whilst Matt, another senior member of the team, cautiously hedged his bets.

"Bad for the stock though," said Matt, tapping furiously on his Bloomberg terminal to check GL's latest share price.

"Gee … Well spotted, genius," replied Harriett. She removed her glasses with a swift gesture, wiping the lenses with the sleeve of her cashmere cardigan methodically. The heavy frame had left two deep indentations below her light brown eyes. She rubbed the soreness away slowly and pushed the glasses back into position.

She had not said a word during the team meeting, Henry had noticed the out of character silence. Harriett had been patient, positioning herself within the firm for the past three years and now stood to be made an MD at the next promotion round as did Matt. Of course, the merger could still ruin their plans and so could any unfortunate associations with a losing leader. Henry was under no illusion that they had joined his team for no other reason than because he could guarantee high visibility. But the death of Anthony Albert could only mean 'issues'. Henry sat at his desk outside his office. He surveyed his team one more time, as an uncomfortable thought started to settle in. He knew them all well, but then again, he knew his people only within the confines of banking. He had seen them weather some tough situations and difficult people, take knocks and come back up, strengthened by the experience. He had seen them compete against one another and other banks to win the deal and the limelight, but this was different. He had chosen them for their complementary skills and personalities and taken risks in welcoming and training these ambitious characters. Whilst he could normally provide an environment where their various aspirations could be fulfilled, the combination of the takeover and this latest drama would put strain on his ability to keep the team together. He needed some space to think. A cup of tea grabbed from his favourite patisserie would do the trick.

L'Epi d'Or was buzzing with customers. Henry frowned at the idea of queueing. He spotted Marianne serving a young woman. She had multiple orders that would most certainly feed an entire desk of traders. He was about to wave when Marianne grabbed a large paper cup and waved it at Henry with a smile. He smiled in return and gave the thumbs up. Someone in the queue turned around and looked displeased. Henry recognised Cindy, McCarthy's PA. He shrugged and mouthed 'sorry' with a grin. Cindy collected a large paper bag and walked past him.

"H, you're incorrigible."

Henry turned back to see her disappear. He had not seen McCarthy since their flight to New York three months ago. The memory of that last meeting made his stomach churn with anger.

He is there once more.

Henry steps into the Gulfstream G400 full of the confidence an indispensable adviser has. The rich smell of leather rises to his nose. This is the smell of unabashed luxury and power. No matter how many times he has flown in the private jet that smell always excites him.

McCarthy is in his seat, documents scattered around him, a cup of coffee in his hand.

Henry has managed before to hitch a ride with McCarthy for a great many of his own clients' meetings. His deals have profile and McCarthy enjoys that association too. Henry's last $3.5 billion convertible bond issue has been yet another exceptional success.

But times have changed and when McCarthy lifts his head, he presents a tired face, deep lines etched onto his forehead.

"Hello Henry, how are you?"

"Hello Doug, haven't seen you for ages," Henry says.

"I know, should've been in touch sooner but I have been considering various options … we'll talk later … Christie at the back will fix you a drink."

To McCarthy all stewardesses are called Christie. Henry has never had the nerve to ask him why. He assumes that remembering the name of an air hostess is fairly low on McCarthy's priority list.

The plane has been in the air for about thirty minutes when McCarthy signals Henry to approach. Henry has opted for a seat at the back of the plane, judging by his boss's demeanour that he does not want anyone around. Time to himself is precious for McCarthy, whose involvement with the Bank's affairs is a constant, gruelling 24/7 schedule. McCarthy has been reviewing his diary for what would be a typical visit to the New York office. The aircraft phone rings and Cindy, McCarthy's PA, is on the phone confirming last minute changes.

"Breakfast at 6.30am with Apple is fine if you tell me that Gary will join us," says McCarthy whilst inviting Henry to sit down.

"Good. Calls and meetings after that fine but I am not giving up on consolidation time … I need to review the CDO file … don't care if Steve needs a quick answer. Tell him I am reviewing the figures and that I understand our position on the AAA tranches."

McCarthy scribbles some notes on the side of his timetable and glances at Henry.

"Yes, I'll take a late call from the Asian office as long as it does not compromise my dinner with Paulson … At what time does his flight from Washington arrive? Table booked at the usual place? No agenda in writing please, just say collateralised debt obligations."

McCarthy hangs up and takes a mouthful of coffee.

"This market is too fucked up for words. One day I am gonna lose the plot," mutters McCarthy.

Henry does not envy McCarthy's CEO position. Rather, he relishes the role of éminence grise, that of favourite counsellor in keeping with the feudal ways of the City. He feels certain that no essential decisions will be taken without his consultation.

"Henry, we need to talk without being disturbed. I'll get straight to the point. I have been speaking to Roy, our Global Head of Debt. You know we are very stretched at the moment in terms of core capital. We have missed one very large trade and are about to miss another one … you know the story … capital cannot be freed easily at the moment … the situation will not in my view improve … unless you tell me otherwise?"

Capital, capital, capital, *Henry knows* – lifeblood of any company from multinational to small cap. He nods, *there is very little he can add since one of the transactions being turned down is one of his own.*

"Well, Doug you know that my team and I have been working on this $5 billion structured convertible for months. We can only innovate and convince the market if we take a fair chunk of the deal ourselves. The Hedge Funds want to feel that we believe in our mathematical modelling and our pricing before they commit—"

17

McCarthy interrupts by waving his hand in the air with a snappy gesture.

"I know all that Henry. I am trying to find imaginative ways of stretching our capital and there are none. We can't come to market, we would be slaughtered, the share is pricing at US$13.47 down ten per cent. We have used a number of structures to reduce our capital exposure but off balance sheet products can only help so far. The Securities and Exchange Commission and the FSA are going to start asking difficult questions soon ... so ... what's next?"

His voice is impatient. He is rehearsing his arguments, a dry run for a future intervention in front of the Board. Henry shifts on his seat, conscious of the uncomfortable distance established by McCarthy.

"I know you know Doug and I am also aware that we have sold all the assets we could," Henry says with some equal impatience. The subprime investments wrapped into CDOs GL has kept on its books are pulling them down and Henry has warned them about it.

"Are you only now trying to tell me that something major is about to happen, such as a sale?" His voice remains calm but his face has lost some of its colour. If GL is being taken over or merged then Doug has not confided in him.

Henry's remark brings a spark of amusement to McCarthy's eyes.

"Well, yes ... I am talking about hanging a 'for sale' sign in the shop window. You admit yourself that your team will not be able to perform unless we broaden our capital base. Even you, Henry, can't bloody well deliver a structured solution despite your experience so what else can I do? We have to take the initiative ... Force a takeover of the reverse kind."

McCarthy's eyes now glow with a mixture of cruelty and excitement at the prospect of what lies ahead. After so many years he is still thirsty for blood.

Henry's heart starts racing and his mouth has gone dry. He has not felt this taken aback for years. The matter of fact statement, the absence of communication, can only mean that he is not in the running, that he and his team are not a core part of the protracted negotiation process. Henry can feel anger gripping him, an incandescence burning in his chest.

Betrayed.

Control is essential. He cannot, will not, allow himself to show the turmoil inside. Henry reaches for his coffee, takes a long sip and sits back. The colour has returned to his face, he is calm.

"Mr Crowne ... Hello?" Marianne's voice propelled Henry back into L'Epi d'Or. His hand had been moving in slow motion towards his pocket, fetching a few coins to pay for his tea. Time speeded up again. Henry gave Marianne his best smile and left with the cup of tea warming his fingers. He turned into Gresham Street not yet ready to rejoin his team. He started walking towards Poultry, drinking his tea slowly. But no matter how good the weather and the tea, Henry could not shake the memory of his NY trip.

McCarthy's voice rings clear in his ear, the arrogance ... the coldness.

"I presume you have a counterpart in mind with deep enough pockets or shall we discuss options?" Henry asks.

"A valid question coming from you Henry!" McCarthy still needs his cooperation in the process. "However, I think our options are limited. I told you, I won't be taken over. I want a reverse, I want to be in the driving seat when I am at the negotiation table ... in the interests of us all of course. There is therefore only one bank that can fulfil that role in my view."

Henry does not volunteer a name. He is still hoping that the forbidden word won't be spoken.

"HXBK is the only one." McCarthy's eyes have not left Henry. The anger is rising again in Henry's chest, much harder this time to control.

"Are you telling me that you are seriously contemplating a merger with this sleeping dinosaur?"

"More like a sleeping beauty, needs to be awakened – and OK some may not see me as a charming prince but what have I been paying my bloody PR consultants for?"

The deal is done, you motherfucker, *Henry knows,* just like that.

"So, what would you like me to do now, Doug."

To be part of the integration committee is vital.

"I am going to ask you one of the most difficult things to do Henry, but I know you well, you will be able to handle it," McCarthy pauses, takes a sip of coffee before putting the cup slowly back in the saucer.

"I want you to do nothing."

Henry goes to stand up. His seatbelt stops him dead. He unbuckles it with rage. He is now towering over the older man who remains impassive. McCarthy looks up into the younger man's face without the faintest hint of emotion. His faded blue eyes don't blink. Had Henry been in a room, a car – dammit even a boat, he would have walked, swum … but at 10,000 feet his options are limited. He sits down again.

McCarthy has organised the meeting wisely. Mind manipulation, also referred to as 'coaching' in most leadership courses, is a strong skill of his and for the seven hours the flight lasts Doug 'coaches' Henry into his way of thinking.

* * *

At home, Nancy was still going through the portfolio of prints, meticulously taking notes on each of them and only looked up when her doorbell rang. She grabbed her BlackBerry to check the time. The bell rang again. It had to be a lunchtime delivery but she was not expecting anything. She gave a sigh and moved to the intercom.

"Yes, can I help?"

"A delivery for Mr Crowne," replied a polished voice.

Nancy was intrigued. It was not the usual coarse greeting of a courier eager to get to his next job.

"Is he expecting you?"

"I had arranged to deliver late morning, so that he could take the time to look at the painting during his lunch break."

"I am coming down," replied Nancy.

Could Henry also be a collector? She arrived at the main entrance door to see a well-dressed young man in a hat. He was carefully balancing a large painting covered in bubble wrap.

"I am happy to take delivery for my neighbour. But you must let me see the piece. A little nosy but well …" said Nancy with an engaging smile.

"Certainly. It is rather contemporary," the young man replied hesitantly. "I am Phillippe Garry by the way."

"The wilder, the better."

Nancy and Phillippe engaged in a lively conversation about galleries and artists, while he unwrapped the piece destined for Henry. He said nothing more, but positioned the painting on one of Nancy's sofas.

Nancy sat down for a few moments, stood up and walked away without losing sight of the piece. She came back, sat down again.

"*The Raft of the Medusa*. A powerful reworking of Géricault. Who is the artist?" she asked, admiring the daring interpretation.

"Tom de Freston. A very promising painter we represent."

"Why the *Raft*? It was a controversial painting in 1819 when exposed in Paris. The story of this shipwreck caused much embarrassment to the newly restored French monarchy. I am right, *n'est ce pas*?"

Phillippe nodded in admiration. He had found an unexpected art expert and French speaker in Nancy.

"Tom enjoys the depiction of epic narratives and draws much from art history."

"Does he believe history will repeat itself?" asked Nancy, turning towards Phillippe.

"What do you mean?"

"Well, so much despair. People plunged into such barbarism. I can't help feeling an association with today's economic crisis, terrorism. Perhaps we are on the brink too. *La fin est peut-être proche!*"

Nancy paused. The idea struck her as a chilling revelation. She shrugged but Phillippe agreed.

"*Absolument*. To be honest it had not crossed my mind but Tom has an uncanny way of seeing the world, of trying to introduce order into chaos."

Nancy was about to launch into a discussion about artists' ability to sense the future but realised she had to prepare for her first meeting. Phillippe left his details and promised he would arrange a lunch with Tom.

As she was getting herself ready Nancy could not help but wonder why Henry had chosen this piece. Was he also stricken by its premonitory power or was it simply an attempt at capitalising on an early talent before Tom's pieces reached unimaginable levels? The question intrigued her. This could surely be debated over a drink. Nancy would extend an invitation to Henry and quench her curiosity.

* * *

Henry was returning from his walk. He had forced his well-trained mind to stop dwelling on McCarthy. Henry had a plan and so far, so good … The weather had suddenly turned cold but the sharp wind was doing him good. His mobile rang.

"Henry Crowne," he said in his smooth baritone.

"Good afternoon Mr Crowne, Inspector Jonathan Pole, Scotland Yard. I understand that you have been informed I may want to speak with you. Would it be convenient for us to talk at some point?"

Henry would have dropped his tea had he not been balancing it on the railing of the pedestrian crossing opposite his office building.

"Well … yes … what exactly are you expecting from me? Anyway, I am outside the office – can I come back to you?"

"We do not need to talk now. Shall I come at 5.30 tomorrow afternoon? I will text you my number in case you need it."

The voice was harmonious yet unequivocally firm. There would be no arguing. Henry knew he would be made available by his firm to the Yard, he had no choice and the voice at the other end of his mobile knew it full well. Inspector Pole would tolerate no setback.

"Fine I'll book a room."

"Excellent, see you then."

The wind that had invigorated Henry was now assaulting him, making him shiver. He rapidly crossed the street and disappeared into the building.

Back at his desk Henry was assailed with urgent calls and emails. The market had moved dangerously again and some of the products his team had helped launch recently were now under stress. The Albert story disappeared in a flash as Henry engaged with the issues at stake.

It was late when he finally reached his home that night. He had jumped into a black cab whilst still scrolling through his emails on his BlackBerry and swiftly replying. At the last traffic light before the cab reached his home, he had stopped. Henry enjoyed this small ritual, a way of preparing himself to let go of the day's pressure.

He entered the imposing yet welcoming hallway. Before he reached the lifts he passed a modern steel and wood table. The janitor was on holiday and his replacement was a disaster. Henry swore in a low voice as he noticed his mail mixed up with that of his neighbour, Nancy Wu.

"If this moron can't put it through my letter box, at least he should allocate it properly."

He separated his mail from Nancy's in an angry gesture and dropped a bunch of letters on the floor. He swore again, this time louder. The little he had seen of Nancy intrigued him. The Chelsea Flower Show Committee had sent her a large envelope. The Henry Moore Foundation had sent her what looked like an official invitation, both letters indicating that she must be a trustee. Another letter from the Inns of Court attracted Henry's attention. He placed his own mail underneath his arm and moved towards the lifts, still perusing his neighbour's mail. Some more mail from abroad, China and France. Henry smiled at his own preconceptions. He walked out of the lift and rang her doorbell. No one replied. How irritating. He could have done with a little company. He could keep the mail and try later perhaps. Nancy had given him her phone number as the mixed-up mail incident was not the first of its kind. Henry realised it was the only time he'd had a conversation of any length with her and been invited into her home. But the mood soon faded. He slid the mail through Nancy's door.

He might not be such good company after all. Besides, Nancy might not live up to his expectations. Henry was about to step into his flat when a white envelope on the floor of the hallway stopped him. His name was elegantly penned across it and underlined.

Henry impatiently tore it open.

Dear Henry,

Your painting, The Raft of the Medusa, *arrived this morning. I was hoping I could deliver it to you but a prior evening commitment prevents me from doing so. I thought you would want to see it as soon as you came in tonight and therefore asked the janitor to be allowed into your flat. I hope you won't mind.*

I could not resist taking a look. I am impressed by the quality of the execution and the strength of the content. Would you care to join me for a drink later on this week? I would so much enjoy discussing this provocative piece with you.

Yours
Nancy

All ideas of grabbing the janitor by the throat for having allowed a stranger in vanished. Instead, Henry felt flattered. He dropped his mail on the low table at the centre of his lounge.

The painting was still wrapped and had been carefully positioned against one of the bigger sofas. Henry had forgotten how large the piece was, not as large as the original Géricault but still imposingly sizeable. He did not bother to change but ran to his kitchen to find a pair of scissors. He placed the painting on the sofa against which it had been leaning and started meticulously unwrapping it. The joy of knowing and yet not fully remembering gripped him until the bubble wrap paper lay discarded on the floor like the abandoned dress of a lover.

Henry took a few steps back. Opposite sat *The Raft of the Medusa*. The shock was intense, the nakedness and the vulnerability, the despair and the savage need to survive. A few days ago death had been a controversial theme that called only for words. Today it had become reality. Why had he chosen such an uncompromising painting?

Henry stood up, incapable of taking in anymore, rapidly covering the piece.

"I am not in the mood," he said aloud, as if it was a sufficient reason.

Henry took off his jacket, threw it on the sofa and unknotted his tie in an irritated gesture. He looked around the room and the elegant antiquities reassured him. They were some exquisite dancing Shivas, a benevolent Buddha and his prize piece, a miniature terracotta warrior from the Emperor Qin Shi Huang's Terracotta Army. All were expensive and suitably safe. Henry had never reflected on the decorative nature of his collection. The pieces had been purchased at a price. He had taken monetary risk, or perhaps that of fraud but what other risk had there been? And was it art?

He climbed a flight of stairs to his bedroom and there again the large Matisse painting on the wall felt kind, a gentle presence, comforting in its origin and execution.

Should art be more than simply pleasing to the eye? Why collect? And why *The Raft of the Medusa*?

Henry shook his head again.

"I am not in the mood," he repeated. He would call Phillippe tomorrow. Maybe this piece was not the hit he thought it would be. Yet he had fought for its purchase against no other than Anthony Albert himself.

Most surprising, they had both been invited to the exclusive preview of Tom's work. Henry's newfound love of contemporary art had led him to follow Phillippe's gallery and its many young up-and-coming artists. When Albert walked in, Henry knew he was there to close a deal. Anything as long as it was a good investment.

Henry had challenged his rival with flair by welcoming him openly.

"Anthony, how nice to see you here."

"Likewise," Albert had replied unfazed.

Henry had turned away towards Phillippe declaring in the low voice of a conspiring man. "I would buy the whole lot but it would feel very Saatchi-like."

"Why, bonus on the decline?" Albert had butted in, unashamed of his uncouth eavesdropping.

"Noooo, but as you know at your own cost, I do not buy in the manner a rug merchant does. I pick and choose!"

Henry had raised his champagne glass in humour and moved on. Albert had then walked straight to Phillippe and asked for a quote on the entire display. But Albert was no Saatchi and Phillippe knew to exercise caution. Henry had become a good client and both men managed to catch up whilst the artist presented his work and was interviewed by the *FT* art correspondent.

"The gentleman you spoke to wants the whole lot," Phillippe had said. "This is unusual for a first-time buyer."

"My fault, Phil. I mentioned Saatchi… but I think *The Raft of the Medusa* is the one I truly want so just tell him I desperately want *Minotaur*. He will buy that one and a few more I am sure."

"Understood. By the way… *The Raft* is an excellent choice!"

And today *The Raft of the Medusa* was sitting in Henry's lounge.

Chapter Three

The room Henry had booked was small but comfortable. He assumed Pole would be coming on his own. He was standing by the large bay window overlooking the City's roofs. The top floor of the newly converted building was solely dedicated to meetings. The place had been given a professional but pleasant feel. Teams of staff were dedicated to the welfare of the bankers and their clients. Henry would press a button on a remote control lying on the small desk adjacent to the meeting table and refreshments would appear swiftly, a well-rehearsed choreography Henry took for granted and hardly noticed.

Biscuits and cakes came to mind … He remembered some of his first meetings where the joke invariably turned on the 'quality' of the snacks provided. It sounded rather frivolous now but the memory made him smile at his own reflection in the window. He was trying to spot the roof of the Bank of England when the phone rang. A male voice announced his guests, asking Henry whether he should send them through. Henry noticed that the plural had been used.

"I'll be with you right away," replied Henry.

Fucking hell. How many coppers does it take to interview one bloody banker?

Inspector Pole was a tall man, with greying hair. Henry noticed that he was also sporting a well-trimmed goatee. His colleague was an equally tall Asian woman.

"How do you do," said Pole whilst extending his hand to Henry. "I am Jonathan Pole and this is my colleague Nurani Shah."

"How do you do?" said Henry.

Henry shook hands with both of them. He had kept his right hand in his trouser pocket ensuring the tissue within it absorbed the moisture of his sweaty palm.

"Shall we move to room sixteen?"

"Certainly. Thank you for taking the time, I am sure you are very busy."

"Well business is not exactly as usual. A merger imposes restrictions on what a bank can do as you know." Henry's voice stayed remote, matter of fact. He had no need to befriend Pole.

"Of course, I suppose the acquiring company wants a period of status quo to ascertain past performances and risk levels in particular in the current subprime context," replied Pole.

"This is not a takeover, this is a merger." The firm's mantra Henry did not believe in would however do for Pole. He pushed open the door of room sixteen.

"Tea, coffee, water?"

Everybody went for tea. Henry placed the order and sat opposite his two unwelcome guests.

The conversation started with a bland exchange of information until refreshments had arrived. This took less than three minutes after the call had been made.

But the biscuits looked sad.

"Well Inspector Pole, I presume you have not come here to enquire about the rate of inflation so let's get on with it, shall we?"

"Certainly, I know that Ted Barnes has given you a quick summary of what happened to the flight Anthony Albert was on. We have also contacted GL's internal legal team to ensure that we can gain access to relevant information. This is important since I am afraid we will be treating the incident as suspicious."

"Do you have any proof of this?" said Henry in a tone he thought too eager.

"Very sorry but I can't discuss this with you Mr Crowne." Pole's voice remained even. "However, in this context we have to try to map with exactitude the movements of Mr Albert. So, tell me, when did you last make contact with him? Is there any information you think is relevant?"

"Sure," said Henry, settling down into his chair comfortably. "Today is Wednesday. We spoke on Monday. Anthony was asking for details of all structured products we were working on. I was preparing this report but wanted a bit more time."

Henry shifted slightly, he was suitably vague, knowing that the subsequent conversation had been made from an anonymised phone in one of the meeting rooms.

"Could you be a bit more precise, was the conversation tense, amicable?"

"Well this is a difficult merger, it is not easy but in the current context it was professional and sufficiently courteous."

Anthony Albert and Henry had had a courteous enough conversation on the Monday, however the subsequent call had degenerated into an almighty row. Henry knew the game too well. Under the pretence of 'future cooperation' and teamwork, Albert was trying to find out what the competing team was working on. His aim was also to adapt his own pipeline of product development and tailor it accordingly. The idea was of course to look at least as good if not better than Henry. They had exchanged information but both camps had surrendered ideas that were already known to the market. The cutting-edge technology that made Henry's team so spectacular remained hidden.

"I understand that you and Mr Albert were not particularly friendly," said Pole.

His eyes rested on Henry and he let him feel their weight. Pole was in the game of information gathering, an opponent worthy of Henry's attention.

"Well, this is a tough environment, banking is hugely competitive, at best people may respect each other …"

"Would it therefore be fair to say that there was respect between you and Mr Albert?"

"I think that is right," Henry gave a soft roll to his r. Pole did not seem to blink at Henry's first lie.

"Could we now show you a number of documents that have

come to our attention this morning? We recovered them from Mr Albert's computer."

* * *

To: Roger Kodorov Global Head of Equities Trading
Date: 08 September 2008
From: Anthony Albert European Head of Structured Products

Subject: Henry Crowne

Roger,
A quick mail as agreed to update you on the latest conversation with Crowne. I simply cannot understand the man. He suggested we fly together to Switzerland tomorrow and now he has changed his mind. He will not take the plane with me! He was the one who suggested we take the company's jet so that it gives us some privacy for a discussion about the teams which I thought was the first reasonable idea I have heard from him so far.

However, Crowne is now too busy, this is frankly a lame excuse. Anyway, I will see you later in Geneva. At least and at last ... Crowne has prepared some documents I can work on. I will pick them up myself so that I can work on them on the plane before we meet.

Best
Anthony

Anthony Albert, ACA, FTII
European Head of Structured Products

* * *

Henry read the note once, and again. He finally pushed the page back to Pole with two fingers. He folded his hand on the table, lifted his head and took a moment to speak.

"I do not understand this email at all, he had mentioned a trip to

Switzerland but never firmed up on it."

Henry's mind was now working quickly and in anger. *Why would this crazy fucker want to send such an email?* Henry had expressed surprise but had he been convincing to the well-trained eyes of Pole?

"You have no explanation why Mr Albert wrote this mail?"

"None whatsoever."

"What about the papers Mr Albert mentioned in his mail, would he have really come to pick them up or send for them? Why not email?"

Henry had delivered some papers but all had been done by mail and the latest batch had not been ready on time hence the row with Anthony Albert. Henry knew he was late and pressure had been mounting. The game had to be played with precision, too much resistance and he would lose the hand.

"Well, the papers were ready but he never picked them up," Henry's voice dipped a little – his second lie.

"You mean there was a bundle to be picked up prepared by you, specifically for Mr Albert, with all the required information?"

"No, not printed, but that could have been printed had he asked for them. He never did."

"Well, we have another email dated two days previously asking for the documents to be delivered, what do you make of this?"

"Can I see it?" asked Henry slowly sinking into the half-truth that made survival in his job possible. His answers would not be incorrect but would always be open to interpretation.

Control at all cost.

"The documents refer more, I believe, to general figures about P&L."

"OK, but I presume P&L can be gathered from your accounts department."

"Yes, but we also have projections."

"Now Mr Crowne, what do you make of this mail?" said Pole moving around pieces of papers so that they landed precisely in front of Henry.

This time the mail was addressed to Albert's PA. It was asking her to confirm the booking of one of HXBK's private jets and inform security of Henry's identity and details. Albert was also giving specific instructions about Henry's pick up at his home address.

"I have absolutely no bloody idea, Inspector. I can't give you any answer to this apart from the fact that Albert and I never discussed this trip in detail ... and I mean never." An alternative reality was unfolding around Henry. He was part of it ... yet a powerless spectator.

Remember, Control at all cost.

"But I thought you said Mr Albert had mentioned a trip?"

"I mean we never firmed up on it. It was not even a discussion more ... a vague suggestion. Absolutely nothing more."

Pole sat back in his chair, looking at Henry, sizing him up. Henry knew exactly what Pole was thinking ... Yes, this man was intellectually arrogant, an excellent negotiator. Probably hideously ambitious, but could he kill for it?

Pole took his time, giving Henry space to measure the impact of his thinking and what would come next.

"Understood, but we will need to talk to you again. You realise that the gap between your account of the facts and what we have as evidence is let's say ... unreconciled ... I am afraid Mr Crowne I am about to become a regular feature in your timetable."

Having shown his two unwanted guests out Henry grabbed his mobile and speed dialled number one.

"Pam, I need to speak to you urgently!"

"Darling, you always need to speak to me urgently," purred Pam in a husky voice.

Pamela Anderson had worked with Henry on most of the complex deals he had put together since joining GL. Her name had been a constant source of sarcasm, mixed, of course, with the inevitable dirty joke. Pam had cleverly used this unfortunate homonym to her advantage, playing for or against it according to circumstances. After all, it was a name to remember and she certainly made sure that her contacts did exactly that. Pam was tough. Some argued that the City had taken its toll as it did on so many women. Truth be told, Pam simply paid lip service to the female condition but enjoyed the company of men more. She was one of the few equity partners at Chase and Case, the largest law firm in the City. Equity partnership meant sharing in the revenues of the firm, an enviable position with a foreseeable substantial income. This of course came with large responsibilities too, a state of affairs which many City critics preferred to ignore. But Pam had more than it took to preserve her position.

"Pam, do you have a good criminal lawyer in your contact list? There is a crazy situation developing at work and I may need to check a few things … in private …"

"Where are you?" interrupted Pam, switching immediately to her professional voice. "Has someone screwed up on one of our deals?"

"No, no, not a deal Pam … something more personal … I'll explain."

"I am completely stuffed at the moment but I could squeeze in twenty minutes for coffee at 4 o'clock."

"I'll be there."

Henry looked at his mobile in disbelief, anger … a constant companion as faithful as a dog, as hungry as a wolf.

Fuck … No, I did NOT screw up. How could she be so bloody quick off the mark? She has collected enough fees from me, been so goddamn ass covering in each transaction. She was bleating away to me when one of the partners opposed her elevation … and without me where the hell would she be?

Henry could not stay mad for very long at Pam. He would not question that feeling of slight helplessness whenever they started a new deal together, getting used to her proximity again after a few hours. But the keen anticipation would always be there after a few months of separation.

* * *

Inspector Pole settled at his desk, stretched his long legs and waited for Nurani to free up the only other chair in his office. She dumped the files at her feet and sat at the edge of her seat.

"So, Nu, what do you make of our particularly exciting case?"

"You mean Crowne? Interesting. What I expected from the City … with something extra …"

"And what would that extra exactly entail? Apart from the fact that he is single, probably a millionaire, rather presentable," teased Pole.

"You mean frankly, sexy …"

"Great start … a frank assessment of The Banker of the Year 2006, 2007, 2008 … You look surprised Nu, but we have here quite a pedigree animal," said Pole.

"Not very politically correct, Jon, we are not at a dog show," Nurani grinned.

"And addressing the sex appeal of Mr Crowne is not exactly PC either… Is he sexy?" Pole mused.

"I thought we were staying strictly professional, avoiding any crude sizing up of Mr Crowne."

Nurani was still smiling wryly at her boss.

"Quite so my dear … quite so. Anyway, the question with Mr Crowne despite his numerous attributes is—"

"Has he got the gumption to commit murder? Could he literally pull the trigger? I am sure he has done so at least in his mind many times in the past, you don't get to be where he is without having slaughtered a few opponents on the way."

Nurani whilst speaking was firing an imaginary gun at the level of someone else's head.

"Well, this is the preconceived idea anyway, you assume that he has had to do some pretty bad things to get where he's got to, but has he? And as you know we are not in the business of assumptions but facts so …"

The phone rang and Nurani picked up

"Some preliminaries from forensic, I'll go. Shall I also call the team in?"

"No, just bring the results back to me. We'll have a look, you and I, before drumming up the troops."

Pole watched Ms Shah (her preferred title) as she disappeared down the lift to the basement. Nurani had been his first choice when the case had come through. What she lacked in experience, she made up for in sheer determination … no one in the City could faze Ms Shah.

"And … she can find a needle in a haystack," Pole muttered as he made room on his untidy desk. His office was permanently cluttered, files, papers, various documents strewn across the room or mounting in piles of various heights. The department's common joke was that any piece of missing evidence would be found in this ridiculous mess.

Pole didn't care. "My favourite detective is Columbo," was the equally common reply given to anyone attempting to introduce their order into his chaos.

He moved a couple of piles with precision, uncovered a blue file, reached for document three, pulled it out with a small flick of the wrist. He had exactly what he wanted. Pole sat down again while surveying his office with a contented grunt.

Pole enjoyed the job because it was 'totally him'. An odd answer for the many who had not reflected on why they were doing what they were but a highly enlightened one for those who had. Pole's propensity to philosophise was regarded with irritation at the Yard. Yet his ability to zero in on a suspect's motivation and get results were respected in equal measure.

As he started reading, Pole proceeded with impeccable logic, creating an elaborate web of possibilities.

There are a number of hypotheses, he thought whilst scribbling some notes. *First accident or homicide-murder. Let's see what Nurani brings but my gut ... Murder.* Pole wrote the word in the far-right end side column on his paper. *Then ... People known to Albert, either close family friends or within his wider social circle, work ... the takeover, past deals, promotion-bonus ... any other link to a network of influence. Money, power ...a good recipe for a bad outcome.*

Simplicity was paramount as many answers to crime resided in the immediate environment of the victim but the Albert case was already proving different. He had, just this morning, gone through a preliminary interview with Anthony Albert's widow. Pole opened his notebook.

Shockingly calm she was ... a high profile hit job ... Possible.

Pole looked at the far side of the corridor. Nurani should be back any minute now.

Yes ... it's got to be murder, the signs are there, a new plane and one of the most reliable on record, an explosion near the tail of the aircraft where the luggage is stored ... Pole had, however, another niggling feeling, difficult to identify, a vague and contradictory sense that although he wanted to keep matters simple, the way evidence was presenting itself was almost too neat. A thought he would keep in the back of his mind for the time being.

"Yep, 'tis a murder case," said Ms Shah.

She had pushed the door open without knocking and was still reading the report.

"Traces of Semtex were found on some of the remains of the private jet, a fairly common but very effective type of explosive."

"Have you asked for the origin of the sample to be traced?"

"Yes Sir, Forensics are on it. It may take a little while unless it is already on the data bank. The guys from the IAFA have also left a message by the way, hope they will not want to interfere too much"

"You bet ... There is a clear security breach at the airport. It's bad enough at a large airport but how can it happen on a private jet. No guaranteed security for the high flyers ... as welcome a problem as a pork chop in a synagogue."

"Wow, goodbye political correctness ... seriously, Jon."

"First thing ... we need to eliminate the pilot from our potential suspect list," Pole said satisfied with his little bad joke.

"Do you think the pilot could be involved? That would be very odd."

"Everybody is a suspect as you know ... don't assume anything in the first instance. And yes, I understand what you mean. But it is possible ... mental illness, less unusual than you think ... frighteningly so."

"OK, that is definitely frightening. I will speak to the company and do a full background check on him."

"Although I have to admit, with a banker on board, my gut is telling me we won't find anything on the pilot."

"So, what do we do next?"

"Now, we follow the trail Ms Shah ... We follow the trail."

"Motive, means, opportunity," she said.

"Correct. Do we think this guy Crowne is on the list?"

"He hates his rival who may be about to take over his team."

"OK, motive!" Pole said.

"He was supposed to be on the aircraft with him."

"Opportunity, I sort of buy that."

"He might have given him docs to carry, or ... something else."

"Yep … means to achieve his purpose."

Pole was looking through the report without paying real attention to it.

"That is a bit obvious, not a very clever way of covering one's tracks, for a guy who I think is pretty bright."

"Yes but, this is only circumstantial for the time being, he may have involved a pro. I don't see him doing a DIY job on this one, I agree."

"He may lose in the battle for power, but this is common in the City. You live by the sword. You die by the sword … then get reborn and move on to yet another guaranteed bonus."

"Is that right?" said Nurani, incredulous.

"Yep, absolutely. But granted, Crowne may no longer be thinking straight."

"Exactly. Have you seen his face? He looks as if he has not slept for a hundred years and he lied at our first meeting, several times. You said so yourself."

"*Bon.* Mr Crowne, you're number one on our suspects' list."

Nurani opened up her notebook and slowly penned Henry's name. She was about to suggest another name when Andy Todd knocked at the door. The youngest recruit in the squad, he had started two weeks ago and was eager to show commitment.

"Hey, Nu, got the tapes you wanted. Do you want to view them now?"

"Tapes?" said Pole raising one eyebrow in his inimitable fashion.

Nurani blushed a little.

"Yes, I asked to see the video cameras at the entrance of Crowne's place. Just in case Albert or someone else came to pay a visit. Just to make sure …"

"I see, no flies on you Missus."

Pole was grinning at the speed at which Nurani was following her own logical path.

Pole looked in amusement as his little team vanished in the distance. He stood up and closed the door. A sign he wanted no disruption and started meticulously reading through the file.

* * *

Henry was pacing up and down the small cosy lounge of Chase and Case. Pam had said twenty minutes at 4pm. It was already ten past four and Henry was growing irritable. He stopped his restless walk to pick up a newspaper when someone grabbed his arm. Pam placed a peck on his cheek in a mechanical fashion and pushed him through the exit doors.

"Let's go."

She was looking tanned and relaxed in her grey designer suit, having just come back from two weeks in Barbados where she owned a large flat in one of the secluded parts of the island.

"Right, Henry, what is this garbage about a criminal lawyer? You look like shit by the way, you need to rest my friend."

"Thanks. I feel so much better after that reassuring comment."

Henry was staring at his tea, adding yet another sugar and stirring it cautiously. Contacting Pam may not have been such a good idea after all, however here she was. He told Pam pretty much everything including about Pole's visit. Pam frowned for the entire time he was talking, her dark brown eyes fixed on Henry. She said nothing until he had finished.

"The first thing you must do is ensure you have the GL legal team involved, you don't want to say anything unless you know they are. GL's gators are pretty fierce."

"Who?" asked Henry.

"I mean the litigation team, nicknamed gators after the creatures that hunt in swamps."

"Right … right," Henry nodded, not amused.

"Henry, what are you concerned about anyway? You seem to imply you are targeted."

"These emails are strange. I've never seen them, I am pretty sure. I am tired not senile."

"Albert was trying to make you sound like an uncooperative little shit. What's new? It's classic merger tactics."

"Unlikely, he would have been found out pretty quickly."

"Look, I'll have a think, don't panic. It is nothing for the time being, OK?" She glanced at her watch. "Got to go. Hang on in there, big boy."

Henry was one of Pam's best clients. She owed him her elevation to the enviable position of equity partner and would call him a friend. These events were, however, strange and dangerous for a young partner. Pam tapped him on the shoulder and left. Henry watched her energetic silhouette move away and noticed that her hair had become blonder in the sun. She had spent exactly twenty minutes with him.

* * *

Back at Scotland Yard, Inspector Pole was still reading the file when he got an excited call from Andy Todd.

"Boss, I got something. I can come up and …"

"I'll come your way. I need to stretch my legs," said Pole amused at the enthusiasm. *"Ah, to be young and keen again!"*

Pole entered the room in which Andy had been sitting without noise.

"So, how many wine gums packets has it taken you?"

"Er, only three. I mean, I know it's not really mature and all that but it helps the concentration."

"Just kidding, show me what you've got."

They both leaned forward, as Andy rewound the tape and played it back. A man resembling Anthony Albert was pressing a doorbell, hunched over as if speaking into the intercom system, then keying some numbers into the entry door pad. Andy froze the image.

"And now Boss, may I introduce you to Mr Albert," Andy grinned.

"Well done, young man. Keep at it. And have another packet of wine gums on me," said Pole leaving Andy to his task.

Andy punched the air, several hours of viewing not spent in vain. He carried on with the tape to see Anthony Albert walk into the building and come out of it ten minutes and thirty-seven seconds later with not one but two briefcases. Life was hotting up for Henry Crowne.

Chapter Four

Henry decided to walk home. Work was piling up at the office but he could not shake off the events of the past few hours. It was only 5pm and anyone back at base would have called it a half day. He took his BlackBerry out of his jacket pocket in a mechanical gesture and started scrolling down the messages, only paying attention to those that seemed important. The sun was out and despite the bitter cold it felt good to be walking at a quick pace. Henry recognised St John Street. He had somehow given up on the BlackBerry and for the first time in years found himself looking at the buildings in the street. Some of them had been freshly renovated, some replaced by new premises. A strange mix, yet not disharmonious, he was taking the time to notice.

Unlike many City professionals, Henry had chosen to live away from Chelsea, Belgravia or Holland Park. He found these upmarket places stuck up and predictably bourgeois. He had decided to remain in Islington, the area he had moved to when he had secured his first job in investment banking. He had been hunting for the perfect flat for years and had finally found it at great expense. A cash purchase, no mortgage. The estate agent had taken two seconds to persuade the vendor to accept Henry's offer.

A large warehouse with an unusual glass entrance appeared on his right-hand side. The place had been converted a few years ago into a meditation centre for aspiring City MDs. Henry had always resisted the training programmes that might come too close to deciphering who he truly was. He knew he had ambition and that was enough. Henry did not distrust psychology as a science but had little respect for those selling their so-called coaching skills to the banks.

He slowed down as he passed the entrance and shook his head at the thought. He had been in competition with Anthony Albert to win the same client and had engaged in the battle mercilessly. The CEO they were wooing had discovered the power of meditation recently and was enthusiastically visiting this City outpost of St Augustine. Henry could now see himself, kneeling on an uncomfortable cushion trying to stay still without too much wriggling. Albert was sitting a little further in front and closer to their prospective client. Keeping one eye open, Henry was surveying the situation. Albert's heavier body was constantly tensing up. He would not last an hour. To Henry's satisfaction Albert had had to bow and retreat, the cramps in Henry's own legs indicating that he would not last much longer either. At least he could withdraw without his target noticing.

"*Nil points for both of us*," thought Henry as he now saw the line of trees that sheltered his own building.

Tiredness gave way to a warm feeling of reprieve from the events of the day. He was fingering the keys in his pocket. Soon he would be home, a place to reflect and stand at a distance from today's drama.

His solitary life pleased him. The work hard, play hard reputation of City traders was too cliché or perhaps out of date. The eighties were long gone. The days when traders snorted coke at their desks before markets opened had vanished. Banks had decided that the bonuses of their higher paid employees should preferably not disappear up their noses. The expression of power had shifted; expensive tastes of a different nature had replaced the exuberance and carelessness of that era. There were still the second homes in the south of France, the cars, the exclusive restaurants and fine wines but there was now contemporary art, a new battle ground on which to unleash vanity and buying power. Henry's own private collection had moved from antiquities to modern art. He had no interest in spending a fortune on school fees when he could direct his hard-earned cash to the purchase of a masterpiece.

Henry knew that his monastic existence raised eyebrows in the City and so what? Wild speculations about his character fuelled malicious gossip. Was he gay? Was he impotent? Did he have an even darker secret to hide? Henry brushed these aside. Ambition had been his sole mistress and she had never betrayed him.

His mind switched back to the painting sitting in his flat, wanting to close further speculation on his emotional landscape. *The Raft of the Medusa* had not been touched since he had first looked at it. Henry decided to call on Nancy – he felt the piece would be better viewed in someone else's presence. Nancy had mentioned drinks. Why not accept her invitation sooner rather than later? The thought comforted him and the prospect of a conversation with someone in the know presented an irresistible intellectual challenge.

* * *

At Scotland Yard Nurani and Andy had been busy and were now sitting in Pole's office. He was listening intently to what the pair had to say about Albert's visit to Henry's flat.

"So, you are completely positive, Albert came in with one briefcase and left with two."

"Absolutely boss," said Andy. "No mistake! He spoke to someone. You can see him bending towards the entry phone and saying something after he's rung the bell."

Andy kept glancing at Nurani to take his cue.

"Someone else could have been in the flat?"

"Crowne is single, no girlfriend, broke up with someone a few years or so ago, it seems, and the cleaning lady comes on Fridays. His family, well, father is deceased, mother still alive, lives in Asia," said Nurani.

"Did you get a shot of Crowne coming into the building himself?"

"No, but he could have taken the car or simply walked in through the garage door. The CCTV camera was vandalised a few days before, not repaired yet. So we would not have seen him. He takes his car regularly, he's got an MD parking space at the office," replied Andy.

"Anyway Jon, why don't we go and ask him ourselves?" said Nurani. She enjoyed using Pole's abbreviated name when most of his other reporting lines addressed him as Jonathan or Inspector Pole.

"You just want to take a look at how the City bankers live, don't you?"

"Now what would give you THAT impression," she said, not flinching.

"OK, let's go and visit our favourite banker. And Andy, check the log of the GL garage. If Crowne took his car there will be a record of him parking there."

Ms Shah was driving her brand new car, a yellow Beetle with a small flower vase stuck to the dashboard. Today a flamboyant red rose sat proudly in its miniature holder.

"Nu, you don't like this guy but don't let it cloud your judgement."

Pole was right, she did not immediately reply. Pole was one of the few senior officers who had taken time not only to work with Nurani but also to train her; a man for whom welcoming an Asian woman into the force was more than fulfilling the 'diversity' quota. His opinion counted.

"I know Jon. I won't make the wrong remarks. I just think it's such a shame that someone as bright as that should be letting himself down by spoiling his talents in a City job. The only guy I have sympathy with at the moment is the poor bugger who was flying the plane."

Pole remained silent. These two men had died a tragic death, which was now murder. Nothing else mattered. He was not here to judge, that task would be left to the jury. He was here to do his job so that justice could be served. After so many years in the force Pole had reflected many times on the clear difference between revenge and justice, between justice and the law. Profile cases blurred these lines and yet he knew that, to be good at his job, this clear-cut definition had to be understood.

"At his best, man is the noblest of animals, separated from law and justice he is the worst," said Pole.

"Wow, did you come up with that? Profound," replied Nurani with a grin. She had been warned about her boss's philosophical inclination.

"I wish! No, it's a quote from Aristotle."

"Was he not a Greek philosopher?"

"Correct, around 400BC."

"So you are telling me we are here to make a difference?"

"Well I am. And to know that revenge in whatever form is neither law nor justice."

"Right. I will need to ponder that a little if I may," said Nurani, unwilling to be drawn into what she considered a superfluous debate.

Pole observed his young colleague sideways and judged that Nurani was not ready yet for an in-depth conversation. But whether she liked it or not he would one day have that discussion. It was the way he taught.

"Here we are."

Pole opened the door and took time to look at the imposing building. It had been the headquarters of Thames Water in North London at the turn of the last century, displaying sumptuous architecture of heavy stone and classical art deco design. They entered through the gate and walked a few yards, past a series of well-kept grass and flower beds, before reaching the main entrance. The bells pertaining to the flats bore no names. Albert must have known where to go. Pole pressed bell number seven. There was no reply. He moved away from the building and glanced up. There was light in the duplex flat occupied by Henry. Pole persisted and was prepared to ring Henry's mobile when a voice answered.

"Mr Crowne, Inspectors Pole and Shah, may we come in? We called your office, but you had left already."

The main door opened without a sound. They moved along a large hallway of stone, wood and steel. It felt solid and yet light at the same time, a peaceful harmony that was home. Pole and his DS reached the private landing of Henry's flat, and the large door on the far-right hand side opened. Henry leaned against the door frame, one hand in the pocket of his jeans waiting for them to make their way towards him. He looked quite different now that he had changed clothes, more carefree. He had swapped his expensive Savile Row suit for a pair of cheap jeans and an old Dublin university T-shirt. Pole took this opportunity to observe him before the mask of control had time to settle back upon his face.

"Could it not have waited 'til tomorrow morning?" said Henry.

"'fraid not," said Pole, cheerfully.

Henry led the way into the flat. The entrance gave a feel for the eclectic taste of its owner. Sober yet elegant; a small collection of Asian antiquities was displayed round the hallway and as centrepiece a fourteenth-century Buddha from Cambodia rested in a carefully lit niche.

In the main lounge an immense tapestry was hanging on the far wall, it looked old and its distinctive blue revealed its origin to Pole.

"Aubusson," he murmured.

Henry tried to ignore him but felt both impressed and gratified. Pole was not just some ignorant copper to have identified the piece so quickly. Pole glanced at the rest of the room, a few other statuettes had been carefully positioned on dedicated shelves, a large cream sofa with a couple of armchairs added to the peaceful comfort. Henry's lounger in brown leather, matching the frame of the sofa, was surrounded by newspapers and files. A quirky teapot sat on a side table still exhaling the scent of its fragrant tea.

Henry let his tall body slump into the chair, he vaguely gestured to his guests to take a seat.

"We are intrigued by a visit we suppose was for you, Mr Crowne. You did not mention it at our last interview."

A faint smile brushed Henry's lips at the word 'interview', which had in the banking world a much more exciting meaning. Pole took out of his pocket a CD, Henry thought he recognised the initials AA on the cover.

"Do you think we could play this for you?"

"Be my guest."

Henry leaned backwards and grabbed a small compact remote, a large screen appeared over the fireplace. He took the CD from Pole and shoved it into a dark sliver below the screen. Some scrambled images shot across the screen, then froze to present a picture of Anthony Albert speaking into the ground floor intercom of the building. Henry had not had time to sit down and any desire to do so was stopped by the scene. He spotted the date and time at the bottom of the screen 08-10-08//21.57.03. His mind raced back to the time only a couple of days ago, trying to remember whether he was still at the office, at a client's. He needed ... an alibi, a word he thought would never enter his vocabulary.

Pole let a couple of minutes pass, he was in no rush to break the silence. Henry felt Pole's focus was total, he was reading his reactions, absorbing every detail, studying the lines on Henry's face, the tension in his body, all information useful to harvest.

"Well it seems to me that Mr Albert was trying to invite himself to a decent bottle of wine," said Henry finally.

Humour always saved his day. But this time the attempt at levity failed. In the silence that followed, Henry heard himself speak,

"Why do I have the feeling Inspector Pole that you do not believe me?"

"Play the DVD further, you will see my dilemma."

And so it was that for the next few minutes Henry witnessed, incredulous, Anthony Albert buzzing his doorbell, entering the building and finally walking out with not one but two briefcases. The images finally vanished, leaving a grey screen. Pole waited, again in no hurry to suggest a possible scenario. Nurani had made herself invisible by studying the surroundings with great care. Henry followed Nurani's glance. She had noticed the large parcel still in bubble wrap lying against the wall at the far end of the room. It looked incongruous in Henry's well-orchestrated décor and *The Raft of the Medusa*'s power shook Henry's confidence.

"What is the crazy asshole doing? He was not supposed to collect them himself, anyway."

"What was the a-hole not supposed to do?"

Pole sounded amused by this sudden lapse in political correctness.

"The papers I told you about yesterday. He was not supposed to collect them himself."

"Well, Mr Crowne, it looks as if he found them after all."

"Correction Inspector. What he found was a briefcase. God knows what was in there," Henry struggled to regain control of the situation. After all, he was right. Who could prove what was in the case?

"Point taken. But you must admit this is rather strange."

"Strange as it might be, I certainly did not see him that evening."

Pole sat back in his seat. The amazement on Henry's face was genuine enough, he felt he had passed that test.

"So where were you that evening?"

"I was here. Later that is. What was the time again?"

Pole grabbed the DVD case.

"Time 22.57."

Henry had seen Liam that evening. He had no intention of saying any more for the time being. Liam was not the type of character he wanted to discuss with Pole. He needed to leave him out of the discussion at all cost.

"Yes, I was back at home."

"From where?"

"The office actually." This was not a complete lie since Henry had dashed back into the office to grab some documents he needed for an early morning meeting. One of the trainees had stayed late to prepare the pack for Henry.

"You are not going anywhere in the next few days I presume. We may need to talk some more," said Pole. "We need to understand what Mr Albert was doing at 22.57 … at the bottom of your building."

"Absolutely Inspector."

* * *

Henry was walking back toward the lift. He had insisted on accompanying Pole to the door of his building and watched the two speak as they entered their car. He had not performed well and suspicions would be mounting. In a strange way, Albert was suddenly in control of his life. But Henry shrugged, Albert was dead. He was about to press the lift's call button when a voice stopped him.

"Henry, what a happy coincidence," said Nancy as she walked towards the lift herself.

"Nancy, how nice to see you," replied Henry, forcing a smile.

"Would you care for a drink? That is if it is not too late of course."

Henry took time to assess his neighbour. He liked her energy and elegance.

"Excellent idea, I could do with a drink and a good chat," he said. Nancy smiled amiably.

"Let me bring the wine if I can be that forward as to come to yours. I would love to take a second look at your new acquisition."

"Something tells me that you are not going to take no for an answer," said Henry, seeing the humour in the situation. His flat, his sanctuary would be invaded again although he had to admit he was looking forward to this latest intrusion.

By the time Nancy entered his lounge, Henry had positioned the painting on the sofa again. He had not removed the bubble wrap. She thought it strange but said nothing. Henry poured two glasses.

"Are you a collector yourself?" asked Henry.

"Yes, but I also support a small gallery."

"I thought you were a lawyer? The head of Chase and Case mentioned your name a while ago," said Henry intrigued.

"I was, a barrister to be exact. It feels like a lifetime ago and no longer that interesting," replied Nancy.

Henry was torn for a moment between the desire to know more and that of speaking about his own collection. Surely a successful lawyer would not give up such a lucrative career.

"We can talk about my old profession some other time if you are interested," said Nancy, relaxed. "How about discussing something that matters much more: YOUR collection."

"Absolutely," replied Henry.

Had he been that transparent?

"I must say … This is a daring piece to acquire."

Nancy drank a little wine and carried on.

"Do you have a particular affection for the original?" she said as she stood up to move towards the painting.

"In truth, I have never seen the original. I mean, I have seen it in books but not in the flesh, so to speak, and … I don't see why it makes any difference," said Henry failing to hide his annoyance. This was not an art history course.

"I agree, a painting can have an immediate effect on the viewer but in this instance, it presents a background story with considerable significance."

"Which is what exactly?"

"Well, Géricault's *The Raft of the Medusa* depicted a tragedy that shocked the world and reinforced in France the distrust in the old monarchy."

"I still don't see the point."

"The *Medusa*'s wreck was largely attributed to the incompetence of its captain, Viconte de Chaumarey. He was perceived to be acting under the authority of the restored French monarchy."

"Why would the monarchy be involved in such an appointment?"

"*Absolument* and a very astute question indeed," acknowledged Nancy. "It is almost certain that King Louis XVIII had nothing to do with it. But remember the whole affair happened at a point in time in French history where democracy, as defined by the revolutionaries of 1789, has failed and yet monarchy is still unable to make a full come back."

"The event was pretty horrific. How many survived?" asked Henry, sensing the potential of the original story.

"Only fifteen out of the one hundred and forty-seven crew survived. And those who did had to suffer starvation and cannibalism, murder, despair."

"Do you see an analogy with the way French people saw the monarchy?" said Henry.

"I see two analogies. Yes, I see the incompetence of the French captain confirming the view that France had of its monarch but," said Nancy, pausing as if to find the right words.

"And the second?" said Henry, eager to put forward the idea that had just dawned on him. "Are you going to tell me you see a parallel with what is happening in the markets?"

"Artists have an uncanny sense for what comes next. *Il me semble*," said Nancy.

"Nancy. This is only a painting."

"Then why do you want to buy it?"

"It is well executed, and the theme powerful."

"It is not enough, Henry … it has meaning for you, not an intellectual one, a deeper one. *Oui, quelque chose de profond.*"

Henry poured some more wine in the two empty glasses, searching for a response and trying unsuccessfully to summon his French.

"There are a number of other pieces that represent the *Raft*. To me this is significant. The collapse of the old, the coming out of the new," finished Nancy.

50

"I don't see it myself but then again I have not spent ages intellectualising this purchase, *et puis, je parle mal francais.*"

Henry had hoped for a diversion from today's events but instead found himself dragged into a philosophical debate he did not want to have. Nancy sensed the mood. There would be nothing to gain in arguing with a very tired Henry.

"You might be right, I might see too much in this piece," replied Nancy. "But I hope you will indulge me if I speak French, a necessary contribution to my mixed cultural background and reminiscence of intellectual pride." She smiled at Henry and the intelligence he read in her eyes struck him. She had defused his anger with unexpected calm.

Nancy changed the subject and spoke about the coming Frieze Art Fair, the latest big names who would be displaying their work. Henry finally relaxed. He could not resist a few good insider tips.

Chapter Five

The global structured equity 7am conference call had just finished. All participants from either Asia-Pac, Europe or the US had left the call but Henry was kept behind by one of his nosier colleagues. He was keen to gather information about the 'Albert case' as he put it. Henry had no intention of volunteering anything meaningful but had not moved quickly enough from the room to avoid him. Despite claiming he had an urgent appointment, he was unable to shake the limpet who accompanied him for part of the way to his phantom destination.

Morag saved the day when she spotted Henry's attempt to extricate himself from the little man.

"Henry," she shouted across the floor. "Your call. Starting. Five minutes ago."

She walked over to them, ignoring altogether the other man. She looked annoyed at this lack of punctuality. The limpet let go, not wanting to be accused of wasting Henry Crowne's valuable time.

"Well done. That guy is such a moronic prick! Why do we bother keeping people like that?"

"His father sits on the Bank's board. He is such a leech too, always trying it on. Anyway, you had a few calls. I've left messages on your desk."

"Anything from Pam?" asked Henry

"Nothing, but internal legal called."

Henry nodded and swiftly entered his office. Since the plane crash, he had spent more time there than he usually did. This was very unlike him and would not remain unnoticed on the floor for very long. As a rule, Henry liked to be among his people. He always sat at the same bank of desks as they did and was content for his office to be used for calls or meetings. The Floor could be noisy when activity flared up, to the point where no decent amount of thinking could be done. Most people who had spent time working there could cope with it. Some even claimed they could never work in any other environment such was the energy emanating from it.

Henry sat down and flicked through his messages. Pam had not called. Did it mean anything? He would give her a couple of hours and call again. This lack of contact was more upsetting than he liked to admit.

James Radlett knocked on the glass partitioning, Henry waved him in. It would be good to talk business, something familiar he knew he was good at.

"Hi, do you have a minute?"

"For you James, always," smiled Henry.

Out of his twenty-three strong team, Henry had chosen James as his number two. James had had a very unusual career path which made him ideal for the job. James had started in the army. He had joined the Intelligence Corps and had been deployed alongside the 2nd Rifles, but an injury during his time in Kosovo had cut short his time on the field. He had decided to change his career altogether and found himself on a 'programme for mature students' at GL. His training in the military had multiple advantages for his reporting line which Henry had immediately recognised. He respected the chain of command and showed Henry absolute loyalty. James could withstand pressure better than most, having had to face the prospect of death for a meagre army salary, but never spoke about his time in combat. In return, James demanded absolute transparency from Henry, which Henry gave him unreservedly.

"So how is the deal with Google doing? Last time we spoke the strike on investors' put options was still under discussion."

"Still waiting for back-test results, the Quants team is reviewing the model. I think we are close; probably a one-year and a three-year put with a 110 and 130 strike."

54

Henry arched his eyebrow. "Quite a risk for the issuer."

James nodded feebly in agreement, showing he was not particularly interested in pursuing the discussion on their $5billion star deal.

"Henry …"

Henry stopped juggling with his pen, startled to hear James call him by his full name rather than the usual 'H'.

"What is happening with this AA story? People are starting to gossip. Some really screwed up rumours are doing the rounds and the team is getting worried."

"Such as …?"

Henry straightened himself up in his chair.

"Well, speculation as to who would gain the most from his murder. I am sure that the guys at HXBK have put your name in the hat. Such a bloody good opportunity can't be missed."

"And what do you think James?"

His voice remained calm but his entire attention was focused. He was not prepared to take any of this fucked up crap from anyone, certainly not his own team.

"You tell me, Henry."

James had remained equally calm in his response.

"Do I understand your question correctly? Are you actually asking me whether I —" (the words stuck in Henry's throat) "have bumped off Albert?" His hands stretched over his desk as he was speaking, his body leaning forward. One move and he could reach James.

"A valid question," said James leaning forward as well. "It is direct but I have seen some bloody awful things in service."

"James, firstly we are not '*in service*', secondly what do you think I am about to say? Even if I had done it, which by the way is completely ridiculous, I certainly would not tell you the truth."

Henry's voice had gone up one notch, the burn of anger setting fire to his throat. But James' time with the Intelligence Corps had taught him all about information gathering. Was he already onto something?

"I had to ask, you know I like to get to the point," replied James as he sat back in his chair. "By the way, I disagree with you on one point. We are at war."

"James, let's take a reality check here shall we? I have worked with you for what – six years? You know me well, do you really think I could dispatch a guy just like this? OK, OK, we are talking about AA, Mr Recovery Man, I know, but still. This is a completely different ball game. I know we use some pretty shit even murderous language on the floor but it stops there! Bloody hell, you know that as well as I do."

"Fine, fine, but be aware that rumours are starting to circulate. Everybody knows that with the IRA's arms decommissioning it is not that hard to dispatch someone, as you say."

A chill went down Henry's spine. Although he had not given it much thought since he had acquired dual nationality, Henry still held his Irish passport, his nationality of origin. And of course there was Liam. Henry was about to reply but thought better of it. James stood up slowly as if to give his last remark time to sink in.

"We will not have any further discussions about this, James. I mean, this is not only bloody ridiculous but also frankly unacceptable."

Henry had got up as well, James left without another word. Henry followed and shut the door. He knew he had not handled the situation as well as he could have but it was now too late to call James back in. He would let things settle a bit and go out for a good bottle of wine; anything could be settled over that. The idea reassured him somewhat. He looked at the various clocks in his office marking the time in different time zones, chose the NY one and subtracted five hours, a silly game he loved playing. It was time to chase the elusive Pam again.

* * *

Young Andy had now been officially appointed to the case. He had spent the last few hours with a permanent Cheshire cat grin on his face, to the annoyance of his colleagues. His first assignment was a full background check on Henry, which he had initiated with enthusiasm.

Pole was having breakfast at his desk when Nurani entered his office.

"I have the transcript of our interview with Albert's merry widow. Shall I leave it with you?"

"Please, we need more time with her. I also want to know what is in Anthony Albert's will, including insurance policies and the like," said Pole.

The first task when opening the case had been to inform the family. Pole had gone to visit Anthony Albert's wife as soon as he could to offer support as well as collect the necessary information. When he arrived Adeila Albert had already been informed of what was considered a 'great tragedy' by the head of Human Resources at HXBK.

Anthony Albert had recently moved to one of the most expensive parts of Belgravia. One of Albert's main objectives in life must have been to become part of the establishment Pole had surmised. The purchase of a large property there was a decisive step in the right direction.

Pole had asked Dolores Patten, the team's psychologist, to join him. He had delivered the same dreaded message so many times and yet he still hated doing so.

On arrival Pole pressed briefly, almost shyly, at the doorbell. The door was opened a minute later by a small woman, dressed in black. Mrs Albert had already decided to rise to the occasion by choosing the appropriate dress code. The sobriety of black was, however, undermined by the ostentatious jewellery. Two diamonds, too opulent to be fake, hung from her earlobes. The necklace of solid gold reached her waistline; the various rings she wore on her left hand dwarfed her modest wedding band.

Pole offered his condolences as he entered the house, introducing his team in the most tactful fashion. Mrs Albert mumbled an inaudible thank you, interrupting him to ask whether they wanted some refreshments.

"We would not want to cause you any unnecessary work," said Pole.

"Absolutely not. I just dashed to Harrods to buy some food when I heard you would be coming."

"Well, that is very kind."

She disappeared into the kitchen. Pole and his team looked at each other in disbelief. The wait was interminable. The team used that time to observe their surroundings in silence, noticing the collection of antiques that left the place feeling cold and heavy. Adeila Albert returned with a large silver tray, on which sat a delicate bone china tea service. Pole stood up and helped her, placing it on the low table in front of them. It was more a high society tea party than a distraught family gathering. He patiently took his cup and waited to speak, again, at what he thought would be the appropriate moment.

"I am sorry to be intruding at this difficult time but we will need to know more about your husband."

"How could he do this to us? Anthony has always been so unreliable. How am I supposed to cope with all there is to do in this house?" Adeila Albert spat angrily. She was furiously twisting her wedding band round her finger.

Dolores Patten, the police liaison officer, softly intervened.

"I am sure your husband was unaware of the danger he was in."

"And how would you know?" Adeila replied.

"We know this is a difficult moment," said Pole again trying to exercise patience and tact.

"You have no idea! I have two children to look after because Anthony refused to send his beloved daughter to boarding school. That is a fatal mistake. The child needs discipline."

"Mrs Albert, we do need, if at all possible, to ask a few questions about your husband."

"Ask away, ask away," said Adeila Albert with a small disparaging wave of the hand.

"Are you aware of anyone who may have a serious grievance against your husband ?"

For the first time Adeila Albert seemed to pay attention to what Pole was saying.

"Why do you ask?"

"Well, certain preliminary tests have led us to believe that this plane crash may not have been accidental."

Pole paused to let the devastating piece of news sink in.

"I know it is yet very early days but we need to inform you of this," he continued.

Adeila Albert stayed silent for the first time. Pole carried on.

"We need to establish whether there was anything troubling him? Did he confide in you? Are there any indications you can give us at this stage? Of course, you can think about it and call us later if you would like."

"There is the takeover of course, Anthony was very busy, and, well, concerned about it." Adeila Albert's voice sounded less confident. "He had mentioned some other person who wanted him out. Anthony is not the most courageous of men you understand, Inspector, but he sounded more scared than usual."

"Did he mention any names?"

"Some Irish person. I don't really remember. Henry – Brown – no, Crowne?"

"Anything else?"

"I have given you a name. Is that not enough? Anyway, Anthony was working in the City."

"So, there was no one else, in your view, either in the City or outside?"

"No."

Adeila Albert brushed her hand through her hair in a seductive fashion.

"More tea?"

Without waiting for an answer, she poured tea into the half-drunk cups.

"We should probably leave Mrs Albert, Inspector," said Dolores Patten softly. Pole nodded.

"If you need any assistance please call me, this is my card," added Dolores.

"I can cope perfectly well on my own," said Adeila, ignoring the card.

"And this is mine," said Pole, leaving his card on the table in a determined gesture.

Adeila rose and walked her guests to the door. The interview was over.

* * *

Henry had left the door of his office closed.

Time to call the elusive Pam.?

59

He could not stay annoyed with her for long. She was, after all, a 'very busy girl' as she liked to put it. The scent of Chanel N°5 floated out of nowhere in his room. Henry's pulse jumped a beat. He had not seen Pam for a few weeks. Time spent apart always gave her a more intimate presence. Something he had learned to tame but felt hard to control today.

Pam's PA answered. She recognised Henry instantly and apologised profusely. She would nudge Pam again. She knew it was urgent. Henry grumbled a vague thank you and frowned. What the hell was Pam playing at? He needed her now. He grabbed a large deal tombstone lying on his desk and read the text inscribed on it. Their first deal together. He looked at his watch. He would call her mobile in thirty minutes.

* * *

Pole was rearranging his tallest pile of documents, fishing for a file he knew was near the bottom whilst Nurani updated him on progress.

"Meeting this afternoon with the IAFA at 2pm," said Pole.

"Background check on Albert in good shape. Started on his wife and family, will have more late afternoon. I have prepared a request for the court to grant us permission to hold and question Crowne plus remand in custody if necessary."

Pole ruffled his goatee but said nothing.

"I have updated the list of people who saw Albert a few days before the crash. We have a few more to see but he seemed to have very much kept himself to himself, at least in the past few months."

"I've also made a list of people close to Crowne, team, colleagues, friends and foes. Will call on them as well."

"Good, what else?" said Pole finishing a cup of coffee that was precariously resting on the side of a notepad.

"Nearly finished the background checks on the pilot. Nothing coming up. As you rightly predicted, Jon."

Pole shook his head, flattery would never get anybody, including Nurani, very far with him.

"When are we going to have the pleasure of interviewing Mrs

Albert again? Can't wait," carried on Nurani, carefully wiping a crumb off Pole's desk.

"I have left a message on her answer phone. No reply yet. We may have to invite ourselves for tea again," replied Pole. "Block out some time in both our diaries. I want to have a good stretch to go through all the info with you after this afternoon's meeting."

"Will do Jon."

Nurani paused.

"Anything on your mind, Inspector Shah," asked Pole leaning towards her with an over-serious face.

"Not yet Inspector Pole," she retorted, leaning forward towards her boss, mimicking his gesture. She could not hold it for very long and started laughing.

"I'll tell you later. Suspense is key."

Chapter Six

Henry finally got an answer from Pam. She had placed a heavy caveat on her choice but had at last given him a name. The barrister was a certain Harold Wooster QC, a specialist in Corporate Criminal Law. Even Henry had heard of him. He had been material in successfully defending a couple of investment bankers in a notorious insider dealing case. Market manipulation of share price had occurred on a large scale, resulting in a quoted company on the LSE declaring itself bankrupt. The trail led the regulator straight back to the door of the well-known institution and yet Wooster had demonstrated that the evidence gathered was not beyond reasonable doubt. The traders had walked free. Holding Wooster's address had pacified Henry somehow, and yet the conversation he had had with James lingered.

What evidence could have pushed James to suspect he could be involved? Yes, it was true that the City was a cruel and unforgiving place and thinking of 'murder' could indeed take place in many forms. It happened every day, battles for positions, battles for transactions. James was right, in a sense they were constantly at war. He remembered one of his colleges saying arrogantly, "My mind is my sword, my will my armour", as if to introduce some semblance of chivalry into his selfish attitude to work. What a lot of bullshit. Maybe fifteen, twenty years ago ethics still meant something to people in the City but the increased domination of the trading floors where the stakes were unimaginably high had put an end to this.

He had done what he had to do. First to survive, then to grow and finally to reach the position he so desired. He admitted he was ambitious, in fact fiercely so, but he never saw anything wrong with it. His childhood in Northern Ireland had not been easy, then again it had not been disastrous either.

Or had it?

It had fostered in him the desire to live intensely, to take risks, to challenge himself, find his limits. He never wanted to feel fear again.

But the old question came back to him.

Could he *actually* kill?

Could he bear the sight of the body torn and lost? He was ruthless, he knew. He had removed people from his team who did not perform to the highest standards he imposed on himself. He, Henry Crowne, had done so in what he considered to be a tactful and humane way. But the choice between the black bin bag and the quiet chat on the side was the only attempt to appear considerate. The careful words selected to make the point that, *"you did not make the grade"*, or *"sorry you batted for the wrong team"* were always the same, picked more in an attempt to avoid a lawsuit rather than to show compassion. He pondered, but then again there was Belfast. Henry forced the image of his native city out of his mind. He once more focused on the ways of the City, the subtle back-stabbing, the gossip and opinions directed at colleagues or competitors to gently discredit them. An activity repeated every day, so common that it became hardly noticeable after a while.

Henry was still deep in thought when Morag tapped at the glass partition.

"I am off for the day. Do you need anything else tonight H?"

"No, that will be it. Thanks." Henry smiled.

Morag had been superb, not a word about the events of the past couple of days, business as usual. Amazing.

He had not noticed the time or the fact that the desks were already deserted. At 7pm it was rather unusual, then again the past few months, certainly the past few days, had been anything but. He was himself glad to be able to escape early. He made his move.

* * *

The meeting with the IAFA had been predictably tedious. The question of the breach of security was clearly on everyone's mind as no new details had emerged from the interrogation of personnel at the airport or from the pilot's background checks. Pole had decided not to mention the second briefcase until it was clear it was a material piece of information. He wanted to gather more but also force the IAFA investigators to dig deep on their side, a strategy that could backfire. He was prepared as ever to take the risk. Pole was unhappy at the cosy way evidence was lining up and he was willing to stretch his luck.

Nurani had not attended the meeting. She was to fully concentrate on the background checks. Information was starting to arrive thick and fast. It was time for Pole to carry on completing the picture of the murder he had started to formulate.

There was a great deal of activity at Pole's office when he arrived. Nurani was on the phone, frantically taking notes. Andy was organising documents on the meeting table. The team had been busy in his absence and Pole felt invigorated at the thought of plunging into the nitty gritty of the case again.

"Hi gang," said Pole cheerfully.

"Hi Boss," said Andy.

"What have you got for me?"

"Followed your advice and got my own thinking organised on the white board and then file. Hope you don't think I am, sort of, lacking initiative," blurted Andy.

"To give orders it is essential first to know how to receive them. That's always my first piece of advice to you young people," smiled Pole.

"You like training people," said Andy.

"Is that a question?"

"No, no, I can see that and I sort of really like it."

"Well, I am sure you have been told that I am a bit of an oddball. And don't worry, I don't mind a bit," carried on Pole. "Just tell me if I start acting like your dad though."

"Boss, I can tell you there is zero chance you'll be like my dad." And with that Andy closed the discussion.

Pole nodded, he would elucidate Andy's last remark over a more convivial pint of beer.

Nurani waved as she finished her conversation and put the phone down. She looked triumphant.

"The travel agent confirms they sent the tickets."

"OK." Pole dumped his mac on his chair. "Rewind will you. Which travel agent and which ticket and where?"

"Sorry. Plane tickets to go to Zurich on HXBK's private jet were delivered to Crowne's flat the day before the trip. The travel agent says someone signed for them. I have asked for the documents to be scanned and sent to us."

"Very good. Bring them along as soon as you get them. Andy, what have you got for me?"

"Quite a lot actually, Boss."

Pole was about to ask Andy to stop calling him Boss every time he opened his mouth but thought again.

"Right. Shoot."

"Background check on Albert and his family nearly completed, lots in there. Statement from the integration committee – they have been willing to release this before they do so to anyone else but it's very general. We'll need a lot more detail. Finally background on Crowne, I have not got all the basic but there are a few bits that may be interesting already."

"Sounds excellent. Let's begin with Albert."

Andy adjusted his thick glasses on his nose and started flicking through the tags he had arranged in Albert's file.

"For a start, his original name is not Albert but Albertini. His father was an Italian immigrant. He owned a small pizzeria near the train station in Southend. He and Albert's mother never got married and it was a real struggle for him, I mean the father, to stay in the UK before the EU. We have a wad of applications for work permits and so on. He died when Albert was very young, five or so. The mother never married, she had a small allowance from her family but was always on the breadline from what I can tell."

"Is she still alive?"

"No, died a few years ago."

"So, Albert had no money as a kid, no real family around him and what does he do next?"

"Well, he gets into accountancy. Safe job and all that. He is a bright guy because he gets his diploma with distinction. He gets married to someone else on the course and as soon as they are married he changes his name, making it more English, I suppose."

"So, from Mr and Mrs Albertini, we now have Mr and Mrs Albert."

"Right, then." Andy was flicking through the file. "He spends five years at Arthur Andersen, works as an adviser to City Group for some of their structured products and makes the big move into banking. Spends another five years there and gets headhunted into HXBK for the small guaranteed bonus of US$200,000. That was thirteen years ago, not bad."

"Actually, not that great Andy. Even thirteen years ago some of the big boys earned a damn sight more! So Albert did not negotiate his welcome pack into HXBK that well, probably because he moved from Arthur Andersen after the Enron scandal. Please check … What else?"

"His wife stopped working eleven years ago. They had their first kid, a daughter called Anastasia, now age eight, and a son Alexander, age four. They only moved to Belgravia two years ago, before that they lived south of the river," said Andy flicking through his notes more vigorously. "Aaannnd … a few more bits. He and his wife may have had some marital problems – they went to see a marriage counsellor about five years ago."

"Before the second kid was born?"

"Yep."

"Had a second kid to try to shore up the marriage. Anything else in that vein could open up possibilities, in particular if he is the one playing away … oh, and for that matter is she playing away?"

Pole remembered how Adeila Albert's attitude had changed during their first encounter when he had mentioned potential enemies. He was about to call Nurani to check on their next meeting with Albert's widow when Ms Shah appeared in his office.

"Got the scanned documents. Don't recognise who signed for the tickets. Might be the janitor but we need to check. I will give him a call to see if he remembers slotting them into Crowne's mailbox."

"Regrettably, it looks as if the delightful Mrs Albert will have to wait for a while," said Pole.

"So we think Crowne got the tickets. That would confirm Albert was expecting him but does not confirm Crowne had agreed to be on the flight."

"Maybe but why would Albert send the tickets then?"

"To force Crowne to be on that very flight, in particular if he, Albert, wanted to have a meeting which the other guy, Crowne, was trying to avoid."

"Surely Crowne would have made an excuse even at the last minute – unless … unless Crowne did not want people to know he had agreed to be on that flight."

"That's a point."

Pole pondered this for a while.

"What happened to the second briefcase? Albert would have wanted to open it before the flight to check the contents. He would have wanted to look at the presentation or whatever Crowne was supposed to deliver to satisfy his curiosity, and anxiety. Why take a second case full of documents if you can't open it?"

"So, we need to establish whether he opened the bloody thing," said Nurani.

Andy, who had not said a word, raised a timid hand.

"Yes," said Nurani turning towards him, unhappy at the interruption.

"If I remember correctly, from what I saw on the CCTV camera, I should be able to tell you what type of lock it is, I mean, was."

"Can you?"

"If it is a simple key lock, then it is easy enough to open even without the right key. If it is a combination lock well, then, it is much more difficult."

"Excellent, go and find out. I need to know whether there was an issue with opening the case. Did Albert try to contact Crowne to get it open? We did not spot anything on email, Nurani, so check for text messages, voice messages. I want to know whether Albert was carrying a case he had not and could not open."

Both disappeared leaving Pole to immerse himself in the fast-growing case. This would be a welcome late night.

* * *

It was 6am when they came for him. Henry had just switched off the alarm when there was a ring of the main entrance bell. Henry knew immediately who it was. The sound of his doorbell had the effect of a cold shower, he was wide awake, his mind totally alert. Inspector Pole and Ms Shah stood in front of him as soon as he opened the door. They had a search warrant for his apartment. There was no point in protesting, so he moved sideways with a welcoming gesture as if to invite them in.

Irony ...

The only way to remain in control. Henry got dressed quickly and grabbed the piece of paper on which he had jotted down Harold Wooster's telephone number.

Nurani had spent a good part of the night searching through various emails, text messages and phone records to find any piece of evidence that would link Henry, Anthony Albert and the second briefcase. She had been rewarded for her efforts with the discovery of a text asking for the PIN number of a briefcase, textbook evidence. Andy had also confirmed, through his work on the CCTV videotape, that the briefcase lock was a combination one. It could not be opened unless the PIN number had been entered into the lock. The text read, *Number invalid, please resend code.* There had been no reply from Henry.

The accumulation of evidence necessitated a formal chat with Mr Crowne. Henry was also a flight hazard and Pole was not taking the risk.

Henry sat down without a word, finding space at the back of the police car. Pole took his seat next to him. Both men remained silent until they reached Scotland Yard. The smell of early morning disinfectant assailed Henry's nostrils as soon as he entered the building and was suddenly back to being a boy in Northern Ireland.

He is no more than seven. It is the first time, but not the last, he ends up in the nick – no ... the paddy! Some street fight with another gang of kids descends into chaos, bricks thrown, windows smashed. The police are called and catch up with them pretty quickly. In those days any scuffle attracts an instant police response. Belfast is not a playground for young boys. After a couple of hours, his mother comes to collect him. A quiet English woman, she came to Ireland as a teacher, married his Irish father and decided to stay. But she has never managed to find her place among the Irish, and found herself shunned by the English as well. Why does he have to hang around with the Irish mob? She tries and fails to scold little Henry. He remembers her crying. On that occasion he feels ashamed but anger prevails ... always.

Pole's voice had shaken Henry back. He had directed him towards the interrogation room. Henry had barely noticed he had been processed in the *customary fashion*. Pole had offered a drink.

"A good cup of tea would not go amiss," said Henry with his usual hint of irony.

His renewed confidence at holding Wooster QC's address, had pushed him to start without his lawyer. There would be plenty of time to call at a later stage. Calling him too early might indicate guilt and he had no intention of giving Pole ammunition.

Inspector Pole started the interview with Dolores observing. A trained psychologist was helpful now that serious questioning was underway.

Both men went over old ground, the sequence of events, the CCTV tape, the takeover, Henry's relationship with Albert. The answers came back identical. The interview had been going on for an hour and a half when a text message flashed up on Pole's mobile phone. He excused himself and left Henry alone in the room. Dolores waved as Pole appeared in the observation room.

"Are you taking five so that you can see how he will react on his own?"

"Yes and no. I've received a cryptic text from Nurani, more evidence rolling in and it was time to take the pulse with you. So, what do you think?"

"On the surface, self-assured, focused, excellent memory. He is going to use the same words for the same questions no matter what.

He has formidable self-control. If you go deeper and I mean much deeper, there is a lot of anger."

"Interesting, you mean old anger coming from way back?"

"Yes, past events, not surface aggression."

"OK, keep up the good work. I will be back."

"Count on me. Don't often study a specimen coming from one of the largest trading floors in the City."

Pole was about to make his way to his office when Nurani appeared. She could not resist the temptation of observing Henry in the cage and had come to deliver her piece of information to Pole.

"I was on my way."

"I know, but this is massive Jon. Henry has some connection with the O'Connor brothers, Liam and Bobby."

Pole's focus became absolute.

"Any recent contact?"

Nurani nodded slowly as if to emphasise her response.

"Two days before the crash."

Chapter Seven

Pole resisted the temptation to go back into the interrogation room and savage Henry.

Was he getting soft?

If Henry had the serious IRA contacts he seemed to have, anything, absolutely anything was possible including taking a plane down. After the IRA decommissioning, the O'Connors had remained on a small list of hardcore operatives; a recent fusion of three IRA splinter groups meant reinforced vigilance in Belfast and London.

Anger was not part of his temperament but Pole was angry. Angry at himself for having given Henry the benefit of the doubt, but more importantly because he might have made a fundamental mistake, one which an officer of his rank and experience should never make. He kept asking himself why as he walked towards his office, but could find no answer.

It was unlike Pole to ask anyone in his team to get him a coffee but nevertheless he asked Nurani to fetch him one. He always looked upon his colleagues who abused their juniors with disdain. But Pole was annoyed, he wanted space. Nurani left him, deciding on a particularly good coffee shop. Inspector Pole needed a treat and space to brew.

She came back ten minutes later and placed a cup of coffee in front of Pole.

"Here we are Jon, strong latte, one sugar."

His fist was still clenched in front of his mouth. He was not looking at the file.

"Thanks, Nu, much appreciated. Give me the lowdown on the Irish connection."

"In the background check, we noticed that Crowne had gone to school with the O'Connor brothers. This rang a bell and so we tried to see whether we could trace any contact they may have had after they left school. Crowne and Liam O'Connor shared the same house with a number of other students when they went to college in Dublin."

"They could not have gone to uni together. I thought Henry's mother was English. And after his father died she looked after him on her own," interrupted Pole.

"Correct. Crowne went to Trinity, which would have been very usual in those days. The O'Connors went to UCD but they shared the same house."

"Did Crowne leave straight after uni to come to London?"

"Correct again. It seems that after uni, Crowne saw them far less but whenever he went back to Ireland, he called Liam and they might meet, with or without Bobby."

"How do we know all this? Was he under surveillance?"

"No, not him, but the O'Connors were."

"Obviously," said Pole. "Henry must have known that his friends would be tracked. He can't have been that naive."

"Perhaps. Or maybe he didn't think the Counterterrorist Squad would find anything. I don't know but he met with Liam again about six months ago. Now, the amazing thing is that it was after the closing of a large transaction in Dublin and guess what? Anthony Albert was there as well."

"Crowne and Albert hated each other's guts ... a meeting on Crowne's turf. We need to know more."

"Albert's team had little to do with the transaction but I get the feeling that he invited himself to the party anyway. It was a very big ticket – $3.5billion."

Pole could not help smiling as Nurani used the term *ticket* like a pro from the banking world.

74

"Don't think I am going mad, I did get the number right. I guess Albert wanted to be part of the glitz. May have cost him his life, of course."

"Are you not jumping to conclusions a little fast here?" said Pole.

"Well, hear me out, this is NOT the end of it," she said emphatically. "Liam hardly comes to the UK for the reasons we know. He did, however, visit last week, arrived on Sunday and left Tuesday night for Dublin. On the Monday he had a drink with Henry." She was about to carry on when Pole lifted his hand.

"So, he has lied to us again. How did we find out about the meeting between these two?" he said.

"Liam is not involved these days, apparently, in anything too dodgy but since the IRA decommissioning some of the old members have remained active," Nurani replied.

"Liam? Now a faction IRA member?" said Pole dubious.

"Well, I'm not sure, but Bobby may be one of them, the Counterterrorist Squad was a bit vague. They keep an eye on Liam as he could be a go-between."

"So, they were following Liam?"

"Yep, although again they were a bit circumspect about this but I gather they have continued tailing Liam ever since the IRA gave up on their terrorist activities."

Pole stood up abruptly.

"Time to reconvene with Mr Crowne. Want to join the fun?"

Henry had been sitting by himself. He knew that behind the tinted glass someone was observing him. He was still relaxed. Waiting games were common in the banking world, in particular around the negotiation table when final terms were being discussed during closing sessions. He had been taken aback by the delivery of the so-called tickets. Then again, the replacement janitor was not the sharpest knife in the drawer. Something he thought would need to be discussed at the next landlord's meeting. If he can't do the job well, plenty of competent people can. Just give the moron the sack.

Henry decided to control his anger by reflecting upon his successful career. He did not want to allow his mind to wander, to feel the pressure of the moment. He chose to go back to the closing of one of his most impressive deals. *People have a vague idea of what goes on in the City*, he thought. Large bonuses and expenses paid were all that was ever spoken about in the papers. The unacceptable level of risk, sometimes irresponsibly taken, was also a favourite subject. Of course, the high level of technical knowledge, the heavy regulatory environment, the sophistication of the entire machinery that enabled an investment bank to exist was completely ignored by the media whose appetite was solely for scandal and scoops. Henry was proud to be part of what he regarded as an elite of 'thinkers' who could apply their mind to finding innovative financing structures and do it properly. He had to admit that the greed and stupidity of some idiots might one day bring the entire system to its knees. Cracks were already appearing in the Credit Derivative Market but he was an Equity man and thus keen to distance himself from the bullshitters who sold CDOs.

The trading floors were places of innovation where astronomical amounts of money transited every day, but they also created an environment where egos flourished untamed. Making money had become the sole purpose of the floor and the sense of service that had once been at the centre of banking had disappeared. And yet it had not always been so. Henry remembered, at the beginning of his career, the words 'ethics' and 'client service' had meant something and had mattered. His first interview had been with a grand old bank, now long gone, absorbed and dismembered by a number of takeovers and restructurings. There were two men interviewing him, a young chap marginally older than himself, who had been hired to expand the trading capability of the bank, and an older gentleman whose attitude as investment banker and relationship manager was diametrically opposed to his younger counterpart. Henry had hesitated to fulfil his ambition and enter the banking world. He had sensed the voracity and harshness of the youth, the face of tomorrow's banking. The older man had been running the interview with professionalism and consideration. He was focused on assessing Henry's capabilities but nevertheless strove to be fair. Henry remembered how thick his Irish accent was then, a matter that had long been remedied. He had felt clumsy in comparison to the well-polished and sophisticated interlocutor. The young man had been, on the other hand direct, explaining what he wanted and immediately pressing Henry for weaknesses, challenging his power. Little did he know, for Henry had had more than his fair share of challenges in Belfast, a mistake that would soon cost this cocky little chappie his job. In the fight for supremacy, Henry was a winner.

Yes, today he recognised it – he was the man in *The Raft of the Medusa* climbing on dead and live bodies in order to survive.

The slam of a file on the table brought Henry back to the here and now. He lifted his eyes slowly to meet Pole's. Pole was standing in front of him, his hands resting on the back of a chair, his body tilted forward, controlled anger showing on his face.

"Henry, how about an honest conversation about Liam O'Connor?"

A quote Henry had seen on Bloomberg sprang to his mind 'Always tell the truth and you won't have to remember what you've said'. But truth was about to become Henry's worse enemy.

* * *

The plane had been delayed by two hours. DMac had experienced delays before but this particular episode was testing his endurance. The head of Legal at GL had called him on his emergency number at 1am in NY. McCarthy had hardly gone to sleep when the news of Henry's arrest arrived on his BlackBerry, guaranteeing a sleepless night. Whether Henry was guilty or not was not a consideration for McCarthy. Henry had by virtue of his involvement in Albert's murder case become a liability that needed to be dealt with swiftly. He called his PA Cindy and asked her to ensure his private jet would be ready as soon as possible. Cindy called back fifteen minutes later, departure time would be 6am EAST. His next call was to Roger Pearce, Head of Corporate Communications. GL had to be ready to make a formal announcement. It was imperative at this critical stage in the takeover that they wouldn't lose the upper hand. Any argument would be used by HXBK to establish dominion over its rival and he, Douglas Sullivan McCarthy, CEO of GL would not tolerate it. McCarthy's next call was to Ted whom he had to extract from yet another meeting of one of the integration subcommittees.

"Hi Douglas, what can I do for you? All on track, as discussed. I am doing my best to—"

"Yes, yes, Ted, you are working on the integration of the two businesses – Albert's and Crowne's – are you not?"

Ted gave a very slow, "That's right."

"Good! I will be back from NY in seven hours. I want to see you then, come to pick me up at the airport, contact Cindy, nothing moves on this before we have spoken."

McCarthy had hardly finished his conversation with Ted when his BlackBerry flashed, announcing new mail. Roger Pearce had been at work, a short statement from GL was ready for McCarthy's consideration. The old man smiled. He could certainly get his people to produce. He started reading, satisfied with the speed and quality of response of his management team.

* * *

Pole was sitting opposite Henry. Nurani to his right had also taken a seat.

"I am waiting Henry."

Pole was tightening his grip over the man opposite him and he would not let go until he had the truth.

"We went to school together in Belfast," said Henry, his eyes shifting quickly away from Pole.

"Henry, you should stop playing this smug game of yours right now. You may be excellent at negotiations, you may be the king of the big deal, but that game is over, understood? I want to know everything and make no mistakes, I will."

Pole paused to face Henry full on.

"So, now, I want everything on you and Liam O'Connor and if I can't have it the easy way, I will have it the hard way. Are we clear?"

Henry nodded, his expression unperturbed. He knew that it was time to call his lawyer. Henry duly made his request. He would stay put until his lawyer arrived. He was disappointed at Pole's calm reaction when he announced that Harold Wooster QC would represent him. It had not been the bombshell he had expected.

Pole was becoming a serious adversary. Henry felt the fever of the hunt. He had thought through everything, all the better if the opponent was of a serious calibre.

* * *

McCarthy's plane had landed at Biggin Hill. His delay had cost him a meeting with the Global Head of Legal, and his counterpart at HXBK wanted an immediate face to face as soon as he arrived. This meeting, if unprepared, could undermine his current position, strategising was essential. The outcome of the integration committee, including past deliberations, were critical too and should be reworked to indicate a choice of candidate that left no place for argument. McCarthy was creating as much distance as necessary between the bank and Henry.

Ted was waiting for him at the small airport gate. From a distance McCarthy could see the small silhouette of Ted, a young man of Henry's age but with a tenth of his intellect, a fortunate state of affairs in the current circumstances. He would have no problem in getting from Ted what he wanted.

"Integration committee still on standby?" McCarthy had no time for small talk.

"Hi. Yes, yes as you said."

McCarthy entered the limo and closed the partition inside the car, isolating the driver.

"Any record, deliberations or any other documents relating to the choices to be made for the new head of the combined structured product business?"

"I will need to check, I am not sure."

Ted was trying hard to recall the events of tens of meetings.

"This is a yes or no answer," exploded McCarthy. "Are you on that committee or not? Unless you have been missing meetings?"

"No, yes, I mean I have not missed any meetings," said Ted retreating in his seat.

"So, do I need to repeat my question?"

McCarthy's eyes were on Ted, drilling into the young man's.

"I am sure that there is nothing in writing."

Ted was unsure but had decided to give his boss the answer he wanted to hear.

"Check again and report to me, no phone calls or emails directly. I want a definite answer in the next hour."

McCarthy's limousine pulled up in front of GL's headquarters. Ted disappeared in an instant, eager to fulfil his task. The car carried on into the MDs' car park and parked in the CEO's allocated space. The driver got out, opened the door. McCarthy did not move. He was still weighing up the odds that Ted would deliver. At the time that the committee was formed Ted had been the right choice, bright enough but more importantly scared of losing his job, and of McCarthy – an ideal element to manipulate. Ted knew his limits, he knew he had exceeded the level at which he could comfortably operate a long time ago. His only chance of survival was to squarely stay in McCarthy's camp.

The parking space was directly opposite a private lift. McCarthy exited his car and started the ascent to the penultimate floor of the building, exclusively reserved for top management.

Cindy was waiting for him as he walked through the doors, the driver always rang her as her boss entered the elevator. Everyone would be waiting for the 'Big Man' as he walked in. She took his coat and went straight to business.

"David James-Cooper has called again himself, he wants to see you ASAP."

"I know, I need you to give me time, find some credible excuse."

"I will. The head of communications wants confirmation that the text concerning Mr Crowne can now be released."

McCarthy noticed that Cindy had switched from H to the formal Mr Crowne, self-preservation in the corporate world was already at work.

"Confirmed."

"Some reports on the various integration committees have arrived."

McCarthy stopped as he reached the door to his office, his steely gaze on Cindy.

"Anything on structured products?"

80

"No."

"Thank you, Cindy."

McCarthy opened the door and sat at his desk, he had hardly slept in the past thirty hours. He dialled Ted's number, Ted answered before the end of the first ring.

"I am ready to come up."

McCarthy put the phone down and waited. He knew with certainty that Ted would do what he had to.

A few minutes passed before Ted appeared. He sat silently, his small frame looking lost in the large armchair facing the CEO's desk. McCarthy interlaced his fingers, and rested his hands on his desk, observing Ted as he spoke.

"You are positive this is the only thing in writing that we have, nothing on email?"

"Yes," nodded Ted.

"Good – good." McCarthy leaned back in his chair.

"Are you able to antedate a document?"

Ted gave a small gasp of panic as the impact of what was asked of him registered.

"Yes, it can be done but—" faltered Ted.

"This is not the time to show lack of guts, I reward guts as you know. Ted, shall I ask someone else to help?"

"Well, I suppose the conclusions of the report were not final and we still were discussing I mean, although, of course Henry was the clear favourite and—"

"Ted!" interrupted McCarthy. "Do you think I give a shit about who thought what? I want the right conclusions to have been reached at the right time. Can you deal with it, yes or no?"

"The committee will remember …"

"Are you running this committee Ted?"

Ted nodded.

"Good. Then IT will remember what is good for IT and what you tell IT to remember, right? What do you think the proposed appointment of a murderer will do to our share price?"

"Henry has not yet been—" Ted had no time to finish his sentence. McCarthy was already reaching for the phone.

"I'll speak to Archie, he can take over."

"I could alter the document in that way," said Ted hastily throwing one hand towards McCarthy as if to stop him short.

There was no reply from McCarthy, his hand was still in mid-air.

"I will alter the document in that way."

Ted had spoken slowly.

"Let me know when it's done."

Ted was looking down and McCarthy knew his hesitation. Ted was thinking about Henry who had been a good friend, thinking about the task ahead, thinking that any other course of action would mean the end of his career.

A slap on the desk brought Ted back in an instant and McCarthy met Ted's scared look with the cold gaze of his faded grey eyes.

Ted stood up and left the room without a word.

* * *

As Ted was walking out of McCarthy's office, Henry was contemplating his next move. He was allowed to call his lawyer and had been left on his own to do so. He took out of his jeans' pocket a scrap of paper on which was written Harold Wooster's number. Henry reached for the phone and dialled slowly, making sure he composed the number correctly.

A male voice answered promptly.

"Harold Wooster's chambers, may I help you?"

To his surprise, Henry felt embarrassed.

"Hello," said the voice with impatience.

"Yes, may I speak to Wooster QC please? My name is Henry Crowne. He is expecting my call."

There was a short silence.

"I very much doubt that is the case, sir."

"Well, Wooster QC may be very busy but I have a personal introduction from Pamela Anderson of Chase and Case," replied Henry, irritated.

"Are you certain?" insisted the voice.

"Absolutely," Henry was about to lash out when a terrible thought entered his mind. He broke into a sweat. The words that came next hardly surprised him.

"I am indeed surprised that Ms Anderson" (the voice trailed slightly on the name) "would have managed to reach him. Wooster QC is currently on a sabbatical. He will not be back until next year."

"Who are you?" were the only words that managed to escape Henry's blank mind.

"Harry Lewis-Cooper, his clerk."

Numbness overcame Henry as he dropped the phone down on the table, a small tremor coursed through his body – unbearable panic, then an explosion, a wave of raw anger carried him across the room. He slapped his hand so hard against the wall that his entire body shook. How stupid had he been, the great Henry Crowne, the number one negotiator, fucked – fucked like a beginner.

A distant voice was calling, "Hello? Hello?"

He walked back to the table and slammed down the receiver with hatred.

Ms Anderson had been too busy to make the call or was it that she had not wanted to make the call? Henry's rage had to abate before he could think straight. There was little time left. Pole would soon walk through the door, asking for confirmation of who the lawyer was. Henry felt pain cutting through him, he would look moronic, ridiculous, a joke.

Henry closed his eyes. He forced himself to breathe, to regain some stillness in which he could think outside the predictable pattern; friends and estimated colleagues would have vanished by now.

Henry opened his eyes. Picking up the phone once more, he started dialling.

Chapter Eight

Henry was waiting for Nancy to answer the phone. It had rung five times and he suddenly wondered why he had dialled his neighbour's number. He was about to hang up when Nancy answered in her warm yet firm voice, happily surprised to hear from him.

Henry wondered, she was rumoured to have been a first-class QC, but their last encounter had put a dampener on this image.

"Nancy, I am not around. I was wondering whether you could check on the flat for me?" said Henry.

"Of course. Tell me what you need me to do. By the way, I am horribly nosy. It's my old profession, you see. I hope you won't mind me asking where your travels have taken you."

"Ah." Henry marked a pause.

If he had had a coin he would have probably tossed it: heads a lie, tails the truth.

"Scotland Yard, small dingy interrogation room."

It would have been tails.

"How uncomfortable," replied Nancy unfazed. "Tell me what needs doing but first let me grab pen and paper."

Henry did not have time to reply before the phone went quiet. He remembered that Nancy had purchased an old fashioned 1930s telephone which she was using in her lounge.

Henry hesitated. He did not know her that well and yet he had made the impulsive decision to rely on her to find a defence lawyer in what was rapidly becoming a turning point in his life.

"Actually Nancy, I may need a bit more than just help with the flat."

"Are you referring to my previous expertise as Queen's Counsel," she said, in amusement.

A door had opened, Henry rushed headlong through it. He summarised as best he could the events of the day.

"I am on my way. You do not say or do anything until I have arrived," ordered Nancy.

"I certainly won't," replied Henry, hoping his voice did not betray his gratefulness.

"These bad boys never change."

As the phone went dead Henry wondered whether he had heard the last remark correctly. He managed a smile, she would be an unusual ally.

* * *

James was speaking to one of the option traders when Ted entered the trading floor. Ted rushed into his office and closed the door. He looked pale even from afar. James hovered, speaking to some of the people he knew well. Everyone had a story to tell, the market was diabolical. Ted left his office again and walked quickly towards the gents. James suspected that Ted's rush had little to do with a bad curry but rather a discussion with McCarthy. After all, James had been part of the Intelligence Corps during his stint in the army. He had learned to read the signs. Ted's PA had just disappeared with a wad of documents, James noticed. She would be busy for a while. There was an opportunity.

James dialled his PA's mobile. "Morag, I am sending you a text." Morag knew the drill, a text when James was only a few paces away meant something important was afoot.

Create a diversion for Ted, I need five minutes after he gets out of the gents. Text me when he is on his way.

Morag stood up and James knew she had understood.

James casually entered Ted's office and closed the blinds of its bay window. He moved swiftly to Ted's desk. He was in luck – the PC had not yet gone into sleep mode. Ted's working documents were open for scrutiny.

James shook his head. *What a cretin.* He sat down and inspected the files. Ted was working on the P&L reports of Henry's team but also and more surprisingly Albert's.

"Motherfucker. What the hell are you up to?" murmured James.

James had worked on the P&L figures with Henry. He knew them by heart. He would spot any changes. Yet, the task of amending these papers was not straightforward. Part of the text in the report had to be modified but more importantly so had the figures. Such a change would be more problematic. The final numbers referring to the P&L of the Crowne and Albert teams came from data prepared by the finance departments of their respective banks. James flicked through the screens and consulted his watch, only three minutes to go. Audited figures of the past years were difficult, if not impossible, to amend.

"Bastard. You're going to change the current year and projected figures aren't you? Much easier than the audited," exclaimed James.

Only two minutes to go. James pressed the print button and paper started to spew out of the printer in Ted's office. He was about to get up when he spotted a yellow Post-it. *Andy Todd from Scotland Yard asking for you, it's about who you know.* Henry? Was Ted truly about to commit the unthinkable?

Only one minute to go. His mobile flashed – a message from Morag. He grabbed the documents on the printer, stuffed them into his shirt, opened the blinds again and got out. Everybody was too busy salvaging their job to have noticed him.

James walked back with no rush to his desk.

"Well done," he said to Morag. She simply smiled. Ted had entered his office and closed the door. James waited a few more minutes before disappearing into Henry's office. He needed to take a look at Ted's reworked numbers. The police were looking at gathering evidence, anything that could provide a motive. James pondered on what this all meant. *Ted is working under orders, McCarthy's? ... Got to be.*

But how could he get away with such falsification? Once the documents had been sent to the police there was no turning back.

James concentrated on what was lying on the desk in front of him.

The first document showed deliberations about the merit of both candidates, the profile of the teams together with previous, current and projected income figures. The second document showed tables of figures and had been used to feed into the first one. These documents were sensitive, disclosing insider information. They were kept in a separate drive, which only a small number of people had access to, including Ted and the other four senior members of the integration committee.

"So, Ted has been granted the IT privilege to go into Henry's drive as well as Anthony Albert's," muttered James, incredulous. *"This is bloody unbelievable."*

Ted would have to open the original documents and make the required changes without arousing suspicion.

"But the system logs any amendments made with names, dates and time of changes. The log would therefore show that Ted, had made some modifications. It would not show where. Mmmm. Maybe the little arsehole has not thought about that." This cheered up James until he noticed a note left at the end of the document.

Documents printed and sent to Scotland Yard re Henry Crowne enquiry.

"Shit, shit," said James through greeted teeth. *"Ted has left a note on the docs so that people think he has only sent them but not amended them."* A very valid move if questions were asked as to why he opened these reports. All Ted had to do was to make the modifications of text and figures after he had called Scotland Yard and all would look above board.

Henry's face, laughing at one of Ted's jokes, flashed in front of James. He flicked through the documents again. A sudden urge to go in and savage the little git grabbed James, but no.

You want to play with the big boys, fine. Let's see how far you go. James took out the USB key that never left his trouser pocket. Opened the relevant original files and saved them onto it. He would disclose these when the time had come. Revenge was a dish best served cold.

***

Cindy knocked at the door of McCarthy's office and entered without waiting for a reply. She had a way of banging on the door which meant matters were urgent. David Cooper-James, CEO of HXBK, had called again. Cindy had gained time by inventing a call from Whitehall but it wouldn't be long until he called back.

McCarthy smiled, revealing that he had been a handsome man, before the City had claimed its price.

"Well done, the pompous arsehole must have been impressed. I am ready to talk to him, wait another half hour and call him back and don't make it easy to find a slot."

McCarthy was preparing his strategy and indeed would make a call to his contact at Whitehall. He left his office and started towards the lift. The place was silent with activity. The floor was reserved for the members of the executive Board as well as their PAs. Most of them were in meetings frantically preparing for the imminent takeover. DMac took the elevator to floor four, which was dedicated to Mergers & Acquisitions. He needed to find a meeting room the phone lines of which would not be recorded as was the case on the trading floor. He also did not want to leave a trace – dialling from his office or his mobile was out of the question. He turned the corner, ignoring the glances from a couple of employees who recognised him. One of the rooms was empty. He dashed in, pulled the blinds shut and flicked the sign to *occupied* on the door. McCarthy looked at his watch, it was 11am. Exactly the right time to call his contact for an update. He swiftly dialled the number he knew by heart.

"Douglas," exclaimed a voice. "How timely of you to call, I believe we must catch up."

"I could not agree more," replied McCarthy.

"Well, how about this evening at the club? There will be a couple of people joining us, Timothy from the Treasury and Edwina from the Bank of England. Shall we say 6.30?"

"Very well, I will see you there."

"Good, good. Oh, by the way, since I have you on the phone, do you need anything done on the slight issue you are facing at the moment? Such an unfortunate affair."

"Crowne – it is under control, at least so far, but we need to discuss some of the ramifications."

"Certainly, I'll make sure we have time."

McCarthy walked back to his office by the back door, climbing four flights of stairs without taking a break and finding that his stamina was still very much with him. He was now ready for a particularly demanding task, a meeting with his rival, the CEO of HXBK.

* * *

Henry had sent a short text to James twenty-four hours ago, asking him to *look after the shop*. Since then nothing.

Unusual, worryingly so.

James noticed Ted coming back from the executive floor where McCarthy sat. He must have been reporting to McCarthy that the task of amending the P&L had been completed. James still found it hard to believe but the evidence was there, securely locked in his desk.

The words of Gordon Gekko in *Wall Street* still rang true after all these years: *"If you need a friend, get a dog"*. A pitbull would have been better than a friend like Ted.

James was right. It was war. It was war every day, without the much-needed camaraderie expected between brothers-in-arms. James' experience of the army was that of harshness and bullying. He felt these were just as present in the banking world if only more subtly evident. The City was feudal. People formed clans, allegiances, in order to protect their positions; a small cluster of people looking after each other's interests, come what may. It was not unusual for these clans to move together. The leader of a team would be headhunted and would inevitably, either immediately or over time, bring across his own people. This generated seismic shock waves for the unfortunate employees whose boss might have been replaced. Some survived, most didn't. Everyone in the square mile would have a view on the amount of money that might have been paid to move the new team. Numbers would be running high, reaching in some cases into tens of millions of dollars. Would the team work in their new environment?

90

The gossip would carry on for months. Despite wanting to establish its reputation as a place of strong intellect, the City was a place of tawdry gossip where reputations and abilities were constantly trashed by competitors who sought to undermine their adversaries at every possible opportunity.

James tried Henry's BlackBerry one more time. He was sitting in Henry's office, playing with his pen, swinging it across the back of his hand, round his thumb and catching it again before it fell. A trick he had learned from his boss, he smiled at the thought. James lifted his head. Someone was watching him. Matt had been observing him and stood up abruptly to mask his distraction. Lack of information was quickly destabilising the group. The usual banter had stopped and people had become unexpectedly quiet, even guarded. Morag herself, Henry's PA, who took no prisoners when it came to nonsense was subdued. Henry needed to be back soon, or at least to communicate. Henry had to know that the team would not hold together for much longer, and as importantly he needed to know about the P&L but Henry's BlackBerry rang engaged, the mailbox was full.

Chapter Nine

Nancy had not bothered to change when she arrived at Scotland Yard. She was still wearing her old faded jeans and gardening T-shirt as she walked into the interrogation room. Henry had not been expecting her in person. He had wanted a professional reference. Both men looked at each other in disbelief. Pole could hardly contain his amusement, whereas Henry looked momentarily horrified.

"I believe you intend to interrogate my client again," said Nancy without greeting Henry.

"That is the idea," replied Pole.

"May I remind you, Inspector, that you started questioning my client twenty-four hours ago and collected him from his flat ten hours ago, without proper representation."

"Your client, Ms Wu, was very willing."

"Understood," said Nancy lifting her hand to stop Pole continuing. "But unless you can show more than circumstantial evidence, my client and I will be leaving you to your conjecture."

"Are you still practising, Ms Wu?" said Pole squaring up for an argument.

"Sir, I have done enough criminal law in my time to know what I can and can't do. To answer your question, yes, I still belong to chambers." This was not exactly an answer but it would do for the time being. "I need some time with my client, now, if you will."

Pole had not expected anything less from a decent barrister. He and Nurani withdrew, leaving Henry and Nancy alone in the room.

"Don't worry," she said, laying her hand on Henry's shoulder in an appeasing fashion. "I will find someone for you. What matters, now, is that you say nothing and you get out of here."

Henry shook his head, uttering a relieved, "Thank you."

* * *

"So, Andy, ready for your big conf call?" said Pole.

"Yes Boss, ready to go."

"OK, put us on the loudspeaker. I won't say anything but will be there in case you need me."

Andy grinned and released the mute button.

"GL, Ted Barnes' office."

"This is Andy Todd from Scotland Yard, he is expecting my call." If there was to be no courtesy, Andy was going along with it. Pole was impressed.

"Mr Barnes, Andy Todd. Many thanks for sending me the information I requested. I have a few questions if I may." Pole gave Andy the thumbs up.

"Certainly, Andy, shoot," replied Ted.

Pole narrowed his eyes. His face said it all, this conceited little git was too clever for his own good. Young Andy gave him a nod. Ted's elation did not last long. Young Andy started to ask searching questions, on the process of integration, the documents required, the people involved, demonstrating that he had been well trained in the art of extracting information. Pole pressed the mute button whilst Ted was trying to answer as best he could.

"Make him feel like the interrogation room is around the corner."

Andy depressed mute.

"Mr Barnes, I am still a little confused on processes. Surely you can't arrive at these conclusions without consulting the heads of team and yet it seems neither Mr Crowne nor Mr Albert have been heard. Maybe you should come to our offices and we could discuss this more extensively."

Pole mouthed *Brilliant* without a sound. Andy was on a roll.

"No, no. No need," blurted Ted. "Why don't I send you some more docs and you can decide whether this is what you are looking for?"

"Good idea, it will save us both time, for now."

Pole had detected Ted's uneasiness. He was fearful.

"You realise I will have to run all this past my 'gators," said Ted trying to assert himself by mentioning GL's legal team of litigators.

"Of course, I have cleared this call with them already, but be my guest."

Young Andy scored another point as Ted had not asked whether Andy had cleared it, before speaking to him. Pole signalled to Andy to hang up. He did with minimal courtesy.

"Well done, Andy. This guy is not telling us all he knows."

"And he is scared out of his wits. I'll chase him in a few hours. Can't let him think I don't mean business."

"You mean business all right, keep up the pressure," said Pole, with a kind shake of Andy's shoulder.

* * *

James had been observing Ted's moves in and out of his office. Ted had come back and yet again promptly closed the door of his office behind him. James thought about the defrauded P&L. But now was not the time to give Ted a bloody nose, further intel gathering was needed. By now Henry's future must have been discussed extensively and the revised number would not help. James walked decisively across the floor and knocked at the glass partitioning of Ted's office. Ted jumped and looked up.

"Hey Ted, what's up?" said James as he opened Ted's office door.

"Busy, good. You know …"

"I was wondering whether you'd heard from Henry. Can't get hold of him."

"What do you mean?" demanded Ted abruptly, fidgeting with his Montblanc pen.

"Nothing more than that Ted. I can't get hold of him."

James had sat himself in front of Ted's desk in one of the leather chairs, attitude relaxed and mind alert.

"Well, I haven't either, sorry but I've got tons to do, you know." Ted gestured vaguely.

"Sure, sure. Well, if you hear anything let me know. How is the integration committee going anyway?" asked James boldly.

"What do you mean? I can't talk about it as you well know," said Ted with disdain.

"Of course, you can't give the specifics but surely an indication. Our P&L results have been bloody good despite the crisis," said James.

"What? What do you mean? How do you know?" replied Ted, on the verge of losing his cool. James had scored better than he thought.

"No worries," replied James as he slowly stood up.

James took his time to leave his office. He stopped to chat with one of the traders, a burly chap with a large paunch – a little too much beer with the lads. James kept looking in the direction of Ted's office. Ted was speaking to his PA, no doubt instructing her to let no one in before closing his door again. James had seen fear in men's eyes so many times; Ted was terrified.

Henry was in deep trouble and the firm was about to cut him loose. James pondered over the expression 'cutting loose', a mountaineering term, the last man on the rope may have to be cut loose if his weight became a danger to the team of climbers above. An extreme act of last resort in the close-knit community of climbers, alas a technique frequently used in banking and Henry was its latest victim.

* * *

Nancy and Henry were alone. She was sitting opposite him, her dark brown eyes resting on him with a sense of calm and something Henry had not felt for a long time.

Kindness.

"So, Nancy what is the game plan?"

"As I said, you need to get out of here first, then we decide on strategy. We'll discuss it in the privacy of my pad."

Henry liked her voice. It was smooth and yet authoritative. Henry wanted to ask her the question that was burning on his lips when Pole entered the room. Pole's face was closed to scrutiny, his voice neutral.

"I am prepared to release you on one condition. You must surrender your passports."

What? Henry's reaction was one of anger at the thought of giving up his freedom. What if a client needed him? He was about to protest but Nancy read his mood.

"My client accepts your conditions, Inspector."

"I do not," burst Henry.

Nancy stopped his sentence short with a sharp move of her hand and a glare that cut him to the quick.

"Yes, you do," she replied.

Pole left the room to prepare the documents. Henry turned towards Nancy, his chair screeching on the floor, his body leaning half way across the table..

"What the fuck is the matter with you?"

Henry blushed for the first time in a long time as he realised he had insulted his neighbour, a woman he hardly knew, and more importantly someone he needed to rely on. Nancy paused before replying with a mixture of humour and implacable determination.

"This is no longer the trading floor, my dear fellow. You do not make the rules. I do. And I know this will be mighty hard, but you do not swear at me either."

"But my passports? What if I have to see a client urgently," replied Henry without conviction.

"I doubt you will be let near a client in the next couple of days. Don't you think?"

"Why the hell not?"

"Because YOU are involved in a murder investigation, Henry. GL will have taken notice of this somehow. Don't you think? And so will your clients."

Henry stood up but Nancy had not moved.

"You won't be allowed outside the country. Get used to the idea."

Henry gave a conceding grunt.

"Good, this is your get-out-of-jail card. We play it and we move on."

Henry felt reassured by the 'we'. His experience in the City had taught him to detect lack of substance. Nancy had plenty of firepower and he liked that.

Nancy looked at her Chanel watch and stood up. Henry raised a quizzical eyebrow.

"The papers are ready," she said.

Henry looked towards the door, doubtful. The door opened. The papers were indeed ready.

* * *

An hour before, Dolores Patten had taken a phone call that could change everything.

Jon, need an urgent chat with you, a significant development in the Crowne–Albert affair, read the text to Pole.

Dolores was working at profiling Henry from what she had so far seen but Pole knew it would take time before she could deliver her findings. It had to be something else, something major. Dolores was not the sort to get him out of an interrogation with a prime suspect for nothing.

Chapter Ten

Pole had left Nancy and Henry. He had swiftly turned towards Dolores' office after receiving her text. Pole saw her in the distance waving at him. Her face, which usually reflected calm and composure, was concerned.

"I know you are keen to go back but I truly need to speak to you," she turned towards her office and sensing Pole's hesitation looked back at him.

"It's urgent."

He followed her. She gathered notes scattered on her desk, Pole perched himself on a side desk that leaned against the wall, his preferred spot when speaking to Dolores.

"I just had a long conversation with Anastasia Albert, very disturbing."

Pole frowned.

"You mean Albert's daughter?"

"Yes, I do. I have taken a copious amount of notes, we can discuss this later but in a nutshell she believes her mother is responsible for her father's death."

"Are you serious?"

"Absolutely, it was a very distressing call. She managed to speak despite the tears. A courageous little girl."

A heavy silence settled. Pole took a deep breath and let his head lean against the wall behind him, closing his eyes.

"Is this credible or is she overreacting to his death?"

"I can say two things for sure. She knows this is a murder case. She is absolutely convinced her mother is involved, bear in mind she is only eight years of age." Dolores stopped again. "She has also had, in my opinion, a traumatic childhood that leads her to think this."

Dolores looked at Pole. He tugged at his goatee.

"I am listening," said Pole and jumped from his perched position, to sit in a chair in front of Dolores.

The situation was grave enough that he owed it his full attention.

Dolores explained the details of the conversation. Mrs Albert had, according to her daughter, a lover who sometimes visited when her father was away but whom she also visited often, leaving Anastasia and her brother alone, terrified. The details given by Anastasia were far too vivid to come from her imagination. When Dolores asked tactfully how she was getting on with her mother the little girl erupted. She had had to grow up too fast, pushed by the demands of overzealous parents, who wanted her to be what they had never been and more importantly could never be. Dolores stopped for a short while, allowing Pole to take the information in. She had worked with him long enough to know that cases involving children always disturbed him.

He stood up and moved a few files on her desk, then sat down again.

"So, you think that there is enough content in this little girl's call to investigate?"

Pole knew the answer but braced himself for the reply.

"Yes, Jon, I do. This is not only the trauma of a major loss speaking here."

"Don't go anywhere please. I know you are on half day but I need to dispatch Crowne first. This latest development forces my hand. I'll be quick."

Pole found Nurani and Andy processing fresh data and keen to share their findings. Pole interrupted his two assistants courteously but unequivocally.

"Yes, I will need to review them with you but before we do this could you please prepare the documents for Crowne's release."

Nurani and Andy exchanged a glance of disbelief. Henry was getting away.

Whilst his team was following the release procedure, Pole went back to Dolores' office. She was reading her notes again, making some additions here and there, ensuring that nothing of her conversation was lost. Pole had not bothered to knock at the door and Dolores did not mind. She lifted her face and shook her head.

"There is a lot in this conversation. We are looking at some serious psychological abuse I fear."

"How old is Anastasia again?" asked Pole.

"She is eight." Dolores clasped her hands underneath her desk and leaned forward. "The procedure for interviewing minors is very rigorous, I will have to talk to social services. Her mother is no longer fit to be the adult present at her interview I fear."

"How can this happen in an environment that is so privileged?" said Pole. "I know it shouldn't surprise me but after all these years it still does."

Dolores smiled at him.

"That's why you still do your job so well after all these years, Jon. You still care about the human soul."

Pole coughed, not knowing how to react to this compliment.

"Anyway, to answer your question. I can think of many reasons unfortunately. A powerful combination of mankind's worst features, greed, vanity, devouring ambition, you know these as well as I do. You keep up with colleagues," Dolores said, "the neighbours, you move up and up and you become so obsessed by it to the point where you fail to ask yourself the real questions, dead to the values that should really matter."

Dolores lifted her face towards Pole. Her dark eyes resting on him, her head tilted so that her mass of heavy dark locks fell to one side. Pole had never asked her why she had chosen the job.

"I also presume that no one in their environment would have noticed anything."

"Unfortunately, it is hard to be honest with yourself. The pressure of what others will think, the need to comply and be accepted. This means not allowing for signs of dissent to appear as much as possible."

"When are we going to get the OK to pay Mrs Albert a visit?" said Pole deliberately moving back to the case.

"I need to follow procedure, call social services. You know the drill. I will do this now. We won't get an answer until tomorrow morning but I don't think the little one is in immediate danger."

"Your call, Dee."

Dolores nodded and started ringing her contacts.

* * *

Henry shivered in the open air when he stepped outside Scotland Yard. Nancy had wrapped a bright orange pashmina around her shoulders, it barely sheltered her from the cold October wind. Her walk was alert – a woman at ease with herself. Henry slowed down and let her move a few paces ahead. He could not quite believe his present situation; the prominent City banker, walking out of the Yard, accompanied by a retired QC who just secured his release, albeit without a passport.

"I'd laugh at the situation, if it weren't mine," said Henry.

"Humour is a powerful tool, don't lose it just yet."

She grabbed his arm and pushed him into the cab she had just hailed.

"Yes, Mum."

Henry grinned at the familiarity he had just displayed to someone he still considered a perfect stranger. Nancy smiled in return and gave their address to the cabbie.

They rode home in silence. Henry was enjoying his freedom. He had thought he would feel exhausted after his lengthy interrogation but he only felt joy. He was free. What mattered, he discovered, was the moment. The cab took a wrong turn, it was going to take longer to get home. Henry would have normally jumped at the cab driver and got him to change his route; not today. He swallowed what would have been a heated argument. It was of very little importance, after all.

Henry took in the scenery. He *saw* the embankment for the first time in years, admired the square clock of the Savoy Tower, spotted King's College disappearing on his right as they went through Aldwych. It felt good simply to be alive and able to take it all in, not needing to block out all that was happening around him, always projecting towards the next meeting, the next deal to close, the next battle to win.

* * *

Nancy pulled a yellow pad out of her orange rucksack and started writing. An old habit from her lawyer's days she had never lost. She took notes on everything and arranged them in folders fastidiously organised in her office. Her note-taking method was renowned in the profession. She captured the words of course but also the minor details she observed, those that made all the difference. Communication of vital importance was always the non-verbal she had observed.

Henry dropped his guard as soon as he entered the cab. His body was relaxed, slightly slumped in the corner of the back seat and his attention focused on the magnificent spectacle that constituted the building outline along the Thames. Nancy gave Henry a side glance. Without knowing yet why, she felt sympathy for him. She trusted her instinct as to Henry's character but also knew something personal was afoot. *The Raft of the Medusa* had told her so.

Vivid images of Paris materialised. The original painting hanging at The Louvre, then The Sorbonne Law School final year results. The students smoking *Gauloises sans filtre*, terrible taste but so trendy among her left-wing friends. She was part of that community that rebelled. She had escaped communist China with her parents at the time of the Cultural Revolution and felt welcome amongst *la gauche française*. The young woman standing in front of the panels with all her friends had undergone such transformation. Nancy wondered whether it could have been different.

The cabbie used his horn and swore at a cyclist. Nancy's past evaporated as quickly as it had surfaced. She went back to her pad. Henry had not moved, still savouring his release. Nancy read what she had jotted down and added one final comment.

Check Jonathan Pole, know the name.

As they were approaching home, Henry noticed that Nancy was looking at him with an amused smile.

"Freedom is good, *n'est-ce pas?*" she whispered.

Henry nodded. Nancy exuded an unusual mix of confidence and empathy. Henry could never trust easily but today he seemed more at ease with her than any of the numerous friends he had in the City.

103

Nancy had stopped writing and relaxed in silence. Time for an in-depth conversation would come later. She let Henry enjoy a few moments of peace. The hard work was still in front of them.

* * *

McCarthy walked out of the building and jumped into a cab. He enjoyed these few moments of complete anonymity away from the well-orchestrated timetable that Cindy laid out in front of him every day; the penance of a CEO he often said. He enjoyed meeting with the UK political elite. Unlike their American counterparts, the British still had a sense of decorum and cultivated the cosiness of exclusive gentlemen's clubs. By some quirky twist of the law, the Club that McCarthy visited was still reserved for gentlemen only, something that he approved of wholeheartedly.

His taxi turned into St James's and stopped at the corner of Jermyn Street. He would walk the last few yards on foot, as was customary. McCarthy left the cab driver with a reasonable tip. He did not want to be remembered either for tipping too much or too little. He disappeared down a small passageway. The door of the club was open and the small plump doorman, who was waiting at the entrance, recognised him. With a short nod of the head and the customary *Good evening sir*, he ushered him into the club's lobby. McCarthy was led through a series of rooms where gentlemen sat in small comfortable meetings. He finally reached a corner of one of the smoking rooms and was left to settle. McCarthy was a tad early. He pursed his lips, a fault in protocol. He knew his contact well enough though to avoid playing games about timing.

At 6.30 on the dot McCarthy's contact entered the room and came to sit opposite him in one of the deep leather armchairs.

"My dear Douglas, I hope I have not kept you waiting long."

McCarthy stood up rapidly and, with a grin, extended a short energetic hand.

"I've just arrived."

"Good, good," the other man said. He turned towards the waiter and then McCarthy.

"The usual I presume?"

"Yes please." McCarthy felt a slight pinch of pride that his contact remembered his taste in beverage.

"Two Glenfiddichs, as they come, Martin, thank you." The man settled comfortably into his chair and joined his hands in front of him, fingertips touching.

"So, Douglas, where is this market going?" asked the slender gentleman without any further niceties. "We entered the subprime crisis nearly a year ago now. There are some signs of optimism which I don't believe will last. How bad is the housing market in the US? You are the expert." He gestured with deferral at McCarthy.

McCarthy pushed his stocky body into the chair and considered his answer. There was no point in trying to sell William bullshit. He had been in government for far too long not to recognise the smell of it.

"Yes, it is going to get a lot worse. We are only at the beginning I am afraid," McCarthy paused.

"And? I feel there is an 'and'."

"And GL has already incurred a heavy loss," said McCarthy clearing his voice.

"So you invested in that market too? Billions?"

McCarthy nodded.

"Tell me more about Collaterised Debt Obligations," William asked.

"They are instruments that use mortgages as investments."

"Like subprime?"

"Correct, but they have tranches of risk." McCarthy replied.

"And you believe that the rating agencies have verified each investment that goes in there. There must be thousands?"

"I am – not sure," said McCarthy promptly taking another mouthful of whisky.

"I see. But GL is the master of the CDO business, right? Any risks of contamination to the UK?"

"Quite possibly, in fact almost certainly. US CDOs sold to UK investors and of course you, in the UK, have your own subprime market!" replied McCarthy almost defiant.

"Mmmm, thought so. Timing is obviously appalling for the Labour Party. Gordon will not survive this crisis but then again a change in the governing party after twelve years is overdue."

"Are you not worried?" asked McCarthy dubious at this even-keeled response.

"No, I am the glue that keeps all governments together," said the man with a distant smile and a spark of humour in his eyes.

"I see." McCarthy paused for a moment before deciding to be unequivocally frank.

"To continue on the subject of subprime," said McCarthy. "We are going to see a spectacular collapse at the lower end of the market very soon, certainly before the end of the year. I don't think the banks know exactly how bad their inventories of subprime products look yet."

McCarthy paused, took another mouthful of whisky.

"Hell, I don't understand some of it myself, CDO squared, CDO cubed," he uncomfortably volunteered.

"Neither do we," the man replied after an equally lengthy pause. "As you know, a number of economists during the Blair era warned us of the impending crisis. The mortgage rates were too low, the level of borrowings too high, etc. John was quite vocal about it but then who in government would volunteer to stop the fun? Gordon got into a world of his own. Intellectual arrogance and stubbornness are unfortunately the main character traits of successful politicians. We received a number of reports from the Bank of England that were sounding caution. Of course, no one had the appetite to do anything about it."

"What about the FSA?" ventured McCarthy.

"Come, come, Douglas, buffoons as you well know yourself. Most of them have a salary one tenth the size of the salary of those they seek to regulate. A farce really."

McCarthy smiled.

"I am aware."

His contact reciprocated the smile.

"The difficult thing here is that all of us are to blame, including the public, but who will be frank or crazy enough to tell the story? It is much easier to concentrate on the obscene amount of money made by the banks."

McCarthy was about to protest when his contact raised a hand.

"I know you don't want to hear this but how many people earn $10m bonuses? Not even the president of the United States, and yes you are going to tell me you work terribly hard, but then again so does he. The banks have been irresponsible but then so have we and so have the regulators. We all know that bankers are bad boys! What the government is not doing is acknowledging the snowball effect of it all."

"The public was equally quite happy to consume without checking whether they were doing so above their means. And the regulators content with mortgages exceeding by a ridiculous amount the value of property."

"True enough but here again Douglas, when you earn £20,000 a year, have to feed a family and want to provide a roof over their heads, I can sympathise," said the other man with some feeling. "How many billions will it take?"

"By the time we have finished probably over one trillion."

McCarthy's Whitehall contact stared at him for a few seconds. McCarthy had created the effect he wanted to create. His contact was assessing the information. Was McCarthy bluffing? Was he implying that GL was too big to fail? Was he expecting some help with the takeover that would involve giving McCarthy support? McCarthy was not yet sure that any of these questions merited a yes but they might soon do.

"Some people are going to brandish the spectre of the Great Depression in front of us. My latest conversation with the Fed convinced me of it."

"I wouldn't be that dramatic," replied McCarthy. "But yes, the papers are going to have a field day."

"Murdoch is going to make even more money, how depressing. One trillion you say?"

"Yes, as far as I can tell from our own exposure, it may be more."

"Your bank is very long in this type of debt?"

"Enough to sink us, unless I can close the merger on time."

"Will you?"

"Definitely," said McCarthy putting his empty glass down. "As long as this story between Albert and Crowne does not derail the process, matters should proceed quickly."

"I expect you have the upper hand at the moment?"

"I have, but – and there is a *but* – " said McCarthy.

"You said there were some ramifications you wanted to discuss."

"As you can imagine very few of HXBK's top management will survive."

McCarthy's contact seemed unsurprised.

"I think it is cruelly ironic. But the combined structured product team would have gone eventually to Anthony Albert."

"That is truly surprising. Do I want or rather need to know the reason?"

"Albert was involved in a lot of subprime structuring. He sourced the majority of these loans and GL is on the other side. He knows or rather knew where some of the skeletons were buried. One of them is Northern Rock and you need to keep an eye on other UK banks too."

"I see," said the other man putting his near empty glass to his lips.

"I will do all I can to control matters at my end however ..." finished McCarthy.

"I need to do my bit – understood. Did Anthony Albert know too much?"

"It is no longer our problem, is it?" replied McCarthy.

"Northern Rock is only the beginning, good to know."

McCarthy said nothing, he had given enough. He felt it was his turn to be on the receiving end.

"Your views on the US elections? Obama? McCain?"

"Obama."

McCarthy did not comment. If he had his finger on the pulse of the financial market, his contact had his on the political arena.

"Timothy and Edwina will arrive in a minute," said McCarthy's contact. "Are you ready for a spot of dinner?"

"Most certainly, William," replied McCarthy.

The time for confidences was over.

Chapter Eleven

Nancy had insisted that Henry come to hers before retiring to his apartment. She needed to understand more about the background, more about Henry whom she knew too little before choosing the right QC. She had dashed into the kitchen to prepare a cup of tea, something the British presented as a remedy to all ills. She smiled. She was not all that British after all, but perhaps keen to feel she was, a good cup of tea was indeed needed.

Henry had nodded his approval and sunk his tall body into one of Nancy's comfortable armchairs. For the first time since he had met her, Henry was looking around. She owned the opposite penthouse to his and had already been there for a while when he moved in. Although Henry had visited her a couple of times, he had never bothered to pay much attention to her home, his mind always racing in another direction.

One of the walls exhibited a painted mural representing a stylised bamboo forest, a *camaieu* of greens (Henry remembered this French word with pride) that gave the room a clear sense of space. The mural had texture and an inviting depth, enough to make him want to wander through the exotic landscape. Henry's eyes moved slowly across the room, noticing the sofa's fabric in intense green, embroidered in various shades of the same colour; large and luscious tropical flowers were enticing birds of paradise to suck their nectar. The other walls were white, it should have been a severely minimalist room and yet it exuded a sense of peaceful welcome, a rich tranquillity. Nancy had arranged on opposite walls two massive paintings, two single canvases in shades of a single colour – white.

Henry smiled. Could it be, he wondered, Pollock? Rothko?

The small clunk of a tea tray interrupted his wandering gaze. Nancy sat down on the same sofa and began pouring the tea.

"I know you need a rest and that you have already spoken at length about the story but I need to form my own opinion. You understand?" she said whilst handing over a cup.

Henry bent to grab his tea, took a sip. He drank his tea very hot just as his mother did.

"I understand," his voice had regained its composure.

"Good, now before you give me the details of what has or has not happened, I need to know more about your connection with the O'Connor brothers."

Such a bold question showed Henry unequivocally why Nancy had been a brilliant barrister. She had within minutes identified where the weakest point of his defence lay. Then again, Henry felt that he should not make it so easy for her. After all, he was out and his instinct told him that Pole had another lead. Henry had so far played his hand rather smartly. And why had Nancy agreed to help him so readily? Nothing was ever given for free in his world.

"Is this relevant?" He sipped again at his tea.

Nancy stopped him taking another sip with a kind but uncompromising gesture.

"Henry, you are out and you feel the pressure is off and maybe you are right, but if you are not, trust me, you need to work at your defence, and right away."

She paused as if she could sense his anger rising.

"I know," she carried on. "You are tired, you are used to being in control, and you may not be willing to speak to someone who is not bound by the conventional client-lawyer confidentiality."

"People do not make decisions for me," said Henry.

"It goes without saying. However, you need to decide right now whether you trust me and, if so, please, give me some credit for my knowledge of mounting a defence."

110

Henry leaned back into the sofa and studied Nancy. She let him.

"I don't trust people easily."

"That comes with the territory. You can't be working in the City and be a friendly, trusting sort of guy, agreed, but you are way beyond your everyday negotiation, Henry. I am sorry to have to break this to you so abruptly, but life will never be the same again. Not now, not ever."

"You have no idea where I come from and how much I am able to sustain."

"I know it takes a lot to have risen to pre-eminence as you have but let me repeat this, you MUST focus on the here and now."

"We are not going to have a philosophical debate."

"Henry, you have chosen to speak to me because you may not trust people but you trust your instinct. I know what I am talking about and you know I know."

Henry was silent, he suspected but he had hoped. When he had left Scotland Yard a few hours ago he had tasted freedom and it was sweet. He had felt safe again, as if it had all been a big mistake, a deal gone wrong that he had just managed to fix.

"Henry?"

He did not like to be pushed. No, he would not be pushed. Everything he knew about influencing, negotiating, manipulating, flooded back to him. He was a master at it, and practice at the game had made him perfect.

"I will fix this too, Nancy, mark my words."

"And when was the last time you spoke to your team?"

Nancy had done it again, gone straight to the point. Henry realised he had not spoken to his team for twenty-four hours. He had been completely engulfed by the events of the past day and by now GL would know about his interrogation. His team would not have seen him or heard from him for a ridiculously long amount of time by City standards. Nancy was right, his life was rapidly unravelling in front of his eyes. He put his cup down. He needed to make contact with his people urgently.

In an instant the comfort of Nancy's home became suffocating. Henry needed to escape this flat and its art. He wanted to rewind the tape of his life and forget about the stranger in front of him. Nancy's voice came as an irritation to him.

"You can call them if you like and in fact you should but I can assure you that, by now, you will have received a number of messages from Human Resources asking you to call them. I would be surprised if GL allows you to go back at all, Henry. At best they may allow you in for a clean transition but in the middle of a takeover–"

"A merger," interrupted Henry forcefully.

"You know I am right but please call, do whatever you need to do and when you are ready we can talk again but I say this to you: the more you delay the worse it will get."

She poured some more tea into his cup, an invitation to stay. Henry was torn. A part of him knew that she was right and yet the thought of losing his team, *his* team, was unbearable. He had reached his goal, he had earned respect, he could impose his ideas, his enemies feared him. He stood at the centre of his world, his will unchallenged, his mind in absolute focus. He had forgotten at long last what fear felt like.

Henry stood up and looked at Nancy. Despite the Asian skin, the difference in personality, she reminded him of his mother. It was the look in her eyes, the same expression of concern. Henry had not noticed he was still holding his tea. He bent forward to put the cup back in its saucer, reached for his BlackBerry in his jeans pocket. Looking finally at the screen, he saw that he had fifty-eight missed messages.

* * *

Pole had spent over two hours with Dolores going through the details of her telephone conversation with Albert's daughter. Although sceptical to start with, he now felt as sure as Dolores that this was a serious lead. Pole was still struggling with the prospect of having to conduct an interrogation on an eight-year-old girl. He was grateful that he had had to deal with very few cases involving children, thanking a God he did not believe in.

"When will we have the OK to," he paused, looking for the right words, "bring her in?"

"Tomorrow morning, at the latest," replied Dolores.

"Doesn't leave me a lot of time to prepare," muttered Pole half to himself.

"I know but we need to act quickly."

"I am not contesting that."

Dolores nodded. She knew he would be as tactful as he needed to be.

"I am here, remember."

Pole shook his head and left her office. He took a left turn and moved rapidly towards the open-plan area where his team was working.

"Nurani, any further info?"

"Yep, more in the direction you wanted us to look into."

"What precisely?" said Pole, irritated.

She hesitated, taken aback by Pole's uncharacteristic grumpiness.

"There is a man on the scene. I don't even think they have been that discreet to be honest, or not until more recently that is. The neighbours talk about him, as do AA's work colleagues, they all talk of a marriage on the rocks," said Nurani, placing a fist on her hip in a disapproving manner. "Some of these guys talk about a marriage on the rocks as if it were a drink."

"Compassion comes in short supply in the banking world."

"All that feels more like an acknowledged lover than a secret affair until a few months ago. Matters seem to have cooled down quite a lot or, at least, become less visible."

"And the gentleman is ...?" said Pole with a small elaborate movement of the hand, indicating he was expecting more.

"Brett Allner-Smith, works with Sotheby's. He is an antiques' dealer specialising in classical stuff." Nurani was a little vague, ill at ease in the arcane world of rare antiquities.

"He is not married, although divorced twice and has private wealth coming from his family, his mother more precisely. Got a picture, rather stuck up if you see what I mean."

"Any convictions? Divorce case ruled against him?"

"No convictions apart from the odd speeding ticket. Actually, he likes speeding apparently. He lost his licence a few years ago, and yes divorce ruled against him, naughty boy it seems, was conducting a number of affairs and eventually shacked up with another bird."

"The very technical terms the court was using too, I expect", said Pole amused.

Nurani pulled a face.

"Not quite. I am giving you the condensed version."

"In short you are telling me that Mrs Albert is having an affair with a philandering, speed-loving, rich-but-now-poor-because-of-his-two-divorces bloke who flogs antiques?"

"Eh, yep," replied Nurani, putting a pen to her mouth to suppress a grin.

"Interesting, interesting," said Pole. "How poor has he become?"

"Well, he now owns only one house in Belgravia," hesitated Nurani.

"All is relative, Nu, I have one house in Clapham and that is more than enough for me but …"

"If you have been used to being rich." Nurani was picking up on Pole's idea.

"It might be a tad hard to let go of the habit."

"Yep, very true." Nurani opened the file again. She usually could give Pole a complete and detailed account of events without any help, having committed it all to memory.

"He had a house in Exeter, mansion, sold to his half-brother, then he lost the house in Grasse, south of France, pretty exclusive."

"True, where perfumes are made. Lovely part of the world and unbelievably expensive too."

"… and a flat in New York – apparently he does a lot of business in the States, and," Nurani carried on leafing through the file, "… a fleet of sports cars, one Aston Martin DB9, one Bentley – no two Bentleys, Bentayga and Mulsanne, aaaand a little Porsche."

"This is getting more interesting by the minute," said Pole, moving from his chair to join Nurani and look at the file over her shoulder. "Do carry on."

"A collection of drawings by Leonardo da Vinci, a painting by Vermeer called *Woman seated at a Virginal.*"

Nurani kept reading from her notes.

"This is unbelievable." Pole stopped Nurani mid flow. "In fact, jaw-dropping."

Nurani stayed silent. The prices of the various items had been submitted as undisclosed and she was starting to understand why.

"I can see why someone losing all this might get tempted to do something really stupid to get back a fraction of what he owned." Pole could hardly believe it. "These pieces belong to a museum."

"Well, Jon, you have your wish. Yes, they do now. This guy Brett managed to lose everything."

Pole burst into roaring laughter.

"This is incredible," he repeated. "OK, we need to have a look at the will as soon as possible, including any recent changes made to it. We also need to know whether Mrs Albert was aware of its most recent content."

"The solicitor dealing with this will never let us see it before the formal opening date in front of the beneficiaries," said Nurani confidently.

"That is what you think, my dear," replied Pole, absorbed again in the pages in front of him, "and strictly speaking you are right of course. However, I don't need the text, I need a direction. I need the number of Albert's solicitors. Let's try to get a meeting today."

"Done. I'll call the solicitor straight away," replied Nurani. "And Jon?"

"Yes Ms Shah, I feel a burning question coming my way."

"How come you know so much about art?"

"Ah, yes, why would a copper like me know about these things? Well, believe it or not I was brought up in an artists' family, destined myself to become one of them."

"What happened? It must have been a hell of a shock when you told them."

"A story for another time," replied Pole ruffling his goatee.

The phone rang. Pole looked at the screen, it was Dolores' extension. She had an answer for him he might not like.

* * *

Henry was pacing up and down his lounge, impatiently listening to his voicemails. He had left Nancy's flat in a hurry, with a few mumbled words of thanks, preoccupied by the time he had already lost. The first message was from James Radlett. The familiar voice had pacified him. James was being his usual controlled, factual self but it was clear from his messages that matters were not looking good back at base.

He was longing to get back. If he could be there, he knew he would be able to control his team again. He would take the questions they had head on. They might give him a rough ride but he would handle it. Henry decided he would call James first. He needed to reconnect but also wanted to avoid hearing what he could not cope with, a message from HR. James mobile rang once.

"H, bloody hell. I have been trying to—"

"I know, Jamie, I know. Can't explain right now, just wanted to check how things are going with our star transaction?"

"Quite a few technical points to go through."

"Shoot," said Henry feeling the tiredness slip away from him. He was at his best problem solving. They discussed a number of complex points relating to pricing and structuring of an equity linked transaction. James would not want to discuss these with anyone else.

"We need to be cautious," emphasised Henry. "I want to avoid the usual feeding frenzy. You know the sort of crap that goes on with the closure of large transactions."

"And the other teams sticking their noses into our business. Pretending they are part of the deal to get credit. Yes, I know."

"Usual shit. And the traders have lost too much money not to try anything that will give them additional P&L," replied Henry.

"Agreed. H, we also need to speak about the team."

"What about it? Are they missing me?" asked Henry.

"Yep, in particular as they have not had anyone to sign their expenses."

"OK, let me guess now. Matt and Harriett have had a big ding-dong, actually no, by now they have had a number of ding-dongs."

"Yep."

"And Matt has been trying to behave as if he is the head of the team, correct?"

"Correct."

"But you showed him who was boss," continued Henry. *Nothing unpredictable there* he thought.

"Just the way you've showed me," replied James sounding amused. James regained composure for his next question "Have you spoken to Ted recently?"

"No, why would I want to do that?" replied Henry, the association between Ted's name and his team seeding unwanted thoughts.

But a persistent noise interrupted Henry. It was the voicemail reminding him that he had forty-five unanswered messages. Henry cut the conversation short. James was doing a good job holding the team together. Henry was ready for whatever GL would throw at him next.

Quite a few messages rolled through, all uneventful. In the absence of any major calls, Henry started to relax. He sensed the return of his confidence, stronger than before, further invigorated by his conversation with James. He looked at his watch and started calculating how much time it would take to shower, get dressed and take a cab to the office. Then the message from HR came through. The voice sounded impatient, it was someone he did not recognise, his old Human Resources' contact had resigned a few months back, dreading the aftermath of the credit crisis and the takeover.

"Mr Crowne, I am sure you are extremely busy."

What a bloody stupid thing to say.

"But could you please call me back."

And who the fuck is ME?

"It is, as you can imagine, incredibly urgent."

"I am not ignoring your call, you stupid bitch. I return calls within the hour, unless of course I am in the frigging nick."

Henry looked at his phone, he was furious at this lack of professionalism. And then he recognised the number of the off-boarding team. His anger erupted. He wanted someone to lash out at, someone he could defeat the old way, the only way he knew. His fists were clenched. He had not wanted to hit someone like this for many years and had forgotten what it felt like. He started screaming at his phone, obscenities, threats of retribution. The more vulgar and disgraceful, the more appropriate. He screamed until he felt his face distorting uncontrollably, a sharp pain surging in his chest. When he was done, he slowly sagged into his armchair, utterly empty. Anger would not get him out of this mess. His eyes fell on a wrapped parcel he had almost forgotten. *The Raft of the Medusa* sat against the wall. Despite the wrapping, the potency of its images flooded Henry's mind. The image of death and defeat made him queasy. He was exhausted, spent, an eerie calm came over him and for the first time since he was a kid, he felt like crying. He hid his face in his hands. The BlackBerry had dropped to the floor, still scrolling through the messages. Leaving it where it had fallen, he walked through his lounge, across the corridor and rang Nancy's doorbell.

Chapter Twelve

The two police cars carrying Pole and his team had parked in the middle of the street in front of Anthony Albert's Belgravia house. Dolores and another woman from social services shared one car, Pole and Ms Shah the other. Pole said little during the journey. He was concentrating on his delivery. His face turned to the car window, looking out at the rolling streets he did not see. His mind rehearsed once more what he would say to Adeila Albert, to control her, how he would speak to Anastasia, to reassure her. He would never be pushed in a direction he did not want to go, something his superior called lack of vision or at best stubbornness. Pole found that knowledge to be his strength. The understanding of his own limits, the one he wanted to surpass, the one he would never cross, gave him freedom.

Pole emerged from the car first. His team was waiting for his signal. He stood for a few seconds looking at the imposing yet elegant house. He moved swiftly to the front door and rang the bell. As he stood waiting, Pole thought he could hear music coming from inside the house in an attempt to cover the noise of two people screaming at each other. He rang the doorbell with insistence, ready to get one of his men to break the door down if necessary but the music stopped and a few seconds later the door opened. A dishevelled Mrs Albert stood in the doorway, wearing an expression of fury. Pole saw a slender silhouette flying up the stairwell behind.

"Mrs Albert, may we enter?" said Pole already pushing his way through.

"This is not a good time," replied Adeila Albert dryly.

"Whether it is or not, is irrelevant," said Pole. "We need to talk to you and your daughter."

"What is this nonsense about my daughter?" she replied, mad anger flashing in her eyes. "She is a very difficult child. Her father used to indulge her without restraint. Anthony never had any discipline."

Adeila was about to continue when she spotted Dolores and the woman from social services. Her face turned livid. She had been overheard and was desperate to give her side of the story first.

"This may be so Mrs Albert but we would like to speak to your daughter directly."

"I am her guardian and will decide whether or not you can speak to her," said Adeila Albert in a shrill voice.

"I am perfectly prepared to file for a search warrant and I have a protection order Mrs Albert. You no longer decide whether we speak to your daughter. I do."

Pole's calm determination sent shock waves around the room. Adeila Albert stepped toward Pole, ready to do battle, when a small child appeared in the doorway of the lounge in which all had gathered.

"I am here," said a young girl in a shaky but decisive voice.

Dolores moved forward gently and swiftly placed herself between mother and child.

"I am Dolores, we spoke on the phone."

The young girl nodded.

"Would you like to come with me?"

Dolores crouched in front of Anastasia, who was twisting a small hankie in her hands. She had been crying. The little girl nodded and Dolores softly took her by the hand. Mrs Albert leaped forward with a demented scream, but Nurani barred the way. Adeila started speaking in another language, which no one could understand, although there was no need to. The distorted expression on her face and the vehemence of her voice could only mean abuse. Pole moved next to Nurani, both of them remaining calm until the front door of the house had been closed. Pole let the crisis rise and fall, waiting for a panting Adeila to stop.

"Could you please now follow us to Scotland Yard, we have quite a lot to discuss, Mrs Albert."

Pole's voice carried the undercurrent of some unbreakable will. She would follow them and would be questioned. Adeila Albert clenched her jaws and moved with disdain. She would follow *after* she had changed into more appropriate attire.

* * *

The coffee machine was making its familiar grinding and buzzing noise whilst Pole leaned against it, his eyes not seeing the coffee that was being prepared. Adeila Albert had been led into one of the interrogation rooms and offered a tea that she had turned down. She had called her lawyer and refused to say a word until he arrived.

"Your coffee is ready, Jon," said Dolores, squeezing his arm gently.

"Ah, yes, thanks. I was miles away."

"She is a brave little girl, and more resilient than you think," continued Dolores, trying to alleviate Pole's concerns.

"What has she decided?"

"She wants to stay with a foster family, for a while."

"Why do people take it out on their kids? I know it is always complicated and I should not judge but by God – why?"

"Ambition and vanity engulf people without them noticing."

"I know Dolores but it still makes me mad," said Pole. "Then again I don't have any kids."

"Well, you don't need to have any to see the absurdity of all this." Dolores had also asked the machine for an espresso, no sugar.

"Your coffee is ready, Dolores," said Pole with a smile.

She smiled back took her cup and lifted it to Pole in a sign of acknowledgement.

"And what is my excuse?"

Pole finished his drink and crushed the cup with one hand. He had nearly reached interrogation room twelve where Mrs Albert was impatiently waiting when Andy caught up with him.

"Boss, just very quickly, I have reviewed the documents sent by this guy Ted Barnes from the integration committee at GL."

Pole's mind switched swiftly back to the other matter.

"The committee that is in charge of merging a number of businesses after the takeover is finalised, in particular Crowne and Albert's businesses. Go on," said Pole.

"Yes, well the numbers are interesting, plus the comments. I am pretty sure Albert would have got the top job."

Pole lifted a quizzical eyebrow and ruffled his goatee.

"Mmm, *not* really what I was expecting," he paused.

"How old are the numbers Andy?"

"Last year's unaudited and this year's projection."

"OK, get me some figures for, say, the last five years, audited, plus a list of deals closed for the past five years and the one that should close this year."

"I am on it, Boss," said Andy turning around to dash out.

Pole shook his head in amusement, paused and inhaled.

He walked into interrogation room twelve. Nurani was already there checking the equipment that would be used to record the conversation, keeping an eye on Mrs Albert and her lawyer.

Adeila Albert had complained that she needed time to change before leaving for the Yard. Pole had had no intention of indulging her ridiculous request. Considering her circumstances, Mrs Albert was pretty focused on the non-essentials. As luck would have it, she had managed to spill a cup of undrunk coffee on her dress – clever move. There was no alternative but to let her change.

With an air of triumph, Adeila had retired, accompanied by Nurani, to her bedroom and effected at speed the much-wanted switch of clothing.

She had emerged wearing an elegant black and white trouser suit from Escada and managed to name drop the designer when calling her lawyer. She had decided on a pair of classic Chanel shoes to match her handbag. This time neither Pole nor Nurani could avoid recognising the unmistakably intertwined Cs. Her jewellery was equally impressive. Finally, and despite the lack of sun, Mrs Albert drew from her bag a white pair of D&G sunglasses.

Pole observed with interest and some surprise the effect on Nurani, the mixture of disdain and what he suspected was envy. Adeila Albert had walked into the police station as though she were entering a recording studio. The show was on.

Pole started with simple questions but soon decided to cut to the chase.

"How close are you to Brett Allner-Smith, Mrs Albert?" asked Pole.

"We are *good* friends," replied Adeila .

"How did you meet Mr Allner-Smith?"

Pole had picked up on her emphasis but decided to avoid the obvious question for a while. Adeila launched into a description of auctions at Sotheby's and Christie's. How she had spotted an incredible piece of antiquity. How her husband had thought it was unaffordable, of course poor Anthony could not tell the difference between a two-thousand-five-hundred-year-old Grecian vase and a flowerpot from IKEA. She, however, was a natural. Her lawyer looked unhappy but simply expressed his growing unrest by indicating that these details were superfluous. Brett had been marvellous, Adeila continued, spotting her skills at detecting unusual pieces. He had recommended she attend a course he was running at one of the auction houses. She babbled along for a while and Pole let her go on. Her lawyer tried politely to redirect the conversation yet again. Adeila was too engrossed in her world to notice.

"Is Mr Allner-Smith your lover?" Pole demanded abruptly.

"Brett is," said Adeila before her lawyer could stop her. "Anthony was never of the right calibre."

"How long have you been having this affair?" Pole asked in a flat tone.

Adeila's face changed colour, her lips tightened. She abruptly turned towards her lawyer.

"Why did you not stop me?" she spat at him vehemently. "You incompetent nerd."

The older man's cheeks reddened with anger.

"Could I have a moment with my client please?"

"Certainly," replied Pole.

The interview would carry on now, no matter what. Adeila would not get much sympathy from her lawyer.

Good result.

* * *

Brett Allner-Smith had arrived at the Yard. He was coming voluntarily, no doubt very keen to give his side of the story and clear his name. Brett was waiting. He had accepted his cup of tea and looked pretty relaxed. His control was different from that of Henry, softer and yet surprisingly more effective. Pole had asked Nurani to start the process without him, giving her the lead. He would observe for a while through the one-way mirror.

His very English tailoring had made Nurani cringe, the Prince of Wales jacket, the silk cravat, the small moustache and the very blond hair made her feel uncomfortable. His perfectly manicured hands showed no sign of real work and his nonchalance irritated her, yet something about him was intriguing.

Brett had become nervous when she entered the room, but then again this was not a particularly relaxing experience. Brett Allner-Smith was somewhat shaken at the idea of where he was but managed to hide his nerves surprisingly well. Pole detected something else. Until Nurani entered the room, the man was bored. Adeila might have provided a distraction for a while but he had moved on. He needed something new. In dilettantish fashion, he was surveying the young inspector sitting opposite him.

The chase is so much more interesting with a female police officer, thought Pole. He entered the room.

"Mr Allner-Smith, Inspector Pole," said Pole, extending a hand. "I hope you have not been waiting too long." Pole smiled.

"Absolutely not," Brett replied, looking annoyed. "I can, of course, spare the time to assist in these terrible circumstances. What a tragedy."

Pole sat down. A few long hours of hide and seek with the truth had now begun.

124

Chapter Thirteen

Henry rang Nancy's doorbell twice, in short impatient bursts. He wanted to get on with it, wanted to get definitive advice from a *proper* lawyer. She would recommend someone tough, someone who could deal with HR, this entire mess. He wanted to go back to his team, his life. Nancy took what Henry thought was an interminable amount of time to reach the door. He had rested his tall body against the wall, arms folded across his chest, when she finally opened up. She gestured him in, she was on the phone to what seemed to be an old colleague.

She carried on her cryptic conversation whilst Henry stepped into her living room, not knowing what to do. She left him there, going back to her notes. He noticed that she was writing once again on a yellow legal briefing pad.

Reassuring – once a lawyer, always a lawyer.

The room wrapped itself around him. Henry felt it again, this deep sense of peace, unaltered by the charged activity. Nancy had now finished her conversation and looked at her watch.

"I thought it was going to take you longer to come over," she said with an amused smile. "A good sign indeed."

"You mean it took me less time than you thought to admit that you were right," retorted Henry.

"No," said Nancy. "I am not trying to enter into a battle of wills with you, Henry. I am simply glad you have realised that denial works against you. I have nothing to prove to you." Her tone of voice was conciliatory. "I have just finished a conversation with Gavin Pritchard QC, a good friend of mine and ex-colleague. He can take the case on. His record in criminal law is second to none. We have an appointment first thing in the morning."

Henry did not respond. She waited a few more moments until Henry finally relaxed, reassured by the news.

"You now need to think about a number of important things. Firstly, do you want to get a recommendation from someone else?"

Henry opened his mouth to speak but Nancy lifted her hand to stop him in his tracks.

"Secondly, do you want me to still be involved and, if so, how? Your barrister will be bound by client confidentiality. I am not, although I am very happy to enter into a form of agreement tying me to the same rule if you so wish. Finally, you must think about what you are accused of and decide what you want to say and how you want to plead. Telling the truth to your lawyer is advisable, then again you need to decide what this all means to you."

Henry sat down on the sofa, bending his body forward, elbows on knees.

"I need time," he said eventually.

"You have some time but not much, at least to decide on the first two questions," said Nancy.

"Could I stay here a bit to think?" said Henry, feeling awkward at invading her privacy. But he needed to stay away from his flat at all costs, the temptation to call his office still far too strong.

"Sure," said Nancy in a relaxed tone. "I need to tend to my flowers, so help yourself to whatever you need in the kitchen. I make a mean *tarte aux citrons* and there is some left in the fridge."

With this she disappeared into the second floor of her duplex apartment. The idea of a slice of cake made Henry's mouth water. He had not had any proper food for forty-eight hours and decided to investigate Nancy's fridge. The association cake and fridge reminded him of his mother. She too kept cakes in the fridge. *Keeps them nice and moist for you my love.* For years, as a child, he had enjoyed sneaking in there for a slice. He had discovered only much later she had been fighting a losing battle with the various rodents that haunted her kitchen.

The fridge was at least a safer place to store food. Henry shivered in disgust, wondering why he was reminiscing about the past. He helped himself to a large, possibly too large for good manners, piece of *tarte*. He had never tasted such delicious food until he had come to London. There was still some tea in the pot so he poured himself a mug, visited the fridge again for milk and settled in Nancy's living room. It was so easy to be here. He sat back, looking at the unusual decor of the room, took a deep breath and fell asleep.

* * *

McCarthy had been updated by Ted twice already, each time after a discussion with Scotland Yard. Ted had been creative in a way McCarthy had not expected, his friendship with Henry soon forgotten. McCarthy consulted his watch. It was nearly time for another key internal meeting. Ted would be there doing what he was told. This total compliance would have been nauseating at other times but with the takeover strategy to finalise McCarthy needed it.

* * *

Ted also consulted his watch. It was five past two in the afternoon, and his meeting had started already. He had been compiling the next lot of documents to be sent to the Yard. McCarthy would probably want to be updated after the meeting. He had to be ready. Pushing the door of the meeting room open Ted uttered a barely audible, "Sorry, lots to do" and grabbed the nearest seat.

A pile of documents had been distributed, waiting to be opened. Anish Gupta, Global Head of Debt Capital Market at GL, was running the meeting. He had paused briefly to allow Ted to enter before carrying on.

"We are checking our combined numbers with the other team, but the low estimate exceeds $20billion at the moment. It will depend how finance wants to calculate the losses on our complex, illiquid and long dated instruments."

Another young man in the team, with a ponytail and a small beard, got very excited. "The accounting standards are going to bloody crucify us. Any mark to market in the current climate is a fucking disaster."

"I know Nick," said the short Indian man pursing his lips in disdain. "But this is what enabled us to take our profits when the going was good. It is going to take a lot more than $20 billion to get the accounting standards to be changed. So we have to be creative."

"You mean a complete meltdown of the whole effing market," Nick replied.

Heads turned from one man to another as if he had uttered the worst of obscenities. Unperturbed, Anish Gupta carried on.

"We now have on the books a number of mispriced instruments, why? Because the original assumptions on growth, interest rates and sustainability were wrong. The leverage on these is tenfold what it should be. We are not going to be able to sell these on, so the balance sheet is eroding at a speed I have never seen before. In fact, at this rate we will be in default in the next two months."

The people around the table protested loudly at the same time, producing an inaudible jumble. Again, unperturbed, Anish carried on.

"The way I see this, we can accept HXBK's offer now and subsume the business into theirs or we can try to play hardball and miss the boat. We still have the upper hand, no need to deny what is happening. We are amongst ourselves today." Anish paused for effect. "If the deal does not go through now, we will all become the underdogs and the next lot of negotiations will *not* be fun. By the way we can argue until we are blue in the face that our financial models have been reviewed and agreed with the regulator, this will make zero difference if the markets tank once more."

This time the room remained uncomfortably silent. A few shuffled on their seats. Suddenly the door opened, the timing was impeccable as McCarthy made his entrance. Each of the men assembled in the room greeted the old man in their particular ways, vying for attention.

"Have you discussed?" said McCarthy without any other form of introduction.

"We have," Anish replied equally abruptly.

"Then you all know what you have to do, don't you?" carried on McCarthy, this time facing the room full on.

128

The question didn't call for a debate, and the room was plunged into an icy silence. Douglas McCarthy scrutinised faces. There was little his men could hide from him. The room stood still. McCarthy waited to see who would move first.

Ted shuffled on his chair.

"Ted, do you have a question?"

All heads turned towards the young man. Ted's dishevelled blond hair, and wary eyes made a few of his colleges snigger. He was not one of them. It took a few seconds for Ted to realise that McCarthy was addressing him, a few more seconds before he could start formulating a remotely sensible response.

"No! Good."

McCarthy had decided to spare Ted the humiliation of making a fool of himself. Ted needed to do a lot more for him in the Crowne affair. McCarthy spoke again.

"I am expecting you all to push for a close. This means that the final due diligence is to be done swiftly, the contracts ready for signature inside two weeks."

A murmur went around the room, McCarthy lifted his hand. He had not finished.

"If you have issues to clarify I do not want emails, I do not want calls, I want direct face to face contact. If you can't do this because you are travelling, I will make sure that Cindy sets up a secure line through our video call network. I am also expecting you to communicate in the same fashion with the members of your staff that you trust."

McCarthy paused and waited, this time no one moved until he did.

"When it comes to the Crowne incident, I will handle this personally together with the Head of Legal. Any queries I want referred to me in person, no mail, no voicemail."

He did not bother to ask whether there were further questions. He knew there would be none. McCarthy left the room having spent less than fifteen minutes with his direct reports.

An efficient meeting, he thought.

McCarthy avoided the lift but walked the three flights of stairs separating the meeting room floor and his office. He had hardly reached his desk when Cindy entered in her usual fashion, asking whether he had time for Ted. McCarthy had expected Ted would need to speak. The young man was fretting during the meeting.

"When is my next available slot?"

"Tomorrow, 9pm."

Cindy never hesitated to push his schedule beyond the call of duty. She had learned, in all the years she had worked for McCarthy, to identify the people he would want or need to speak to. Ted had become one of them. But McCarthy needed to see Ted sooner. Cindy suggested a rearrangement that disregarded rank and seniority. McCarthy managed a smile – this was why he respected Cindy.

* * *

The phone call with Henry was over and yet James had not moved. As their dialogue progressed, Henry had come back into his own. No one but him could have helped James navigate the complex matter they were debating and certainly not Ted. The intricacy came from a number of angles, one was the mathematical modelling of the embedded option. The technology was cutting edge and only a handful of people comprehended it fully. James understood well enough what his quantitative team, in charge of this new model, was talking about but then again, he wanted to make absolutely sure, never fazed by admitting he did not always know. Henry made a point of encouraging his people to speak freely about their doubts, something that the CDO team hardly ever did.

Henry had little respect for a team that created what he regarded as artificial products. *A lot of bullshit and hot air!* His take on sophistication and risk was simple. There is no such thing as a free lunch. If the rewards were high, so were the risks. Anyone pretending otherwise was guilty of shameful, intellectual dishonesty.

James was invigorated by their chat and almost optimistic, almost. But they had not spoken about Ted. On reflection, the discussion about Ted needed to be face to face. For the time being he would hold the fort as Henry had asked him to. Would GL ever allow Henry back on the trading floor? Certainly not until this mess had been sorted out and possibly not even after that.

130

"Yes, you are in deep shit my friend," uttered James.

He sat back at his desk and started checking his mailbox. One of the messages caught his eye. It was from Cindy Freeman, McCarthy's PA.

James,

Mr McCarthy would like to see you at 7.00am sharp tomorrow morning.

Regards

Cindy Freeman, Executive Assistant to Douglas McCarthy

He read the message again for clues and finally pressed the only button he could possibly press, accepting the invite.

James looked up and saw that both Harriett and Matt were missing. He leaned towards Morag.

"Where are those two?" he whispered.

"No idea," she replied. "I have a feeling that Matt is in New York."

James took in the information, flinching at the thought.

"Doing what?"

"Again, no idea," whispered Morag.

"Harriett?"

"I suspect still at the lawyer's. She is trying to close her deal this week. She was working on it late last night, in fact early this morning. She sent me an email at 2am."

"Who is he using?"

"Pamela Anderson."

In other circumstances James and Morag would have made the expected joke but the mood was missing.

"Find out for me where Matt is please. This is urgent," said James in a low voice.

"Understood, I am on it."

Morag put on her headset and was immediately on the trail.

Chapter Fourteen

Pole spent over an hour with Brett Allner-Smith, talking about his two marriages, his work and finally his relationship with Adeila Albert. He was proceeding gradually, moving in deeper with each question, so he could get a different angle. In this meticulous job that he enjoyed doing, Pole felt like a surgeon moving closer to the epicentre of the disease.

Currently, however, both Pole and Ms Shah had retired to exchange views, leaving Allner-Smith on his own.

"This guy is starting to interest me more," said Pole.

"Why? He is so removed from real life," replied Nurani, dubious.

"Well, you look at him and you think 'antiquities' that few people can afford, at least at the level he operates. That makes him remote. OK, true enough but—"

Pole paused. He sat on Nurani's desk whilst she took the chair.

"It does not mean that he is not after money the good old fashioned way. And that he is not capable of scheming to get back what he has lost or even pushing someone to commit the worst."

Nurani considered Pole's proposition for a few moments before replying.

"I find him creepy in a seductive sort of way," she volunteered. "So, yes, he could manipulate, be the brain."

"It is a simple calculation. Right?" said Pole. "Anthony Albert dies, Adeila gets the money, he moves in or even better he marries her. She probably does not know the extent to which he has lost his own wealth. If all goes well he stays married for a while and spends her money the way he has been used to all his life. Worst comes to the worst, he gets a divorce and asks for a settlement. People have killed for less – he simply needs to put the right idea in Adeila's mind."

"I agree that Adeila is besotted enough with this guy to do anything for him and, well – if her own husband had an affair then maybe. But then again, it is pretty obvious."

"We are dealing with people who are arrogant. Do you think they think we are going to catch them? No, no, no – they are convinced they are going to fox a bunch of dumb coppers like us."

"Yes, Guv," carried on Nurani, crossing her eyes.

"And conveniently, this murder takes place in the middle of a protracted takeover."

"Does Adeila really measure the huge tension between her husband and Crowne?"

"All we have seen of the competition between these two men indicates that this has been going on for some years. She knows. She also is the sort of woman who will want to find out whether her lifestyle is going to be affected by the changes in her husband's financial situation. If he is likely to fail, a life insurance cheque may not go amiss."

They both stopped to assess this latest statement. Neither Pole nor Nurani had noticed Andy standing at the door, listening intently to what was being said.

"Actually, I might have found something … interesting," exclaimed Andy.

"Mmmm," said Pole, his mind still on Adeila and Brett.

"I think Brett Allner-Smith knows Henry Crowne and also Douglas McCarthy, the CEO of GL."

"What?" Pole said with a sideways look. "That IS news, go on."

"I have been checking Crowne's bank account for movements that might be of interest and I've found some large sums of money being paid to Sotheby's. He buys and sells a fair bit of Asian art, so I called Sotheby's."

Andy was about to enter into a lengthy account of his findings when Pole interrupted him.

"And?"

"Sorry, sorry," replied Andy, blushing slightly whilst adjusting his glasses. "Allner-Smith sold a statuette, a Guanyin, in ivory, sixth century AD, to Crowne in March 2004. The statuette came from his own collection but had to be authenticated by Sotheby's, at Crowne's request as far as I can tell."

"Very good. A nice bone of contention between those two," exclaimed Pole. "And what of the McCarthy connection?"

"Allner-Smith always invites McCarthy to all sorts of previews when Asian art comes to auction, but I haven't had time to dig deeper."

"Well done, young man – keep digging and you, Ms Shah, you go back and have a little chit-chat with Brett."

Nurani's face twisted, cringing at the thought.

"I will put Mrs Albert on ice and join you for a more in-depth conversation with the English gentry."

Pole dealt swiftly with a furious Adeila. Yes, she would have to wait, yes, she could have a coffee but no, it would not come from Caffè Nero. Pole rejoined Nurani for a new round with Allner-Smith. Brett was very animated, seeking Nurani's attention. Pole could see that Ms Shah had dropped her guard significantly, admiring with slight annoyance the skill of the other man. Inspector Pole walked straight to the table and slid a picture of an ancient ivory statuette in front of Brett.

"How about giving me an expert description of this particular object, Mr Allner-Smith, together with, if you please, an even more detailed description of its sale?"

Pole's eyes ran over Brett, ice cold. Nothing would escape his attention until the interrogation was over. Brett Allner-Smith took a small pair of half-moon glasses out of an old leather box and pushed them up the tip of his nose.

You can try to buy time, thought Pole, *I am still getting the truth out of you.*

Allner-Smith remained composed, yet Pole detected the man's mood swing, a mix of irritation and disquiet. Pole was satisfied with the reaction he had just triggered. He now needed to tap into its source. Brett finally responded, his voice was low and his lips quivered.

"I used to own this Guanyin," he paused. His fingers went lovingly down the picture as he spoke again. "A magnificent piece attributed to the Tang dynasty. It came from my great grandfather," he paused again his eyes resting still on the picture. "A well-travelled man."

"And you sold it?" interrupted Pole tearing the man away from his fond memories.

"Yes, I did," replied Brett, still composed. "I had to sell it to this – Irish peasant." The words escaped Brett but he did not seem to care. "New money you see," he said in a vague attempt to redeem his outburst. "They think they can buy style or appreciate the finer things in life but what do they really know about the exquisite pieces they acquire?" he finished with a sigh.

The room fell silent, leaving Pole to acknowledge the strange intensity of Brett's feeling for his world of art and aesthetics.

"Crowne, the buyer – after a massive bonus. God knows what unholy transaction he must have done to deserve that one."

Pole shrugged, "And so …"

"It is hard to relinquish such a phenomenal piece to such an amateur," carried on the antiques dealer adopting an expert approach to the argument, still hoping for sympathy.

"Why did you not mention this before?" asked Pole, not letting go of his grip.

"It was a while ago Inspector."

"You must be aware that this is a murder investigation," replied Pole.

"Well, you're the policeman. Details like these escape me."

"Well then, let me therefore remind you of the insignificant details. You received £250,000 from Henry Crowne on the 27th of March 2004 and delivered the object on the 22nd of June, the reason for the delay was?"

"Inspector, you cannot be serious," said Brett barely able to refrain from laughter.

"Do you really believe that that was the full settlement for such an exceptional piece? You must be out of your mind," exclaimed Allner-Smith, his outrage sounding genuine.

Allner-Smith had managed to unsettle Pole. Inspector Pole took it on the chin and sat back.

"OK, enlighten me Mr Smith." Pole consciously dropped the double-barrelled name.

"It cost Mr Crowne the ridiculously low sum of £580,000," exclaimed Brett, now fired up.

"How did he settle the rest of the sum?" asked Pole.

"Ask my accountant," replied Brett, crossing his arms over his chest.

"I will," carried on Pole.

"Now let's move onto another subject if I may. What is your relationship to Mr and Mrs Albert?"

Allner-Smith pushed his chair back in a move to go.

"I am not sure I want to carry on with this conversation, Inspector. I came in good faith and you are now throwing some pretty unpleasant suggestions my way."

"And we appreciate your cooperation greatly, Mr Allner-Smith, as well as your contribution in enlightening us as to the true value of these antiquities."

Pole sounded sarcastic but no matter. Brett Allner-Smith still wanted to get his side of the story across before, or at least at the same time, as Adeila did. Pole now simply wanted to listen, to hear the man speak about himself and the Alberts. But Allner-Smith had decided on another tack altogether.

"Well, Inspector, may I interest you in another relationship? One that was worthy of a Greek tragedy, Mr Crowne and Mr Albert," said Allner-Smith resuming his emphatic tone.

"What about it?" said Pole.

"Ah, well, you must be aware that Mr Crowne and Mr Albert were rivals in many ways?" Allner-Smith paused for effect. "Everyone knows of their rivalry in the City. Although I cannot speak of this as it would only be hearsay on my part but I can certainly vouch for it in the auction rooms."

"Please indulge us and do enlighten us further."

"I have witnessed, as you can imagine, many a battle at both Christie's and Sotheby's but Crowne and Albert had a memorable confrontation a couple of years ago."

Pole stayed silent. Allner-Smith was on a roll. "The desired piece was another oriental artefact, a small terracotta warrior that was almost certainly a miniature version of the larger and well-known terracotta warriors of Emperor Qin Shi Huang, first Emperor of China." Allner-Smith cleared his throat and continued. "We presume that the small version had been used as a miniature copy of what the larger pieces would look like. A sort of proof, to be shown to the Emperor for approval before the production began."

Pole nodded in acknowledgement but Allner-Smith did not notice.

"It is very rare that an auction is participated in by the bidders directly. Usually agents are involved to shield the identity of the purchasers. It is equally unusual to have the bidders in the same room. Exceptional pieces attract bids from all over the world."

"Albert and Crowne were there in person?"

"The bid started relatively low for such an exceptional artefact, at £150,000. Crowne has always had a fascination for Asian pieces and even I have to admit his collection is rather good."

"What about Albert?" asked Pole.

"Albert had not noticed it until the bidding started. I can't imagine where it would fit in his collection. Mrs Albert is not particularly fond of Asian pieces, unfortunately."

"This battle was more a 'mine is bigger than yours', I presume."

"That is a rather crude way of putting it, Inspector! But I suppose yes it was. In fact, that's a rather fitting description of the mentality of the two protagonists."

Allner-Smith had become very animated, the electric atmosphere of the auction still in his mind.

"Crowne immediately doubled the bid to £300,000, a clear indication that the bidder was not going to mess about. It does away with small opponents but Albert added another £150,000 right away, £450,000 – within three minutes the price had tripled."

"£150,000 per minute, the auction house must have been ecstatic," remarked Pole.

"An exceptional piece, Inspector. Still Crowne would not give in; he added £50,000. Half a million pounds, just like that. Adeila was furious. She had her eyes on another object and Anthony was ruining her prospects of getting it. I could see her arguing with him but he was not having any of it. He was on the phone to his private banker. How far could he go?"

"So, Albert increased the price?" guessed Pole.

"Indeed. Albert increases the bid by £30,000. We are talking £530,000. The entire room is on edge. We are all holding our breath, me included. But Crowne was magnificent. I have to admit it, on that occasion, I was impressed. Final bid £580,000. Adeila left the room. She had said only one word to Anthony and the hammer fell. The room did not move, unbelievable. The sale was sealed in less than five minutes."

"Albert must have been gutted," said Nurani.

Pole smiled at the expression. But Allner-Smith shook his head in complete agreement.

"That he was."

"Did he stop because of his wife?"

"I am not quite sure, Inspector. I did not think it wise or discreet to discuss it with Mrs Albert."

"Could you say a little more maybe? The relationship with Mrs Albert and her husband seemed tense."

Allner-Smith relaxed. He had set the scene the way he wanted. He described the first meeting with the Alberts and an evolving relationship that developed through various organised auctions and grand receptions. Pole knew that Allner-Smith had rehearsed his story. He was a good storyteller though. He used his talent to make the events credible and enjoyable, without too much flourish, peppered with plausible anecdotes, deliberately vague or forgetful when asked for details by Pole or Nurani. To an untrained ear it would have sounded honest and justifiably imprecise, suitably depicting Adeila Albert as a highly charged, difficult woman whose marriage was at an end, a deluded woman when it came to other men. In short, he thought her to be a modern Madame Bovary, as he put it to himself. Pole and Nurani listened, nodding encouragingly, letting their interlocutor unfold his story without interruption. Pole saw the art of the conman in Allner-Smith. He modulated his voice, his speech, his body language effortlessly. It was clear that he had managed to convince Nurani of his story. Her first reaction of distrust was now replaced by a neutral or perhaps favourable opinion. She was not enthusiastic but she was finding him plausible. Pole had to rein in his own judgement, consciously standing back.

"Adeila was desperate to buy a new painting, a portrait by a small Dutch master from the seventeenth century. Anthony was not at all convinced. A great shame as the painting was well executed. Of course, events overtook us." Allner-Smith had finished his story. Albert's death did not seem to either bother or concern him.

"Many thanks for this very thorough account," said Pole. "It will help us greatly in forming a picture of the situation."

Pole emphasised the word *situation* in a conciliatory voice giving Allner-Smith the reassurance he was looking for. He rose, pressing a button on his mobile and signalling that the interview was over. Nurani stood up and managed a small smile at Allner-Smith. He responded with a courteous bow, extended his hand towards her, making contact.

"Let me show you out, Mr Allner-Smith."

Pole's voice sounded almost friendly. Brett looked content, hiding his feeling of success.

Both men walked down the corridor, exchanging banalities about taxi availability outside Scotland Yard. Allner-Smith was keen to get back to work even at this late hour; an impending auction needed his full attention. They were turning the corner and descending a flight of stairs, when a small woman dressed in a black and white designer suit and a podgy man passed them, on their way up. Brett Allner-Smith and Adeila Albert came face to face. Adeila could not contain a short shriek, her eyes wide. She might have run towards her lover had her lawyer not prevented it with a solid grip of her arm. She pulled herself together, calling upon her sense of decorum. Allner-Smith was unfazed. He nodded and moved away to let the pair through, hardly stopping his conversation with Pole. The encounter was masquerade, and Brett let the moment pass.

Pole was reluctantly impressed.

Pole went back to his office to take stock of the events of the day. He was deep in thought when a familiar voice startled him.

"A penny for them?"

"My God, Nurani, I have not heard that expression for a while."

"I am old school you know."

"So am I," sighed Pole, "anyway, I think this guy is a cool customer. Our little charade between him and Adeila yielded very little emotion. I think Henry Crowne has just found a serious competitor on our list of suspects."

* * *

Nancy returned to her lounge to discover Henry fast asleep on her sofa. She wasn't surprised. She moved silently closer to observe him at his most vulnerable. His face had relaxed and sleep revealed deep emotions. Henry moved slightly as if Nancy's scrutiny disturbed him. She stood back a little and continued looking at his face. The unhappy arch of his mouth was telling the story of pain, loneliness, certainly feelings that were never expressed. The furrows that ran along his face and gave it its attractive sculpture had deepened, carved by a heavy chisel.

Nancy looked around at the spacious room in all its delicate femininity and contemporary aesthetic. She enjoyed the contrast. Memories of her darker past floated unexpectedly in front of her eyes.

She saw a much younger Nancy walking the streets of Paris and entering the premises of one of France's most controversial lawyers, Jacques Vergès. She had just finished her dual law degree between La Sorbonne and King's College and was looking for an internship. No one had dared approach him but she knew her own cultural background would be key, a Chinese father and an English mother. He had warned her. The Law, in particular the Bar, was not a place where kind souls thrived. Egos flourished there just as they did in the City. He relished it, but would she?

She inhaled deeply and was grateful that the desire for power had left her many years ago. And yet here she was, reconnecting with that past she had so desired to give up. The idea merited some thought.

Henry moved again. She cast a last look at her unexpected guest. He would be asleep for a little while longer. Nancy disappeared into her kitchen, closing the door behind her softly. Time to indulge in another of her favourite activities, cooking.

The cab had dropped him a few yards right in front of his apartment. Brett Allner-Smith entered his building rapidly, not wanting to be noticed, a habit he had developed after the sale of his Belgravia family home. His flat was spacious and comfortable but it was a flat! Brett got in, threw his mac onto a Louis XV armchair and walked straight into his office. He opened the door of a small cabinet and poured himself a large whisky. The tumbler was elegant, part of an antique service he had managed to salvage. It was late enough and the work he was about to undertake required concentration. A small tonic was much required.

Brett placed the glass on a low table and pulled aside the Hereke rug that lay in front of it. He pressed a small wooden square etched into the floorboards and a medium sized opening appeared. He pulled a couple of files from the vault, a small laptop and a USB key. Brett shut the safe, replacing the rug. He walked to the sofa, placing the items he had just picked up on the table next to his glass.

The phone rang, but he took no notice. The voice with a foreign accent recorded a message. His Chinese contact was getting impatient. Too bad he would have to wait. The auction for the newly discovered Ming pottery was in a week's time. He would call after he had finished.

The laptop was now connected. Brett opened the first file entitled Henry Crowne. He chose a couple of pictures and some neatly typed notes. The first picture showed Henry and a friend having a drink in a small inconspicuous pub in Dublin. The second showed Henry and Anthony Albert celebrating the closing of a large transaction, again in Dublin. The man in the first picture was there too. He spread the pictures on the table and took a large mouthful of whisky. He savoured the quality of his drink. He could still afford the best. He closed his eyes and let the delicious malt flavour linger on his tongue. Adeila's image flashed in front of his eyes. He pushed it away. Brett would deal with the woman and this afternoon's events later.

Brett leaned towards the table again and opened the second file. He scrawled through some documents that had come up on his screen. A list of all major sales closed with the Alberts appeared. Brett smiled at the thought of two of his best clients tearing each other apart in

142

business. Competition sent commissions rocketing up, splendid – but Brett Allner-Smith wanted something more substantial. He longed to move his collections into a large house again. He longed for the standing he had lost. His plan had been executed with elegance and the call from Scotland Yard had not surprised him.

The phone rang again. The same foreign accent. Brett sighed. In the meantime, he would answer the phone.

Chapter Fifteen

The homely smell of cooking enticed Henry. He opened an eye and woke up with a jolt. Where was he? It took a couple of seconds to realise that he was in Nancy's flat. She could not refrain from bursting into laughter.

"You were out for the count. I did not want to wake you up."

She was still smiling an amused but kind smile. Her face was so different when she laughed, much younger and much more Asian. The high-set cheekbones that delicately shaped her face became accentuated and her almond eyes gently closed. She was a very attractive woman, maturity seemed to have softened her.

"Was I?" said Henry, his mind still wandering.

"Oh, yes. You were."

"What are you cooking? It smells very good."

"Sichuan chicken curry, my family's special recipe – or so they claim. Most people enjoy it."

"You should not have gone to so much trouble."

Henry felt embarrassed, assuming she was cooking for him and she indeed put him right.

"My dear fellow, it wasn't just because of you. I cook for myself. I simply added a bit more."

She was standing in front of him with a closed fist resting on her hip. She was still wearing her oven gloves. Henry burst into laughter and felt better for it. The scene was so unreal.

"Can I help?"

"Yep, you can set the table, crockery in this cupboard and cutlery this one." She was pointing in various directions as she returned to the kitchen. "And you can select the beer you prefer too. I have some in the fridge."

"Beer? I thought wine?"

"Well, you thought wrong I am afraid. Wine with curry is an aberration. A good beer. Nothing else will do!"

Henry nodded, a good beer would always please an Irishman. Moving towards the kitchen he found that he had not done simple things such as setting the table for quite some time. Most dinner parties he held in restaurants. The friends he kept were always keen to try the latest and the best. If he had dinner parties at home he organised these through a caterer. All he had to do was choose the menu, since staff would be in attendance to wait on them. Yet Henry remembered a time when he had enjoyed cooking. The joy of discovering new types of food in London was still vivid in his mind. He'd never thought food could be so enjoyable, a whole new world of excitement and possibilities opened up to him.

They sat at the small dining table in the kitchen and Henry tried not to wolf down what was in front of him. He had survived on very little since Scotland Yard. He did not quibble at the offer of a second helping. Nancy was also clearly enjoying her meal. As predicted, it was excellent and they both savoured it in the half silence that befits appreciated food.

"Tell me more about yourself, Henry," said Nancy after bringing a plate of fruit, cut and prepared, to the table.

Relaxing, Henry wondered whether Nancy had waited for the opportune moment to plant her question. He looked at her and smiled. He did not mind. In a couple of hours, he would meet with her contact and would include her in his legal team. He cast a glance at Nancy's iPhone and remembered his own BlackBerry had been abandoned on the floor of the lounge but resisted the urge to return and look at his emails. Nancy was right. He had to get himself out of this unforeseen mess before he could reclaim any of his territory.

"Where shall I start?" he said.

"The beginning is usually a good place," said Nancy pushing her chair back and turning it sideways to extend her legs. She was elegantly slim.

"OK," said Henry gathering his thoughts.

"Where did you grow up?" asked Nancy to get the conversation going.

A shadow moved over his eyes.

"I grew up in Belfast."

Nancy could not hide her surprise.

"I know," he added very quickly. "I don't sound Irish at all any more. You won't believe how effective elocution lessons are when you really want to learn. The City eighteen years ago was not exactly welcoming."

"I've had plenty of racist jokes in my time."

"I was five on Bloody Sunday." Again, Henry hesitated but now he could hardly backtrack. Why stop? After all, it was only a piece of history.

Nancy folded her hands in a meditative fashion, her left hand cupping her right in a most peaceful gesture. She was giving him her utmost attention.

Henry had not cast his mind back to his childhood for a long time. He remembered it as a dark place full of fear, anger, and yet he could not say that he had been unloved. He spoke about his mother, a young woman who had come to Belfast to teach English, escaping her family in England. She had wanted to take risks, to establish her own independence, thinking she could always go back if matters did not work out for her. Life had decided otherwise when she met Henry's father, Irish Catholic and strongly militant.

"Forty years ago," added Henry with little emotion in his voice, "Ireland was a nation on the verge of destruction." He sounded remote, an observer of a city long cast away.

"An Irish boy marrying an English girl – that must have been ..." Nancy stopped searching for the right word.

"Disastrous," ventured Henry, with a small sad smile.

"I was going to say dramatic but, I suppose, very difficult at least."

"Yep. I remember two things from my very early years. My father

147

swinging me on his shoulders, grabbing Mum and dancing to some crazy tune, we were all laughing and then …"

Henry grabbed his fork and toyed with a piece of fruit. He no longer wanted to conjure the memories back.

"The shrieks of sirens after bombs had struck, the predictability of the bombs. So much violence ready to erupt for little reason, it becomes part of who you are, you don't even – well, notice it."

A long, drawn silence elapsed before Henry continued.

"My mother and I were on the street that day, why? I don't know, she never said. Anyhow, miraculously, we survived."

"Are you angry?" asked Nancy.

"Wouldn't you be?" replied Henry, without hesitation.

"Yes, I was angry too, for different reasons but yes, I understand that sort of anger well."

"Are you still angry?"

Henry could not imagine Nancy being anything but charming and relaxed. Yet behind her eyes was a light that sometimes lit up. He had seen it when they were both at Scotland Yard.

"Not anymore, I have made my peace with what was eating me alive," she said, serene, "and so should you. Late thirties is the right time to start letting go."

"Maybe. I will have to think about it," said Henry. Anger had filled him with energy for success. He was not prepared to yet let go of such a potent fuel.

"Was your father IRA?" Nancy asked.

The question surprised Henry by its directness, but then again, she knew nothing yet of his complex links with the O'Connor brothers.

"I am not sure. If he was he never said. Anyway, it is irrelevant now. He died many years ago. It was not the cause that killed him I think but the bottle."

"Sorry to hear that."

"I was young when it happened. It belongs to another life."

"What about you Henry, are you IRA?"

Henry opened his eyes wide and roared with laughter, shaking his head.

"Nancy, I know you are my brief but I am not sure what you

expect me to say to that?" He was still grinning at the question.

"The truth, of course," said Nancy in complete focus. Henry's face fell a little.

"If you are referring to my friendship with the O'Connors, yes I knew them as kids and Liam and I went to uni at the same time. Bobby was older."

"Did you know they were involved?"

"It always was a hot topic of conversation with them, although Liam has been much more, let's say, conciliatory of late. Bobby has been a staunch follower of Gerry Adams from the time he discovered who Adams was. However, I am sure you have read the news. The IRA has been decommissioned."

"So, you are Catholic Irish, on your father's side," continued Nancy.

"Yep, my lass," replied Henry in an Irish accent. "Although a little complicated by the fact that my mother was Anglican and in charge of my education."

"Henry, your life is so different now. What keeps you close to these guys?" Nancy asked with genuine interest.

"I have asked myself that question many a time. Maybe old bonds don't die so easily. I don't really know, Nancy," carried on Henry after a while. "We did some silly things together when we were kids. You know, boys stuff. We looked after each other even more so after our fathers died. To them I was not an English brat, the invader that deserved to die. I was their friend."

Memories of his past propelled Henry back to the Troubles. Some lads at school have started calling him names, one spits in his face and soon he is on the ground fighting. The whole class is ready to join in but Liam intervenes. Bobby, always ready to throw a punch even at eight, savages the most vicious of the boys whilst Liam issues his warning: *you mess with Henry, you mess with us.*

Henry inhaled and the memory faded away.

"Mmmm," Nancy said "I am not sure this explanation is going to wash with Inspector Pole."

"Possibly not but it will have to do. In any case I hardly see Liam these days and never Bobby."

Nancy looked at her watch, the conversation was over.

"A final cup of coffee?" she asked.

"Now, let me do that one. I do a mean cup of instant coffee," replied Henry with enthusiasm.

Nancy looked at him in horror. He had pronounced the forbidden word *instant*. Henry clapped his hands and with a wink continued, "Got you there ... Just kidding, let me make a proper cup of well brewed Jamaican coffee."

Nancy face relaxed slightly, still not entirely convinced that Henry's standard of well brewed coffee was up to hers.

* * *

Ted looked at his watch and made his way to McCarthy's office. As usual he would be too early. Cindy saw him step outside the lift and sigh. When would he ever learn?

She indicated to him with a short wave of the hand that he had to wait a few minutes. She was on the phone to New York. Ted made his usual gesture of apology and stepped into the visitors' waiting room. He stood in front of a print, depicting the image of an androgynous man. The picture was a William Blake and featured as one of GL's most impressive pieces of art. He read the text yet again, as he always did, a form of symbolist poetry which still eluded him.

"Mr McCarthy will see you now," Cindy said formally.

Cindy always referred to McCarthy by his surname, preserving the distance a CEO should have with his people. Only a few direct reports enjoyed the privilege of having her refer to him as Douglas. Henry had been one of those people. He was a rising star who would have eventually been elevated to a position as high as that of McCarthy. Ted was a different kettle of fish. But today, as he was about to enter the CEO's office emboldened, Ted looked like a puffed-up sparrow, lots of feathers and very little weight. Cindy walked past him, did not knock at the door in her usual way and introduced Ted. McCarthy did not move. He carried on reading an email.

"I spoke to James," said McCarthy, now typing his reply.

Ted was standing in the middle of the room not knowing

150

whether he should approach the great desk or simply take a seat at the meeting table.

"Oh good," he hesitated.

"Did you have another conversation with Scotland Yard?"

"Yes," mumbled Ted.

McCarthy was waiting.

"They want more information," said Ted.

His stomach did a somersault, in fear of the old man's reaction.

"Not surprising," replied McCarthy.

He stood up and moved towards the meeting table at which point Ted sat down.

"Have you prepared the next set of information needed?" asked McCarthy as he sat down himself.

"Well, I thought we could have a conversation about this, maybe."

McCarthy gave Ted a cruel look.

"Do I have to dictate the numbers to you or will you be able to cope on your own? Should I ask someone else to deal with this?"

"No, no. I can cope, I just need general direction," replied Ted.

Their eyes met and Ted was doomed. The young man had crossed the threshold whence one does not return. There would be no further heart-aching questions. He would now simply think about how to execute the task with ruthless efficiency. Thoughts of Henry, his colleague, his friend, had stopped haunting him. He had tasted real power and it was good.

McCarthy and Ted spent a few minutes on what McCarthy expected and then Ted was gone.

Walking out of his office after Ted had left, McCarthy turned to Cindy.

"No calls or meetings for the next hour. Reschedule. I need to think."

Cindy nodded. Nothing and no one would cross the threshold to his office for the next hour.

McCarthy went back to his desk, unlocked a drawer with a key permanently kept on his own key ring and pulled out an unlabelled file. McCarthy took a deep breath. The contents of this file were only known to him and the head of the CDO team. What it contained was capable, even after all these years, of taking his breath away. He had not checked the latest figures. McCarthy did not bother to consider the rows of numbers and the text that justified the findings contained in the document. He jumped straight to the aggregated figures, one indicating the current loss on the portion of CDOs GL had kept on its books. The second was an estimation of the potential loss going forward should the subprime markets not stabilise. The second figure was accompanied by a number of scenarios. The first figure was already very alarming. McCarthy paused. In his entire career he had never considered bankruptcy of a financial institution the size of GL, a bank of such stature simply could not disappear the way Bankers Trust did. He clenched his fist, his mind racing to find a way out of this predicament. It was then that the second number hit him, $31 billion. He pushed his chair back in horror. He was speechless. He came back to his desk and muttered to himself.

"Who the fuck chose the parameters for this set of projections?"

Still standing, he read the figures again and again, as reality slowly and inexorably began to sink in. Were the markets to move down again, there would be no salvation. McCarthy went back to the text and speed read the content. The complexity of the subprime products that had been designed by his team eluded him but the equation that could cost GL bankruptcy was simple. The level of risk that GL had retained with its CDO business had been grossly miscalculated. Even the AAA tranches, reputed to be the most solid part of the CDOs' tranches were collapsing. The rating agencies had cocked up, the regulator had cocked up, and his senior team in risk management had cocked up. No one had checked the content of what they were selling.

McCarthy sat down slowly, the battles of the past few days now taking their toll. He had to make the call.

Chapter Sixteen

The background checks on Brett Allner-Smith confirmed Pole's suspicions. The suave English gentleman hid well the ruthless dealer. Pole smiled into a stretch, his arms folded behind his head. In a strange way, Henry Crowne had met his match in the antiquities world. A number of deals had been questioned – the value given to certain 'priceless' objects, the authentication of a variety of pieces. There was never enough evidence to conclude that there had been foul play. Allner-Smith, although sailing close to the wind, knew how to protect his rear end. Pole had called in a specialist from another squad so that he could understand the level of sophistication such a fraud would demand.

Eugene Grandel had worked on some of Allner-Smith cases. He was, for his part, convinced that something was afoot.

"This guy is incapable of being completely straight."

"Not surprised. Anyhow tell me more about this chap."

"Smooth operator, extremely knowledgeable and connected. If I were a betting man I'd say secret services of some sort. The little git gets himself out of the tightest of spots." Eugene lifted his hands before Pole could ask for more. "Don't ask me to substantiate – can't. Just the view of an old copper but one thing I can definitely say – can't keep it in his pants. He has a soft spot for the ladies, young ladies."

"How young?"

"Young enough," added Eugene.

Eugene gave Pole a naughty grin and raised his eyebrows.

"How far would he go for money?" continued Pole.

"Very good question."

Eugene crossed his arms and rested his head on his chest. He looked at Pole.

"Murder? Yes, possibly but it would have to be sophisticated."

"Really?" said Pole unconvinced.

"No direct involvement, as I said, but he could be the mastermind. He could manipulate, in fact, come to think of it he would enjoy manipulating. There is a case," he continued, now following his own trail of thoughts, "Might be helpful. Let me come back to you on this."

Eugene walked away, promising Pole more information and soon.

Pole was alone in his office having refused his team's invite for a break. He needed time to reflect. Henry no longer remained the only suspect. And then some disturbing information had arrived on his desk exposing Anthony Albert's transaction pipeline. Albert was involved in the structuring of subprime products. Pole had just started scratching the surface of what Albert was up to at work. There were rumours of enormous deals being closed and astronomical sums of money being made. A billion dollars had been mentioned as the average size for a transaction.

The AVERAGE size – these guys had really lost the plot.

Now Pole had two key targets in mind. He wanted to hear what Liam O'Connor had to say about his friend Henry Crowne. The police in Northern Ireland had been informed and were on his trail. Liam was a smart operator, it might take some time. Pole also wanted to speak to Albert's solicitor. The will would be open and read – soon. Pole would arrange for a sneak preview. Still, Pole was not satisfied. Something else was afoot and he had not yet found out what. He was deep in thought, creating a picture of all that he knew when Nurani knocked at the door. Without waiting for a response she poked her head through the door.

"The guys in Ireland have traced Liam O'Connor," she announced, excited at the thought of meeting her first IRA sympathiser.

"Good work!" said Pole. "That is a bit of luck. Any details on how it happened?"

"He was trying to get out of Switzerland."

"And going to?" asked Pole whose interest had been piqued by the location.

"North Africa, Libya to be more precise."

"Where did they pick him up?"

"Zurich Airport," replied Nurani. "Big banking there. Any coincidence?"

"That would be a very big coincidence," said Pole stretching his arms wide. "How quickly are they going to extradite him?"

"Pretty quickly. I think he should be home tomorrow. The Swiss are keen on banking secrecy but not so much so on terrorism. This is happening as we speak."

"OK. Get two tickets to Belfast, we are paying our friend a visit," said Pole.

"Yes Boss," saluted Nurani.

Pole rolled his eyes. She grinned before disappearing. He settled down, immersing himself once more in the files piled on his desk.

* * *

Henry was back in his flat with a long list of to-dos. Nancy had focused his attention on the task. She hoped the exercise would be long and tedious enough to prevent Henry from contacting GL again.

Nancy for her part needed to follow one of her hunches. She had stored her own to-dos in the back of her mind as methodically as she used to when a barrister. *Old habits die hard*, she smiled inwardly, surprised at the speed at which the dormant QC had resurfaced in her. Her reputation had been built on the sagacity of her observation, her phenomenal determination. She never spoke about her other weapon – intuition. Not to be discussed in this male dominated profession, they might have called her a witch. But she had learned to listen to her inner voice. That voice had made itself louder during the day.

She grabbed her lime green coat, stuffed a pad into her matching handbag and rushed out. She looked at her watch. She had some time. The library on Russell Square would not be shutting yet. Before hailing a cab, she cast an eye towards Henry's window. The light was

155

on. She derived some comfort from it. He was doing his homework, maybe? She pushed that idea aside to concentrate on the task at hand.

The library was slowly emptying. It was much more functional than she remembered, PCs everywhere. Still the smell of books lingered, sweet and subtle. One of the librarians had been particularly helpful. She sat in front of the oldest PC in the room, letters almost erased by so many eager fingers. She started scrolling through old newspapers. She remembered the tedium of perusing the press for information. This was so much easier and yet she had enjoyed the feel of the pages unfolding beneath her fingers.

Nancy had reached the year 1992. She had a date in mind, 10th April of the same year. The date the last IRA bomb had killed in the City of London was linked in her mind to a face and a name: Jonathan Pole.

The search engine threw a number of newspaper articles onto the page. Nancy skimmed them; *The Times*, the *FT*, *The Daily Telegraph* and finally the *Evening Standard*. Here it was, a large front-page article describing the bombing, accusing the Met and the Counterterrorist Squad of poor communication. The article was condemning the lack of efficacy of both forces in failing to anticipate the blast, despite a serious but last-minute tip-off. The same article showed a picture of a young police officer fielding the press as best he could. A much younger Inspector Pole was looking straight at Nancy with a serious look in his eyes. Nancy smiled at the young man. He looked rather dashing, she thought. But no flirting with the enemy or at least not yet.

The printer spewed out two copies of the various articles. She grabbed them and made her way to the coffee shop. The library would close in one hour and was already completely deserted. She ordered Darjeeling in a proper teacup and was pleased to discover that the old crockery had not been replaced. Nancy chose a deep chair and settled in to reread the news articles. The IRA bomb had cost three lives. The usual IRA message had been sent to the Met only thirty minutes before the blast. Slow communication between the Met and the Counterterrorist Squad had been blamed for the tragedy. Pole looked ill at ease in this bad picture of him. The article presented him as a spokesperson for the Met, the liaison officer with the CT Squad.

Not an easy job in those days. She took a sip of tea, refreshed by its delicate aroma. She sat back and wondered whether this new piece of information mattered. Henry was Irish, brought up in Northern Ireland. Should this imply some connection? The explosion that killed Anthony Albert had necessitated access to explosives and an expert knowledge of bomb production.

The cup was warming Nancy's hands. She took another sip. What would Inspector Pole make of this? He had experience of the IRA and its techniques. Pole was bound to create a link between Henry's Irish past and the murder. She finished her tea and stood up.

"Jonathan Pole. It's time to have a little chat," she murmured.

* * *

Pole looked at the clock on the wall. He rolled his head around in a welcome stretch before moving his seat away from his desk. He could see the desks emptying slowly. Nurani and Andy had gone to check some key details with Forensics. The phone rang. Pole frowned. What now? But his professional self tapped him on the shoulder.

"Pole."

"Guv, Nancy Wu is downstairs. She would like a word."

Pole remained silent. How unexpected. The intriguing Ms Wu wanted a word, and why not.

"I'll come down Reg. Ask her to wait please."

"Okey dokey, Guv."

Nancy was standing in the lobby, absorbed in considering the space when Pole reached her.

"Ms Wu, what brings you to my neck of the woods?"

"*Good evening*, Inspector," said Nancy. "I was admiring your new lobby. It's a lot more impressive than it used to be … but could do with a good piece of contemporary art."

Pole smiled at the remark.

"Apologies! *Good evening* Ms Wu."

"Don't worry, I have not come to discuss the merits of the new interior decoration. What exactly was your role in 1992 with the Met and the Counterterrorist Squad?"

Pole's face turned to stone.

"I could try to find out indirectly but why not answer the question yourself," carried on Nancy.

"May I ask why it is of any concern of yours?" replied Pole dryly.

"Henry is Irish, from Northern Ireland as you know by now. I just wanted to decide whether the Inspector leading the case had particular views on this key fact."

Nancy was squarely facing Pole. Her ebony hair clasped with an ivory pin, her almond eyes sparkling with intelligence and wit.

"If you are trying to establish whether I will be biased—"

"I am not implying anything, Inspector," Nancy interrupted "I am simply asking some honest questions. I do not shy away from these issues, in particular if I feel they may be material to the case."

Pole remained silent. Part of him just wanted to give Nancy a piece of his mind, while the other part wanted to yield to the openness she had shown.

"Well, I presume you will find out. I was with the Met but worked as liaison officer with the Squad. And before you ask, it was complicated and mistakes were made in 1992. It was a long time ago, so no, I do not hold a grudge."

"That I can believe Inspector," replied Nancy. "It takes a certain type to join the Squad."

"A compliment?" replied Pole.

"No, a statement of facts," said Nancy unperturbed. "I like to determine very quickly how I can work with people Inspector. I am not trying to be argumentative but I will get to the point and rather quickly at that, if I feel it is in my client's interest."

"Very good, Ms Wu, and I will certainly be more than happy to oblige," retorted Pole, invigorated by this honest discussion.

"We now understand each other, which is excellent," said Nancy. Pole had expected her to bid him farewell but she was not finished. "And to show you I think we can work together, I have come to give you an important piece of evidence."

"Why now? Should you not have come forward earlier on?"

"A valid question of course but I needed to know how to approach this. Are we to talk here or in your office?"

Pole pursed his lips.

"It depends how long this will be."

"Very short indeed. I received post for Henry a day before the flight. The janitor is on holiday and his replacement is quite absent-minded I am afraid. In that post were a couple of plane tickets which I suspect were for the fated trip to Switzerland. I asked the young man to redirect them to Henry and was a little short with him. Probably because I felt guilty I had not done so myself more swiftly."

"In short Henry did not get the tickets on time because you could not be bothered," said Pole.

"A harsh but good summary of the position," replied Nancy unfazed.

"Does Henry know?"

"That is between me and my client, Inspector. With due respect of course."

"Anything else I need to know?" said Pole bluntly.

"Absolutely nothing."

"Fine," Pole grunted. "I will get one of my team to record your statement."

"Thank you for your time Inspector, no doubt we shall speak soon. *A bientot.*"

"*Certainement. Et au plaisir,*" finished Pole in impeccable French.

Pole gave a short nod, turned back, disappeared into a lift and walked back to his office. He went straight to his computer and clicked on the Scotland Yard search website. He entered Nancy Wu's name. He scrolled through her bio quickly and returned to the beginning. Her mixed cultural background did not surprise him, but the history of her family both intrigued him and resonated with his own personal experience. The internship with Jacques Vergès however was utterly unexpected. He jotted a few words on a pad, a reference to the Klaus Barbie affair. Ms Wu must have been fiercely ambitious to agree to be one of the defence lawyers for a war criminal. Pole would not cast judgement on whether Nancy Wu was also devoid of all moral principle to have accepted this assignment, knowing the answer to this question was more complex than it seemed. Then again, she had left France and entered pupillage at Gray's Inn. Her career had been stellar, becoming a Silk at such a young age. She should have been called to the bench but in 2008 Vergès' name reappeared. Pole jotted down a few more words and sat back in his chair. Something important had happened in 2008. The Nancy Wu that had managed to get under his skin a few moments ago was a very different woman to the one he had just encountered on the page of the Yard search website.

Why?

Chapter Seventeen

As Nancy turned the corner of her street, she looked up. Light was still on in Henry's flat. She consulted her watch, it was past 9pm. Henry had followed her advice or perhaps not. There was to be no contact with GL until he had spoken to his lawyer, the notorious Pritchard QC. Pritchard had defended a number of high-flyers in the City. Finance was his domain. If Henry had focused in the way he should have, then his list of to-dos was finished. Nancy anticipated that it would be executed to perfection, with certain omissions of course. She couldn't imagine a man like Henry disclosing all at a first meeting. Then again Pritchard was a man of extreme sagacity. A small pang of anticipation entered her heart. She smiled. Could it be that she was missing the old profession? It only took a few seconds for her to answer with a categorical no, or at least no to the way she conducted her affairs a few years ago. Nevertheless, she had to admit that she was enjoying the intellectual challenge.

The door of her own apartment appeared in front of her. She paused before opening it. Should she check on Henry? Was he actually there or had he left? She decided against it. She would call when she had settled herself back into her flat. Another cup of Darjeeling would do the trick. The flashing light on her answer phone told her that she would not have to call. The small replay button was pressed and Henry's baritone voice filled the room, poised but expectant.

"I have completed my list. But I think I have to come back to you with a couple of questions. One or two points to clarify."

There was a small silence.

"Happy to cook, by the way, although my standards are unlikely to compare to yours – takeaway perhaps. Let me know."

Mr Crowne is starting to come around. She had left the door ajar on the off chance and Henry a few moments later leaned against the frame, knocking inside the door.

"Evening," he said informally.

"Good evening, my dear. How is it all going?"

"I am very clear on most of it," replied Henry as he sat down where he had sat before.

He took the tea that had been poured for him, bringing the cup to his nose. The gentle and fresh scent of first flush Darjeeling satisfied his senses. He took a sip.

"Do I really have to say a lot about Albert? I have to admit I disliked the guy but it feels futile and rather strange to speak ill of him now."

"Speak no ill of the dead for fear they may come and haunt you. That is a tad irrational for you, Henry," said Nancy gently mocking him.

"I don't like speaking of someone whom I can't challenge any longer."

"Fair enough. Why don't you give examples? Show us events that have happened between you and him that you think best describe your relationship and who Albert was. The prosecution will use these too and your defence team needs to be prepared with your version of facts."

Silence.

"I can imagine that you must have done business together, closed transactions."

After some more hesitation, Henry succumbed to the most human of temptations, the pleasure of talking about himself.

"I suppose I could talk about Dublin?"

"I think you should," said Nancy. "You know as well as I do it is an important moment."

"I am sure you are knowledgeable about my speciality," continued Henry.

162

"You mean the fact that you run the Structured Product Team at GL?"

A smile and glance of admiration lit up Henry's face.

"So you know that GL arranges some pretty large deals for its clients?"

"My old profession, Henry, I dealt with a lot of City people. I know your business."

"Well then you will appreciate … My team had closed a particularly large complex transaction, in fact the first of many. It was an accounting play that improved EPS, I mean Earning Per Share, for corporates. I must add that these transactions did not cause any negative effects in the markets."

"You mean this has nothing to do with subprime, of course."

"Absolutely nothing remotely to do with it. In fact, I think those guys got exactly what they deserve but that's another story." Henry poured himself some more tea.

"The transaction had taken us nearly a year to construct and the amount raised was the largest ever raised for a quoted company, and still is, I believe."

Henry stopped, mentally perusing the record of the deals he knew had been done.

"Yes, I am sure. Anyway, we had used HXBK as partners in the transaction. GL had taken a portion of the deal on its trading book and needed someone else to come along that the company would trust. There was no front running, of course. But our Head of Marketing is pretty good. He knew what we had to offer to place the deal with them."

"Was Albert's team involved?"

"They had to review the technicalities of the deal, legal structure, pricing."

"How so?"

"Well, for a start this company had been their client for years. The CFO would derive some comfort if they joined. We were testing our ability to explain the deal and the impact of the parameters of pricing and kept a little black box that would give us an advance on the market."

"You mean, you protected your intellectual property because it did not impact on the buyer's?"

"Correct!" said Henry. Yes, Nancy would have been superb in his team.

"And I presume Albert was livid."

"Oh yes, you bet. We had managed to market to one of his major clients right underneath his nose. Of course, the little motherfucker, sorry—"

Nancy waved her hand. "Go on."

"But, we needed them buying into the deal alongside us. Very few clients enjoy being first to market, let alone with a bank they are not so familiar with."

"I suppose Albert did his best to scupper the deal?"

"To start with he did, but we were confident and GL's structure was very robust. He could do nothing but pretend he was working on a similar idea; pathetic really but so typical of him."

"And why Dublin?" said Nancy wanting to hear about what she suspected was a loaded subject.

"We closed the deal there because we needed an offshore Irish company to structure the transaction."

"So, Albert was at the closing?"

"Well, yes, and bearing in mind that HXBK came to the table and he knew the client. It was very hard to tell him to get lost."

"Who else was there, then?"

Nancy poured herself a fresh cup of tea. Henry measured the impact of the question, admiring Nancy's ability to lead effortlessly.

"The usual suspects. That is, a cast of thousands: structurers, traders, marketers, lawyers, accountants, the client and his own team of course."

"And Albert."

"And Albert," acknowledged Henry. "We all got pretty drunk."

"In a good Irish pub?"

"Wine bar, Michelin star restaurant and then a good Irish pub."

Henry's mind drifted back to that evening.

The face of his Chase and Case lawyer Pam hovers very close to him. They are both laughing. She is teasing him about drinking

Guinness. She grabs his pint and drinks from it, pulling a face. He remembers her words after she has wetted her red lips with the dark liquid. *Henry, babe, how can you drink this stuff?* He can't quite recall his answer but he feels the opportunity, the intimacy.

"As a matter of interest, who was your lawyer on this deal?" asked Nancy, dissipating the last image.

"Why?" replied Henry. Had she read his mind?

"Well, once a lawyer always a lawyer as you must have guessed by now," said Nancy. "I am interested in finding out who the next generation of high profile solicitor is."

"We use a number of law firms at GL but usually for these deals Chase and Case."

"A good choice. And do you have a partner assigned to your deals? It is rare to chop and change. Important to trust your key lawyer, it's fine and dandy when it goes smoothly but when a deal goes sour ..." continued Nancy.

"Well, yes. I agree. It's when a deal goes south that ..."

The memory of the Wooster QC debacle came back to Henry like a slap in the face. He had thought there was something special between Pam and him. Physical attraction, he knew, but perhaps something more. Trust he had relied on and the hope she cared.

"And the lucky partner that looks after you at Chase and Case is?" said Nancy.

"Pamela Anderson."

"Anybody else to help you celebrate the pinnacle of your career?" asked Nancy. She would come to Pamela later on.

"What do you mean?"

"Well, you are Irish after all. And Dublin is a small place. I don't wish to offend you by saying this of course. Are you not bound to meet people you know when you get out there?"

"I know the owner of the pub quite well. I always bring a good crowd when I sign a deal and he gives me good service."

"Was it the pub you frequented when you went to uni?"

"Nancy, really, Dublin was a hell of a different place when I went to uni."

"Mmm, so no uni pals to help you celebrate your big day?"

The ring of Nancy's phone spared Henry. He would not have to speak about Liam and Bobby. Nancy stood up. It was Pritchard QC.

Henry no longer hears Nancy's voice. It is sound rather than words, replaced by the buzzing noise of a pub, glasses ringing, laughter bubbling up.

Henry does not notice his two friends at first. But Liam raises his glass in the distance with a large grin on his face. Henry goes to them cheerfully, inviting them to join his crowd for another round. The moment is too big not to ask his best pals to share in his glory. He feels invulnerable. Liam and Bobby stay with his party well into the night. Who have they been speaking to? He cannot remember.

Nancy was standing next to her 1930's phone when she turned to Henry.

"Pritchard will see us first thing in the morning."

The memories of Dublin lingered in Henry's mind. He stood up as if to shake off the image of his two friends. He bade Nancy goodnight and left.

Nancy waited a few minutes before crossing her flat to her office. She opened her computer and started a search for the pub Henry had mentioned in their conversation. She knew something material had happened there.

Chapter Eighteen

Henry walked into his flat and was about to go to bed. He had nearly forgotten his BlackBerry. He had left it where it had dropped and not looked at it since. But the little red light was flashing in a hypnotic fashion. Henry tried to ignore it and was about to toss it into his briefcase when his last conversation with James resurfaced. What had he meant by speaking to Ted? He looked at his watch. It was gone 10pm but James would take a call.

He dialled without hesitation. James mobile was engaged. Henry sent a quick text and the reply came back swiftly.

Still @ office, finalising docs, anything you need?

No txs, keep going, was Henry's equally cryptic reply.

He could be at the office in fifteen minutes if he took the car. Nancy had told him to stay away but so what? She was not his mother and he had already breeched her recommendations once by trying to call McCarthy. There had been no negative consequences, but then again McCarthy had not taken the call.

Henry turned towards the door but something was holding him back. He hated this state of indecisiveness. It wasn't him. His eyes fell on the wrapped-up painting. He had not looked at it or moved it since the night Nancy and he had had drinks. Henry walked decisively towards the piece and tore the bubble wrap in one violent move. The painting nearly crashed on the floor. Henry held it back and pushed it into position. Now he could see it better. He liked the ferocity of it and its uncompromised violence. Yes, he would once more bend the rules. He grabbed his car keys, tossed them once in the air. He pocketed his BlackBerry and walked out of his flat.

The car park underneath the block of flats was brightly lit, Henry's Aston Martin parked close to the entrance in one of the larger bays. Henry stopped for a few seconds, someone must be in the car park as the light was on. He looked around but could not spot anyone. He was about to deactivate the car alarm when he felt a firm hand on his shoulder.

Nancy was standing in front of him.

"Going for a spin?"

"Absolutely. The car needs to take the air."

"And would that spin take you back to the office, by any chance?"

"Look Nancy, you're my lawyer not my guardian," he raised his voice.

"Frankly Henry, it feels as if I am turning into just that, otherwise stop being so childish."

"What the fuck has childish got to do with it? I need to have a chat with one of my guys. It's strictly business."

"It has zip to do with business, Henry. You just can't control yourself."

"Control myself! What planet are you on? I have a multibillion dollar deal in the pipeline—"

"Stop the crap," interrupted Nancy. "If this is important you can deal with it on the phone. I am sure that you have perfect backup. Your team are not a bunch of incompetent nerds, right?"

Henry did not have time to reply.

"You do what you have to do, I won't interfere again but I will not be working with some chap who is going to annihilate his chances of salvaging his case – clear?"

Nancy turned and walked away.

"And what is my case to you anyway Nancy, hey? An attempt to crawl back into the limelight?" shouted Henry.

"No, a vague attempt at redemption. And since we are getting down to it, I had received the plane tickets in my post by mistake and forgot to deliver them back on time to you. Yes, the police know. Yes, I feel bad about it. And no, I don't give a damn whether you're peed off." Nancy was speaking over her shoulder as she was waiting for the lift. She disappeared into it when it arrived.

"Shit," shouted Henry throwing his keys against the door of the lift.

* * *

McCarthy had checked his mobile earlier in the day and could see he had missed a call. Henry's name was showing on the small screen and McCarthy was only surprised it had taken so long. He must have been informed of GL's decision by HR. McCarthy had not made the time to speak to Henry directly and for a moment he felt regret. After all, Alexander the Great had been known to give the *coup de grâce* to his dying soldiers himself, but then again McCarthy was not Alexander the Great. More pressing matters were requiring his attention besides his philosophical beliefs or Henry's need for explanation. He walked out of his office in search of an empty meeting room. He needed urgently to call his Whitehall contact. McCarthy walked purposely. Anyone meeting him would imagine he was on his way to an urgent appointment. He would not be interrupted. To his annoyance all the meeting rooms were full. This sign of renewed activity did not cheer him as most meetings were internal, his firm was on the brink. His people were starting to get too agitated, the takeover combined with a gasping market that could not find its feet was destabilising GL's well-oiled platform. Disaster scenarios were being run daily. It was now only a matter of time. McCarthy dove into the staircase and went down one floor. Thankfully, a small meeting room was free. He swiftly entered the room and dialled his contact number.

"Douglas," said the voice, genuinely surprised. "So soon! How are you my dear fellow?"

"We urgently need to talk," McCarthy said. There was no time for niceties.

"I suggest lunch tomorrow. I may be a little late. Say 2pm, same place? I'll be there, alone."

"As you see fit, William," answered McCarthy.

"Can you give me a hint?"

"We are on the verge of a global financial meltdown," replied McCarthy without hesitation.

* * *

The rain had started falling in the early morning, a fine drizzle that made the cold even more penetrating. James Radlett shivered as he crossed the street towards GL's offices. It was 6.30am. The trading floor began its day with cash traders on European markets arriving as early as 6am to prepare their day, listening to the analysts' reviews of the economy, reading the financial papers and scrolling through Bloomberg and Reuters. Information was key, not only published but also inferred; each trader trying to create a position of favourable arbitrage before the London market opened, a discipline that most traders would respect.

The derivative people would arrive at 7 or even perhaps 7.30am, their reliance on market data different from their cash colleagues unless the markets were turbulent.

James showed his card to the security guard – since 9/11 GL had introduced drastic security measures. He progressed towards the turnstile in the vast atrium, scanned his card again and moved to the third floor, rapidly climbing the escalator. The trading floor was already full. The subprime crisis was spreading fast, reaching areas of the market that under normal circumstances would have been spared.

One young woman had been working the Asian market and, looking away from her screens, dropped her head into her hands in a gesture of defeat. She could do nothing but lose time and time again.

James logged in, and quickly perused Bloomberg. He was not focusing on the debacle, but rather was hunting for any announcements relating to the takeover between GL and HXBK. Interesting news had the habit of appearing early morning and brusquely disappearing from the news panel as the day moved on. He searched under the GL ticker, then HXBK's then financial institutions. Nothing. He quickly looked at the clock at the bottom of his screen which indicated 6.47. He would make his way to McCarthy's office at 6.55. He had no intention of arriving ahead of time.

* * *

Ted had also arrived at the office early. He had parked his Porsche 911 in GL's private car park, a luxury only MDs enjoyed. The congestion charge did not worry him. His property had had the good fortune to fall on the right side of the line when Ken Livingstone had extended its perimeter. His house in the West End was indeed well positioned. Something he liked to brag about with less fortunate colleagues. Ted reached the elevator and looked at his watch; 6.55 exactly.

When the door opened again, Ted found himself face to face with James. A small yelp escaped from his mouth. James nodded stiffly and stepped into the lift, forcing Ted to rush out.

"*Little fucker, I'll get you one day,*" James said through gritted teeth.

The lift pinged again, reminding James of why he had entered it in the first place. It took him to the executive floor where Douglas McCarthy was expecting him.

Unusually, McCarthy's door was open. Cindy was nowhere to be seen. James was about to wait for Cindy to return when McCarthy's authoritative voice summoned him in. He was seated at his desk and well advanced in his day's work. He asked James to take a seat at the spacious meeting table. James sat down and McCarthy joined him, neither man had greeted the other.

McCarthy's attention rested on James, a heavy weight that the young man felt immediately. His army training and military career, albeit short, had familiarised him with the implacable authority of his commanding officer, and yet the proximity of McCarthy made him uneasy. Whether he liked it or not his CEO was a force to be reckoned with.

"I am sure you know why you are here James," said McCarthy without any further formalities.

"Well, since I have not seen Henry for over thirty-six hours, I think I do," replied James.

There was no point in being coy. If McCarthy intended to have a straightforward conversation with James, James was intent on giving him just that.

"Our legal team informs me that matters look difficult for Henry," said McCarthy.

No reply from James.

"I consequently have a major decision to make regarding the future of the team," carried on McCarthy.

James remained silent. He had prepared himself for this outcome. McCarthy paused once more. James, still sitting straight in front of him, rested his gaze on his CEO. Without Henry or Anthony Albert around, McCarthy had a much broader choice. He held an additional chip that could be played to his advantage. Something that would not have crossed his mind thirty-six hours ago now became a distinct possibility. HXBK's people knew this too. They were on tenterhooks.

"HXBK is putting pressure on me to transition the team immediately. It would be a quick and viable answer but I am not sure it is the right one," carried on McCarthy.

McCarthy was waiting for a reaction. James, still sitting straight in front of him, had folded his hands calmly on the table. He looked at McCarthy straight in the eyes. He would not compromise.

"For the time being, I would like Ted to take control of the team. He will be relying on you heavily, of course, to keep the technical side under control. But when it comes to management decisions Ted will take over from Henry."

James finally shifted. This was preposterous. Ted had neither the kudos nor the market credentials to take control of Henry's team.

"I am sure there is a rational reason why this is so but I am sorry, I just can't see it myself."

McCarthy remained relaxed. He would not employ the same technique as with Ted. In fact, Ted bored him, he was so easy to scare and manipulate, so repulsively weak. James was more of an interesting challenge.

"I agree that at first sight it does not seem a good move. I know Ted does not have, let us say, the same credible image as Henry does but ..."

McCarthy paused for effect and poured a fresh cup of coffee for both of them. James was taken aback by his willingness to explain his decision.

"Ted is heading the integration committee on this segment of our business and you seem to work well with him. He has only good things to say about you."

"I am glad Ted feels comfortable with me," replied James, unmoved by the compliment. Ted had no option but to claim he got on well with James. He needed James' technical expertise to control Henry's team.

James felt awkward. If he had any ambition to succeed Henry, he had to seize the opportunity now.

"Excellent," McCarthy said, turning James' hesitation to his advantage. "Then the matter is settled. I will confirm by email the arrangement."

"Which I am sure is only temporary, until a final decision is made," added James, still seated and not prepared to move.

McCarthy may have decided the discussion was over but James had not.

McCarthy shot an ice cold look at James, but indulged him. After all, it would have been too easy. James glanced at the clocks on the wall. McCarthy had another ten minutes to spare. If he wanted to check how much guts James had, James was up for it. McCarthy was game, he moved back to his desk, checked a couple of emails as he was speaking to James.

"You are referring to the outcome of the merger. I agree," replied McCarthy still looking at his screens.

James was still in his seat.

"I am not sure I am actually referring to the ultimate conclusion of the merger, no," carried on James.

Now or never.

"The first question is, will Henry come back, the second, if he ever does, in what capacity, and finally does it make a difference anyway?"

McCarthy stopped browsing through his mailbox and leaned against the front of his desk, arms crossed, a faint smile on his lips. He was enjoying this battle between ambition and integrity.

"You mean, if Henry returns, does he have a chance of getting his job back? Assuming he is cleared of all charges, his reputation will have been damaged beyond repair. This is *not* something you recover from. Henry is finished. Consequently, yes. I need to make up my mind on long-term succession."

McCarthy stopped there, not prepared to make things easy for James. If he wanted it, he would have to ask, possibly even beg. James would have to descend into the pit, fighting in the mud like all of them.

Despite his rising anger, James felt that maybe, just maybe, McCarthy was right. What right did he have to judge so readily? He had chosen banking and not any type of banking. He had chosen to work on the trading floor of one of the largest banks in the world. These were the rules of engagement.

A sharp pain in his left leg surprised James, his face closed to scrutiny and he quickly pressed his hand upon it to stop the shaking. The wound he had suffered in battle had decided to make itself known again. He mechanically massaged it whilst trying to formulate his next question. A battle scene flashed before his eyes. He stood up.

"When you have, Douglas, please let me know," said James.

The moment had passed. James would never become one of McCarthy's men. He returned to his desk. Usually keen to know what the markets were doing, James would normally stop to chat with a trader. Not today. Morag had kept the meeting quiet, secretly hoping James could take over. Her fresh news about Matt's whereabouts would do nothing to cheer him up.

Arriving at his desk, James sat down without a word. He activated his screens not paying much attention to what was scrolling in front of his eyes. Morag shifted in her seat, still hesitant.

"Yes Morag," said James, without looking at her.

"Do you want the bad news or do you want the *very* bad news?"

"It's going to be one of those days," replied James with a grim smile. "Come on. Give it to me."

"I know where Matt is," she said, lowering her voice and leaning towards him.

"Mmmm," James moved towards her, his solid face now close to hers.

"New York," she whispered.

"And?"

"HXBK's offices."

"Definitely one of those days," sighed James. "OK, fill me in."

Morag passed on all the details she had managed to glean. James walked into Henry's office and shut the door. He looked at the last text from his boss.

Keep going …

Chapter Nineteen

Nancy had rung Henry's doorbell in three short bursts. She could hear, from behind the door, a fumble of activity and it finally opened. Henry had switched his jeans for the expected dark suit, white shirt and, *oh*, a red tie. Nancy took a step back.

"You're with GL, aren't you?"

"I like your newly found optimism Nancy. I thought you might have said, *you were.*"

"I am referring to the colour of the tie my dear. You look very Goldman Sachs. Red tie."

"Correct. I am going incognito. This is camouflage."

"Anyway, I approve."

Henry grinned but did not reply. As they went down in the lift, he observed Nancy. Her elegance was sober yet striking. Her suit was dark grey and the shirt an unusual pattern of soft greys and black. The final touch was a large ring featuring in its centre an equally large pink pearl. Her style made him feel confident. He was dealing with a professional woman who knew how to power dress.

"You mentioned your driver would be here to pick us up. Should you not have checked?"

"No need, Nancy. I have used Charlie for over five years. He is the most punctual person you can ever meet. He would have called if he had been delayed."

Henry opened the door of their building, making room for Nancy to go first. She spotted the black S-Class Mercedes waiting for them. A heavy man with dark glasses emerged from the driver's side. Nancy thought she was meeting Agent M from *Men in Black* and immediately approved of Henry's decision to stick with Charlie.

* * *

The meeting with Henry's brief was going well. At the outset Henry had required Nancy to be included in his team; documents were being drafted to that effect. Henry repeated what he had said to Pole. Nancy gave details about what she had witnessed. One of Pritchard QC's pupils was taking notes. For the first time in thirty-six hours, Henry was feeling in control. He had regained the upper hand. He had also managed to avoid looking at his BlackBerry for a couple of hours. Yet he fiddled with it with the intensity of a religious devotee fingering prayer beads.

"Shall we have a tea break?" Pritchard QC offered.

He signalled his pupil to organise it. Henry stood up and escaped, to be alone finally and scroll through his emails. A sense of new possibilities had given him hope. The call he had received from HR could wait. He could never take these people seriously anyway. But no new emails had come in for several hours. Henry checked again, no emails since 10am in the morning. It was already 3pm and there was only one explanation: his email service had been suspended. The searing burn of anger flared inside him.

"What is that stupid bitch thinking of? Fuck you."

He scrolled through his previous emails and furiously dialled the HR number. Henry exploded on the phone when she answered but she was having none of it. She kept asking him to calm down and listen to his voicemails. Henry decided to shut her up by requesting to speak to McCarthy immediately. He had viewed this request as his ultimate defence. The old man had not responded to Henry's missed calls but then again how could he in the midst of a takeover? Henry would have to swallow his pride and try again. He asked to be put through to Cindy. She would arrange a call with McCarthy to clear up this ridiculous mess.

"Mr Crowne," insisted the woman on the phone in a high-pitched voice. "The decision to discontinue your email service was signed off by Mr McCarthy himself."

Henry could not remember having been slapped so hard in the face, more used to throwing the punches than receiving them. He recovered swiftly, not prepared to admit defeat, yet.

"I want to hear this from him in person," said Henry.

"Well, call him directly if you'd like," retorted the voice on the other end, "but I will not disrupt him for what are clear instructions—"

Henry hung up without waiting for her to finish her sentence. He dialled McCarthy's personal mobile number once more, a privilege he had never abused before. He had just put the mobile to his ear when a strong hand grabbed his arm. Nancy had witnessed the whole conversation.

"This is not a good idea," she said calmly. "What are you going to achieve?"

DMac's private mobile had started to ring.

"WHAT?" she repeated, still squeezing his arm.

Henry was furious. He tried to yank his arm free from her grip. Nancy's hold must have been stronger than he thought. They exchanged angry looks. The mobile was still ringing. This time Henry pushed her hard and freed himself. The BlackBerry escaped his hand, flew into the air before crashing on the ground with a metallic crunch.

Henry's eyes opened wide as he yelled, "No," – a cry of agony. He dropped to the floor where his phone lay in pieces. "No," he moaned each time he picked one up. Nancy's face had reddened, her hand frozen in mid-air. Henry darted toward her, a demented look in his eye.

"I need to get a new phone right away, right NOW."

"We have not finished our meeting with your defence lawyer," replied Nancy with as much composure as she could summon.

"I don't give a shit," shouted Henry. "I need to get another phone RIGHT NOW."

He had grabbed her arm, screaming.

"I understood you, Henry, nevertheless—"

"What the fuck am I doing here? I must be completely out of my mind. I should be at the office and you," he said, pointing at her with a menacing finger, "you have not practised for years, you have no idea what goes on in the City anymore."

His body shook with uncontrolled laughter whilst shaking his head, looking at the bits of phone mangled in his large hand.

"It is just not happening. I am getting a new phone. Tell this lawyer of yours I will come back when I have done what I need to do, you stupid cow."

"And your QC will tell you that he is fully booked until next month," came a curt response from behind Henry.

"By the way, Ms Wu may not have practised for a while but she still is regarded by the profession as one of the best, so you may care to apologise. I will be in my office. You have five minutes to consider whether you want to continue our conversation."

Nancy closed her eyes slowly, still shocked at the violence of the outburst. Now that it had passed she realised she was more *surprised* than upset by what had triggered it. Letting go was never going to be easy for Henry. She heard the bench in the corridor groan beneath the weight of his body. He sat there motionless, staring at some invisible images.

"I am really losing it," said Henry finally, rubbing his hands over his face a few times. He could not face Nancy or apologise.

"You may not believe it," Nancy replied. "I went through it myself. It is hard to give up the rat race."

"Don't say it, please," Henry murmured, eyes cast in the distance.

Shifting on his feet, he could feel renewed anger in the pit of his stomach. He had no time for a lesson he did not want to hear.

Nancy was choosing her words carefully.

"To let go of old anger."

"Is this a lesson in Eastern philosophy?" replied Henry with sarcasm.

"No," said Nancy calmly. "I think you will find the same idea being tackled by most of Western theology."

Henry looked surprised. Nancy had gone down a path that he had never trodden himself.

"Come on," said Nancy, extending her long delicate hand

towards him. "Let's finish what we have started. You can buy another BlackBerry after that. OK?"

Henry stood up and walked into the room alongside Nancy. His expression was inscrutable.

* * *

Nurani had booked the early morning BA flight to Belfast. She had originally hesitated between BA and a low-cost alternative, but Pole was categorical. He was not flying a cheapie airline that almost certainly shirked proper maintenance. So, the great Inspector Pole was scared of flying. She cast an eye at her boss sitting next to her and saw the relief on his face when they eventually touched down. Pole grew positively euphoric when they reached passport control.

A short, ginger-haired man was waiting for them at the arrival gate. Pole recognised his colleague of old and they shook hands warmly, delighted to see each other again.

"It's been a while," said Inspector Murphy in his distinct Northern Irish accent.

"It has," replied Pole still smiling. "May I introduce you to my colleague Nurani Shah."

"Good to meet you," said Murphy. "Couldn't get a better boss."

Nurani smiled in turn and shook his hand, not knowing what to reply to a remark that may have sounded patronising but somehow did not feel that way.

"She doesn't need much of that these days," said Pole.

Nurani blushed at the compliment and they all moved towards an old battered car.

"Don't tell me they can't do better than that," said Pole looking at Pat's official car.

"Na, it's my car. Pay could be better though," replied Pat unconcerned.

"Yep, London's the same. Can't complain too much though. At least I am not trying to raise a family of four."

"Five actually Jon. My little one is already six years old."

"Congratulations Pat, Niamh must be busy."

"Thanks, she loves it though. And what about you Jon. Still single?"

"'Fraid so. I am a lone wolf after all," said Pole, increasingly conscious of Nurani's curious silence.

"And still south of the river?"

"Can't leave the house, too many memories there."

"Plus the artworks she left you. I remember them well."

Pole nodded slowly and Pat picked up on his unease.

"Liam has not been that cooperative, but he's got the message – we softened him up a bit for you," said Pat, tactfully reverting to the case.

Pole cast a somewhat alarmed eye at Nurani. Pat had always had a way of getting what he wanted and sometimes not in an entirely orthodox fashion. He was about to reassure her that all was legal and above board when she poked her head through from the back seat of the car.

"How do you do that," she said, enthusiastically.

Pole sat back amazed. *What, one foot in Northern Ireland and she was ready for some serious interrogation techniques. Ms straight-laced-and-by-the-book shows her true colours.*

"Well," said Pat, now sounding coy, "it takes a lot of – training."

Pole decided to stay out of it, almost miffed that his old chum had stolen the limelight.

Pole recognised the police station from a distance, the same sad building earmarked by years of terror and neglect. The sight of the Troubles' effects reminded Pole of days he still could not forget.

Without much formality, Pole and Nurani were led into a meeting room where Liam O'Connor was waiting. Nurani's face showed her disappointment. Liam did not look like much.

"Less impressive than you may think," whispered Pole, reading her expression.

"Hello Liam."

"What a pleasant surprise," replied Liam. "I've said all I need to say to these guys." Liam indicated to Murphy with his head.

"So I was told but I always like to hear a good story for myself," said Pole.

"If you have time to kill," replied Liam, shrugging his shoulders.

For the next hour Pole and the team took Liam O'Connor through some key facts; his connection to Henry, his job in the Dublin Docks providing IT support to some of the banks settled in the Irish financial centre. The same story was rolled out, which was identical to the transcript Pole had received before he took off for Belfast that morning. Inspector Pole was starting to wonder whether Liam had anything new to offer when a last question on his meeting in London with Henry focused Pole's attention. Liam had a plausible reason to be in the UK, since his company was organising the maintenance of a number of offices situated in the Dublin Docks. He was sent to London regularly to check on clients. Pole smiled at the thought that Liam O'Connor was running quality control checks for a number of English companies. This sounded all very much above board. Pole decided to ask an unrelated question regarding the takeover and its impact on Henry. After all, Liam was also supposed to be in finance.

"Do you think Henry will survive the takeover? His competitor is well positioned, I understand."

For some reason Pole used the present tense and noticed a surprised reaction from Liam O'Connor.

"Well, unless GL and HXBK play the Ouija board, I don't think that snooty bloke will trouble Henry anymore," responded Liam with a hint of sarcasm and smirk in his voice.

"Unless Henry is convicted," retorted Pole, trying to yank open the door.

Liam looked at Pole with ferocity, "You have nothing on Henry."

This was the answer Pole had been waiting for. The game was on. He mentally praised his colleague. Pat certainly had softened up Liam considerably. Nurani discreetly disappeared at the sound of her BlackBerry buzzing. She moved noiselessly, hardly disturbing her chair as she rose.

"Why do you think Anthony Albert was snooty, anyway? Did you discuss him with Henry? I thought you said you hardly spoke business."

"I can just imagine it," replied Liam.

"Why do you think there is nothing to be found on Henry?"

"I don't know. I'm just making assumptions," carried on Liam.

Nurani had returned as discreetly as she had left and placed a number of pages in front of Pole. Pole stood up, turned away and took the time to read through them. Liam could wait until he was ready to continue.

"Let's talk Switzerland."

"Why?"

"You know why," said Pole evenly, producing the document he had been expecting since his arrival. "I am sure you are aware that the secrecy surrounding banking law in Switzerland has been greatly reduced? If you're not, you should be. We are getting much more information from our Swiss colleagues these days. They have learnt the word *speed* when we mention the word *terrorism*."

Liam took it in, but still offered no reply.

"My colleague Ms Shah will tell you more about what we have learned. The world is becoming a very small place," continued Pole.

In front of Liam Nurani placed several snapshots showing him walking out of Zurich Airport, spanning three years. There were also photos of Liam taking the tram and finally entering a bank, a discreet institution specialising in private banking.

"So what? I have a bank account in Switzerland, big deal, a lot of my clients have too," said Liam unshaken.

"Sure," said Nurani. "But how many of them do so under an alias and please let us have a list. It might make for some interesting reading."

Nurani slammed a list of transactions from a bank statement in front of Liam.

"Do they also receive large sums of money from numbered accounts registered in the Caymans, the owner of which is another numbered account from Lichtenstein? If so I really, really, want to know."

Nurani was enjoying herself. She was not going to be intimidated by some guy with or without IRA connections. She was ready to take on the little git. Liam had no idea what it meant to be at Scotland Yard for an Asian woman.

"Well, if you are so clever, why do you bother questioning me at all?"

"I am not. I am telling you," she said vehemently.

Liam's light green eyes had changed colour, growing darker. His round placid face hardened up.

"Another very large sum of money arrived a few days ago, another new client from Saudi Arabia," Nurani pushed a copy of the Swiss bank account details in front of him.

"I have a lot of generous friends."

"Me too. But maybe not of the same calibre."

The change in law had not been part of the plan. Liam had hoped to be quick enough to move accounts around. He had been a little too slow in taking Henry's advice … shame. The great network of clandestine help had started to dissolve in Ireland after the IRA decommissioning, making large movements of cash much more difficult to engineer. But the old links with other terrorist networks had remained. Switzerland still played a part in the money laundering chain. Liam sat back and looked at everyone in the room. There was no doubt in his mind that they would eventually find out, but he would be damned if he made their task any easier.

"I want my lawyer," he said folding his arms over his chest. "This discussion is over."

"Sure," said Pat. "Do you have a name?"

Murphy, Pole and Ms Shah left the interrogation room to recap.

"Do you hope to link Crowne with those payments?" asked Murphy, knowing that Pole would share his thoughts.

"Of course, that would be a major step forward. Although I suspect it won't be all that easy. After all, Crowne is a banker. He uses tax havens to structure his transactions. I suspect he can create enough screens for us to find it difficult to track him down. Then again, even the most intelligent of people make the most obvious of mistakes sometimes."

Pole was now sitting comfortably in Pat's office.

"And you missus," he said, imitating Liam's Northern Irish accent. "I would like you to stay and continue our discussion with O'Connor."

"Great," replied Nurani, her dark almond shaped eyes shining with pride. "Looking forward to this."

185

"I know, I know," said Pole. "Just don't savage him too much, will you? You, on the other hand, Mr Murphy, you're not allowed to teach Ms Shah the many different ways of softening up witnesses or, in other words, beating the bejesus out of them."

Pole waved a reproaching finger at Pat. They all laughed. Other officers in the neighbouring offices lifted their heads at the raucous noise.

They were preparing to go back to the interrogation room when another officer knocked at the door and opened without waiting for an answer.

"We have located Liam's brother, Bobby. I think you guys should get down to central. It's not going according to plan."

The relaxed atmosphere faded in an instant.

"Let's go," said Murphy, his spirit dampened.

He knew what to expect and did not want to cast his mind back to the days of the Troubles.

"Talk to me," carried on Murphy as they all started running towards central control.

"Bobby must have heard about Liam being picked up. He was trying to leave the country following the usual arms smuggling route. Unfortunately for him it did not go as smoothly as he'd hoped. Some of the old guard are prepared to grass on the splinter groups. They don't belong anymore," replied the other officer.

"He has barricaded himself in an office at the Docks. There may be hostages. We are not sure yet. What we know for sure is that he has fired a few gunshots at the local guys."

"Shit," blurted Pat. "This idiot is going to get himself killed with some other poor sods who have nothing to do with the whole affair. He just can't give up."

Murphy and his guests burst into the control room, where other officers were giving directions on the ground.

"Have you spoken to him directly?" asked Pole.

"We have tried but nothing doing at the moment."

"Pat, are you going to engage with him?" said Pole.

"Do I have a choice?"

"I have not done this for a very long time, Pat. You're the man on the ground. I am no longer part of that team anyway and …" Pole hesitated. "Nurani is with you. She will handle it. Just keep me in the loop."

"It will be done and I am sure it will be safe."

This was not what Pole had intended but then again it was part of the job and he trusted Pat implicitly in the affair. They shook hands with no further words exchanged and Pole headed towards the exit. He had a plane to catch.

Nurani wanted a word. Pole wondered whether his decision to leave her behind might be too much too soon and he was about to change his plan when she spoke.

"This could be a breakthrough Jon."

"How so?"

"Well, if Bobby can't or won't give himself up maybe this helps with Liam."

Pole gave a little nod. He knew where she was going. He felt both impressed and shocked. She certainly was the person for the job.

"You want to cut a deal with Liam?" he said, focusing his full attention on her. She had never experienced this before and recoiled under his glance.

"Well, I thought …" her voice trailed off.

"It has to be considered. Bobby's life against the name of the account holders," said Pole. "But," he stressed, "before you cut a deal, I want to know every detail of what it entails. Do we understand each other? I want consensus with Murphy. This is not going to descend into a political disaster or the evidence being tainted by foul play."

"Of course Jon, I would not want to do anything without you knowing," replied Nurani.

Pole relaxed in the knowledge that his stark remarks had hit home. He looked at her with kindness.

"These guys are very dangerous Nu. Don't be fooled by what you see. Even the C-T squad in London is scared about what they can achieve." He turned around, grabbed his bag and disappeared into his cab. Nurani would miss his guidance terribly.

Chapter Twenty

The plane was taxiing down the runway and Inspector Pole was strapped into his seat. He was not looking forward to the flight back on his own. His dislike of flying was usually alleviated by conversation but Nurani was still in Belfast and by all accounts shouldering the considerable task of bringing Liam home to roost. Pole closed his eyes and gripped the armrest when the pilot revved the engine for take-off. His stomach somersaulted as the plane left the ground. Pole opened his eyes again to see the little boy seated next to him observing him with curiosity.

"It's fun to fly," said Pole, embarrassed.

The boy nodded once and went back to his comic book perusing it with the seriousness of a business man reading the *FT*. Pole exhaled deeply and dived into his briefcase which he had placed underneath the seat in front. He was not going to stand up to get it out of the overhead locker. Carrying a briefcase was bad enough. He had never believed in the need to own one and always borrowed the one he had to use occasionally from a willing colleague. He took out a wad of papers he had printed before leaving Murphy's office – emails and reports. A mass of documents he might want to read once more.

Pole sank into the case with the feeling of familiarity and ownership. The first document was confirming the meeting with Anthony Albert's family lawyer the next day. Albert's solicitor had been away but was now back in the office. He would make the time for Pole, although he was asking for a few hours' grace to organise matters appropriately (in his own words). Pole was asking for the rules on confidentiality to be bent and had to give way a little himself.

The second email was from Eugene. He had sent him a long account of Brett Allner-Smith's recent dealings. Pole managed a smile. Brett was a controversial figure who enjoyed sailing close to the wind, in Eugene's words. A number of antiquities which he had brokered had questionable origins. He did not seem to mind too much who the seller was as long as he had a buyer to match. Evidently, Brett Allner-Smith enjoyed a few connections with the underworld of trafficking although there had never been enough evidence to convict him. Pole nodded. This guy was surprisingly good.

The stewardess offered Pole a much-needed drink. A small bottle of red wine would help with a very sad looking sandwich. He was not strictly off duty but needed a bit of help with his air travel. Pole carried on reading the lengthy mail, details of specific art pieces, valuations, contacts. He was starting to lose interest when a piece of information attracted his attention. Allner-Smith owned an account in Switzerland with a small private bank well known to Pole, one of the last strongholds of the much-denigrated banking secrecy. There secrecy meant secrecy. Pole had never managed to get one iota of information out of them and nor had his Swiss colleagues. Pole sat back in his seat muttering to himself.

"Now this is interesting, another coincidence? Mmmm."

He immediately felt the heaviness of another set of eyes on him. The little boy sitting in the adjacent seat did not seem amused.

"Sorry," said Pole with a silly smile.

"Accepted," replied the little man and dived back into his comic book.

Pole was about to make some comment but thought otherwise. *Children these days*, and as the thought crossed his mind, he did feel like an old fart.

Pole returned to his own stack of papers. He started constructing a plausible scenario surrounding Albert's murder. Would Allner-Smith want to frame Henry? Could he frame Henry? It would not be too tedious to find out about Henry's Irish links. He knew about Anthony and Henry's rivalry. Allner-Smith had witnessed it first hand in the auction rooms of Christie's and Sotheby's. Motives were plentiful; greed would always be at the centre of this case, then revenge, power, vanity. All of these qualities Brett exhibited in spades. But then there was the briefcase, Pole stopped. He straightened himself up and cast an eye at the little lad next to him. He was still engrossed in his comic book now furiously chewing on a piece of gum.

Pole smiled, sitting back in his seat.

So where was he? The briefcase. Pole drew a blank. How could Allner-Smith have orchestrated the delivery of this explosive item? *That is a very bad joke*, thought Pole, still unrepentant for having cracked it. Maybe with the help of Albert's wife? That did not sound right either or maybe it was – a switch in briefcases? By all accounts Allner-Smith would have wanted to stay in the background to manipulate Adeila. Discussing the delivery of the briefcase directly with her would give her immense power over him. They would be accomplices, and Allner-Smith operated on his own. No, he would want to be the sole mastermind, or so Eugene said. Then again, he had never, as far as they both could see, gone that far.

Pole stopped, took a sip of wine from the plastic glass and pulled a face. He looked at the label which was claiming a full bodied red exploding with wild berries. In short, a passable plonk. As the plane started to give a couple of small jolts, Pole emptied his glass. He spent a few minutes still considering the motive, there was a lot of money involved.

Actually, how much money exactly?

Pole reached for his colleague's briefcase again and pulled out another document. A summary sent by Albert's accountant of the dead man's assets, *give or take a few £100,000* read the email.

Ridiculous, but then so many things sounded ridiculous at a few thousand feet in the air. Pole shifted. Not an idea to dwell on. Back to the case.

The mail was well constructed and showed in a very concise form what a City senior MD can make in a few years of hard earning.

1) *Belgravia House (latest estimate @ 30/08/2008)*	*£10,500,000*
2) *Art collection (including pieces over £1,000)*	
See appendix 1 for details	*£5,650,000*
3) *Jewellery*	
See appendix 2 for details	*£1,100,000*
4) *Flat in Nice (latest estimate @12/07/2007*	
Fixed @ 11/10/2008)	*£1,750,000*
5) *Investments in Funds and other*	*£9,584,000*
6) *HXBK unexpired options*	*£7,500,000*
7) *Cash on account*	*£70,800*
8) *Aston Martin DB9*	*£115,000*
Grand Total	*£36,269,800*

Pole read the numbers one more time and mused at what he would do with £36 or so million. Then again did he really want that much money in the first place? He could have followed in the footsteps of his grandmother or indeed his entire family for whom art did not mean meagre revenues. He remembered the artists visiting her house, the debates, the excitement and the falling out. Her sense for talent was unique. He could have lived in her shadow, or that of his father, a remarkable saxophonist who still played, at the age of seventy-eight, with the greatest jazz fusion musicians. But he had chosen to be different. Why? Pole looked at his watch and decided to park the question for later on knowing full well what the outcome would be.

So, it was evident that Anthony Albert had done well for himself since joining the banking world. Pole remembered the sum Albert had negotiated when he had first joined HXBK. The shy young man had learned to monetise his talents, fast. Such a quick rise in revenue, however, must have indicated only one thing, a ruthless desire to take risks, and a lot of them.

Large and risky transactions were about to come undone, or so the financial press claimed. Albert was not the sort of man who looked closely at the ethical consequences of the deals he put together. What simply mattered was the bottom line and the bonus he would derive from negotiating such large deals. The idea focused Pole's mind again. In the context of a takeover matters became much tenser. He jotted a note down on the side of the document he was reading. Albert dealt in the subprime market. Andy had collected a list of the latest deals by Albert, with counterparties' identities and revenue streams. He also had a detailed account of Albert's bonuses in the past four years. HXBK's HR had finally provided a list of bonus figures that were as impressive as his total wealth. The last bonus in particular was explosively large both in cash terms and HXBK options.

Interesting, thought Pole. *Looks like HR are dragging their feet. Why?*

Pole was interrupted when the plane gave yet another jolt. The seatbelt sign lit up. Inspector Pole grabbed the armrest. The pilot came on the intercom. They would be encountering some turbulence until they landed at Heathrow which was only twenty-five minutes away. Pole grumbled and prepared himself for a very uncomfortable final ride.

* * *

Back on terra firma, Henry, Nancy and his barrister were about to conclude their findings. The BlackBerry incident had put a dampener on what would have been otherwise a very successful meeting. Nancy's choice of barrister had proven to be very judicious yet Henry could not reconcile the incident. He had lost control but then again, why interfere with his business?

Gavin Pritchard QC's voice brought Henry back to the meeting room, a large space filled with books and faded furniture. The chairs looked as if they hadn't been changed since Pritchard had started his career, which Henry took to be a very long time ago. Yet it felt cosy, even familiar.

"I am feeling clear on all the facts and evidence surrounding your matter," declared the barrister with confidence.

"I will step in the next time Inspector Pole wants a meeting. It is essential. I recommend a solicitor I work with regularly to attend meetings." Pritchard QC leaned forward and tapped his pen on his notes.

"So far WE take the view that WE have a series of coincidences which are fortuitous. WE believe in the circumstantial nature of the events. The police of course will not accept this easily. Pole is a methodical man. Nevertheless, it is OUR intention to pursue the argument."

"Precisely," replied Henry.

He felt drained of energy and knowledge. Pritchard waited a few seconds. His thought process was nearly palpable to Henry. Beyond his tiredness Henry gathered Pritchard might have something else in mind.

"Excellent," carried on Pritchard.

He jotted down a few more notes. Henry had been tense for several hours. He felt a release from pain. *Fight or flight*, he thought, as he gathered himself to stand up. Maybe, just maybe, he could escape further scrutiny.

"One final point if I may?"

Henry's barrister adjusted his round glasses and pushed his body back in his chair. He had kept the meatiest morsel for the end.

"Your IRA faction connections?"

Pritchard had not bothered with the word alleged. To him all Irish men from Belfast had IRA connections.

"What about it?" replied Henry, non-committal.

Pritchard QC looked at his client and remained silent. He was simply waiting. Nothing Henry could say would convince him to drop the question. It hit Henry to see the anticipation of success, the challenge – and what a challenge, a banker blowing a plane out of the sky through IRA contacts. Magnificent. Even more so after the IRA had renounced violence. A splinter group would make matters more complex to defend. Possibly the challenge of a lifetime. Henry suspected he might have done it for free, but Pritchard would know as well as Henry did that money was not only worth the pleasure it gave, it was also a benchmark against which all professionals aspired to be measured. Was Pritchard giving him a reflection of his own image when he himself was going for the kill?

Henry stared at his lawyer, anger burning his gut. The moment passed. Henry kept looking intensely at the face in front of him to make it give in, but the smooth round oval did not budge. The slightly overarched eyebrows, the large forehead etched with waves of lines, all was calm and decisive. Henry inhaled deeply. Pritchard would not take the case unless he knew. Henry sat back in his chair.

"Where do I start?"

"The beginning is usually a good place," said Pritchard picking up his pen once more. He leaned forward with avidity.

"It was a long time ago."

* * *

The officer at passport control greeted Pole with the requisite stern face when Pole handed over his passport. Pole had received news from Nurani by BlackBerry. He was trying to reach her now that matters had moved decidedly forward in Ireland. He was concerned. Bobby was a dangerous man, hardened to the core with a hint of lunacy thrown in for good measure. Pole had tried many times to imagine what the IRA decommissioning would do to such an extreme mind. Bobby was a zealot, his dedication to the cause more a way of life than a political battle. Over the years Pole had suspected that the reasons why had become secondary to the means. Nothing else really mattered. It was all about the fight, regardless of the peace process.

Pole had recognised the impact Henry's upbringing in Northern Ireland had had on him. The violence would have been in the background, a constant present, an unseen filter potent enough to distort all that it touched. Pole remembered reading a book a few years back describing life in Belfast: the prejudices, the people trying to make a living out of so very little, but above all the bombs. The book's description of one bomb blast had made a lasting impression on him. It was not so much the torn bodies and the atrocious violence that made an impression on him. It was the incomprehension, even the absurdity so clearly exposed. The stubborn attitude of the perpetrators, the total disconnect between rhetoric and death. Pole did not believe in God or indeed that the Church had any valid role to play in guiding man on his ethical search but he believed in humanity. The ringtone of his mobile brought him back to the now. Nurani was calling.

"What news?" asked Pole without further greetings.

"Bobby is refusing to talk at the moment," replied Nurani, eager to give her news. "We still don't know why he turned up there, probably to see Liam. However, things are getting more complicated. We are almost certain it is a hostage situation."

"What do you mean by 'almost certain' about the hostage situation?"

"Bobby got in as people were leaving. One person has not arrived home yet. We have to presume he is still in there unless we hear from him."

"Agreed, we are not taking chances," replied Pole now regretting he was in London. "Who is on the scene?"

"The situation is pretty advanced. Pat called his contacts in Dublin. Special forces are there as well as a hostage negotiator."

"Can you deal with it?" asked Pole abruptly, unconcerned about sparing Nurani's feelings.

"Yes, Jon, I can," she replied with absolute certainty.

"Very well, what are you suggesting?"

"Bobby has already fired a few rounds. The guys in Dublin are very twitchy. The Docks are a popular district for business. They are deciding whether to storm the premises or not. The only thing that stops them at the moment is the hostage story. An IRA incident is not what the authorities want at the moment, even if this comes from a splinter group."

"Pat has no jurisdiction over that part of the world though."

"Yeah, but he knows the boys in Dublin pretty well. And he knows the O'Connor brothers even better. The Dublin guys have already asked him for his opinion and they now know that we have Liam in custody – to storm or not to storm?"

Pole took it in. Nurani had accustomised herself to the situation pretty fast. She was hard and uncompromising, she would do well.

"Pat is prepared to cut a deal. Liam gets to reason with his brother to give himself up and gets him out of this alive but–" .

"Liam gives us Henry," Pole interrupted

Nurani coughed.

"OK, do it," replied Pole after another brief silence. "I am on my way to the office and will call you two from there. I want to discuss the terms of this agreement if there is going to be one."

Pole dashed into his waiting cab.

Chapter Twenty-One

Henry was walking home. He had left Nancy behind with little ceremony. He needed to be on his own and desperately wanted to replace his lost BlackBerry. It took some considerable time for Henry to find what he had in mind. He had not previously taken the trouble to investigate the multiple options that were available to him. His PA Morag always chose the most up-to-date version available, irrespective of whether it made sense or not. One simply had to have the latest at GL. Henry never had the time or indeed the inclination to be a 'geek', however the subject matter had become of intense interest to him and the young woman who first tried to serve him did not fare well. Henry could not admit it, thinking himself a progressive, but he had to be very convinced before he relied on a woman for anything technical.

Her boss had spotted the issue and moved in to help. It was too late and Henry had already worked himself into a contentious mood. He was furiously enquiring about functions and apps that he had barely noticed let alone used, and then, of course, the phone was too bulky, the keys too small, the iPhone he was offered did not have the right security protocol. The intervention of another sales assistant only made matters worse until Henry eventually looked at his watch.

He decided upon a particular model much to the disbelief and relief of the exhausted staff. Henry left the box behind, had the SIM card installed, grumbled a final question about mail access and pocketed his phone. He walked slowly down Chancery Lane revisiting his time with Pritchard QC. He would not be a man easy to lie to. Could Henry risk jeopardising the relationship with his defence lawyer? The thought of succeeding gave him a pang of excitement. He had done well but the day was young and he would not presume success.

Henry was about to cross Holborn when he spotted a small cafe on his left. He decided to do what he often did in the City when he needed to take a step back. He settled himself in the window of the cafe shop with a large Assam tea and a biscotti. For a while he observed the passers-by. He tried to guess which firm or employment the men and women who walked past were coming from. The young man with a white shirt, sober but noticeable red tie, and clean-shaven was unmistakably Goldman Sachs, the middle-aged woman with her severe black suit and large briefcase one of the barristers. Henry could not help but notice that none of these people had a smile on their faces. No matter how much he tried to brush it away it kept coming back. He looked at his watch, he should be going home despite a half-drunk cup and unopened biscotti. Yes, home – he saw his lounge, his favourite armchair, the collection of expensive antiquities and art. Henry listed his prized pieces, his beloved Guanyin he had stolen from the shady Allner-Smith and the miniature terracotta warrior he had won from Anthony Albert. What a coup that had been. The savagery of triumph stirred him up. Albert was a coward. He would never have matched him when the price became truly hot and he certainly would never have opposed his wife. But now there was *The Raft of the Medusa*. Everything he had chosen up to now had created a sense of wealth, an easy decor to live with. Had it been all for show? Nancy had made the point and he had to admit reluctantly that she might be right. Was it an attempt at probing what art truly meant for him or a message of doom? Henry shrugged. What a ridiculous idea!

But no, Henry pretended all was good, opened the biscuit wrapper and wolfed it down. He washed it down with the now lukewarm tea. It occurred to him that he had had no desire to see any of his friends. This thought put a derisory smile on his lips, the only man he would want to speak to at this moment in time was Liam. There never would be any confidants among his City pals. Friendships had been built on a show of power or self-interest. He had made particular choices and was not surprised by the result.

200

But then there was Pam. The debacle with Wooster QC's sabbatical had left him raw. Forgiveness was impossible, his throat tightened up. Henry shifted on his chair, struggling with his feelings. He praised his ability to stay detached and clear-headed but was it not a lot of nonsense? Henry had to laugh, he was anything but detached. He simply did not want to admit he cared. Pam was safe, she was his lawyer, she was forbidden territory for a man of Henry's ambition. He saw her face close to his in the pub in Dublin. She had drunk Guinness from his glass and pulled a face. He had moved a strand of hair away from her eyes, hardly brushing the skin of her forehead.

His BlackBerry started to buzz, he hesitated for a second not yet prepared to let Pam's face fade away. He finally pressed the answer button. The voice at the other end startled him.

"This is Henry."

The familiar voice of James shoved GL back into his life, the sea of desks, the constant tension on the trading floor, the highs, the lows, a wild energy that he had found hard to leave behind. Sitting in the window of this small cafe, he suddenly felt the urge to belong again.

"Hey Jamie, what's up?"

"H, bloody hell, WHERE have you been? I thought I was never going to get hold of you."

"That bad, hey," chuckled Henry.

At least James had called him, there must be some hope.

"Have you spoken to DMac at all?"

"Nope, can't get hold of the old man and I had a little mishap with my phone, I'll call him later," continued Henry, trying to sound confident. "In fact, why don't I call him right away and call you back afterwards, I might–"

"H. Henry," said James. "Listen, I am so sorry mate, I am sorry to have to tell you that you're wasting your time. He won't take your call."

"And how would you know?" said Henry now squeezing his BlackBerry to breaking point.

"Because McCarthy called me in to discuss succession–" James had no time to finish his sentence.

"What! I am gone for less than three days and you shits have already decided to screw me over."

The entire cafe went silent.

"Of course not," replied James. "Do you think I decide for McCarthy? Wake up Henry. That guy has always been a selfish bastard and he certainly—"

"I don't give a flying fuck about what you think of McCarthy. I don't believe … I know he would have spoken to me."

"Henry where the bloody hell have you been for the past fifteen years? This is investment banking, my friend. This is the trading floor and YOU are in the deepest shit because you've got a murder hanging around your neck."

James was also shouting.

"And," finished James, "because DMac wants to be the CEO of the combined bank. Do you really think he is going to stick by you?"

"So bloody what! He WILL lead the combined bank," replied Henry emphatically. The sudden realisation of truth punched Henry in the guts.

"NOT if he sides with you he won't," replied James. "Ted has been named head of your team."

A heavy silence fell between the two men. James was about to ask whether Henry was still on the phone when the noise of a smashed piece of crockery deafened him.

"That motherfucker cannot, will NOT, head up my team. I'm coming in."

"H, let's meet outside. We can come up with a plan. We are the A-Team aren't we?" said James trying to coax Henry away from an impending disaster.

Too late, the phone had already gone silent. The whole cafe had been hanging onto Henry's words, no coffee had been stirred, tea drunk nor pastry eaten.

Henry smashed the phone on the small table. He closed his eyes, the beast within was loose. Henry had not yet reopened his eyes when he felt the pressure of a small hand on his arm. He turned around with a jerk.

"The cup is broken," said one of the young female waitress.

Henry did not bother to reply and slammed a twenty-pound note on the table.

202

"And your hand is bleeding," she added, handing over some tissues.

The hand holding the shattered cup was dripping, Henry looked down, used to the sight of his own blood. He had not felt a thing and started laughing. Blood was indeed on his hands.

Henry dislodged a piece of porcelain that had planted itself inside his palm and grabbed the tissues as he stood up to leave. The waitress offered more assistance that Henry ignored.

He walked out of the small cafe without a reply and was transported thirty years back, to a squalid street on one of Belfast's estates.

Three against him, no chance, a rain of insults and then one of the boys starts pissing in his direction. Henry's rage propels him. He strikes the first boy in the throat, the boy falls, his eyes bulging in pain and amazement, the other two stop laughing. Within seconds their astonishment has been turned to Henry's advantage, a quick punch in the head and the nose of the smaller boy explodes, a well-adjusted kick to the groin of the last boy brings him to his knees and then it happens, a frenzy. Henry carries on kicking and punching. He cannot hear the screams. He cannot see the blood. Nothing else matters but this elated release, the joy of inflicting pain, a newly discovered power.

* * *

Nancy was walking at a pace, her hands deep in her coat pockets. The satchel on her right shoulder felt heavy. She had not felt the weight of her lawyer's bag for a long time. It was uncomfortable. She quickened her steps and realised that her high-heeled shoes were hampering her. She stopped at a traffic light. The light turned green. She waited. Some young man grumbled past her. She was in his way. He pushed forward and crossed the road towards Temple Inn. What was she doing? Henry's outburst was predictable. She had known it would come. Could she handle the case at this moment in her life? Could she even be bothered? For so many years she had removed herself from the circle of power. She had done it deliberately, with the utmost determination, a slow process that had finally borne fruit. She liked the Nancy she had become, but was her life sterile? Henry's encounter was a passage she knew, his story a vital moment between old and new. She also knew that the air tickets debacle had shaken her complacency. She could still make mistakes that endangered others.

Her time with Jacques Vergès resurfaced. Defending a war criminal: it had sounded so daring, so impossible. The Klaus Barbie affair in France had made the front page of the papers for months.

The light turned green again. She started walking, wincing in pain. *Damn shoes*, she thought. Her chambers were thankfully very close. She needed to reconnect with her old practice, in a fresh way. She entered the familiar rooms. In seven years nothing had changed. The wood panels, the smell of ancient leather and books. Her sore back relaxed as she spotted that her favourite armchair was free. She sank into it and paused for a few moments. The severe face of her tutor, the first barrister for whom she had worked, materialised in front of her. She had learned from him that appearances were indeed deceptive as he had taught her everything he knew. No fuss, no need for thank you, he simply liked to impart knowledge. And after the Klaus Barbie affair her admission to the Bar was not a trivial matter. She remembered the ambition and disliked now what she was then but it had been a necessary transition. She thought she had moved away from it all and yet here she was. A young barrister brushed pass and apologised, intrigued by this face he did not recognise. Nancy pulled her satchel onto her lap and retrieved her old address book. Leaving her belongings behind, she moved slowly towards an old telephone booth. The old-fashioned devices were still there. Chambers operated in the past, how refreshing.

The number rang a few times and Nancy wondered whether her contact's number might have changed. She had not called Whitehall for a few years. A polished voice finally answered. That voice had remained the same in the twenty-five years she had known him. He was then a young barrister intent on entering the civil service. She smiled at the thought.

"Nancy Wu," exclaimed the man, a little taken aback. "I cannot believe it is you."

"It is good to speak again, William. I should have called you earlier. It must be at least a couple of years."

"Possibly more."

"You might well be right and yet, here I am calling you to ask for a favour."

"Well, my dear Nancy. In the spirit of our old friendship, I take no offence and will make an exception for you. I do not speak much with lawyers these days."

"You may want to know a little more about the subject matter before accepting."

"Very true, how considerate."

Nancy had never abused his friendship and probably never would.

"It is about the Albert–Crowne affair."

The phone remained silent for a moment.

"You have come indeed to the right man," replied William slowly. "Let's meet at Tate Britain in thirty minutes. I make the habit of escaping there to gather my thoughts and grab a tea."

"I remember. The William Blake room."

"The William Blake room indeed."

Nancy put the receiver back into its upright holder. She gave it a tap of satisfaction. Her Whitehall contact had a view.

* * *

"Pat, I am sorry to labour this with you but ..." Pole was going to get what he wanted out of his Irish colleague. He knew Nurani was also on the call and he wanted to reaffirm his instructions.

"Jon, the deal with Liam will be solid. It won't be done in writing, no lawyer present. Liam knows I can only request it from the guys in Dublin but if I don't, all hell will break loose for Bobby."

"Right," replied Pole, still measuring the impact of this next move.

"Liam has gone around the block a few times Jon, think about it. He has always been smart enough to protect his brother and, after all these years, he won't let go. He won't let him down," carried on Pat with absolute certainty.

"I think you're right. Christ, what a choice: his best friend against his insane brother." Pole was now convinced, blood ties would be the strongest.

"Will you do this on your own?" asked Pole.

"Yes. We have discussed it with Nurani," hesitated Pat.

"It is better that way, not an easy discussion," added Nurani quickly

"Fine, we are all on the same page. The floor is yours, Pat."

* * *

The 'chat' with Liam lasted five minutes at most. Pat entered the room alone as planned. Nurani observed through the tinted glass although the sound had been cut off. Liam stood up abruptly as Pat put the deal to him, no introduction, no soft landing. Liam walked to the wall and, facing it, leaned against it, smashing his fist into it. Twenty years of hatred and destruction came flooding back. He sat back at the table. He could not look at Pat at first and when his cold blue eyes locked with his, he uttered only two words.

"Take Henry."

Pat handed over a pad and a pen. Liam started writing.

* * *

Tate Britain was buzzing. The Turner Prize was on display, creating the predictable degree of attention. Nancy was a little early and decided to pay a visit to the new installation that had won the much-wanted recognition. She surveyed the display of Richard Wright's work. Her mind could not quite focus. The piece in front of her had to be intellectualised to be appreciated. She decided she was not in the mood and made her way to the William Blake room. Her contact was there already. She could see the delicate frame of his body standing in front of a favourite piece, an illustration from Blake's book *The Marriage of Heaven and Hell*. Nancy glanced at the room around her, it was a little too full for her liking. She moved slowly forward.

"Good afternoon, my dear."

The slender man had seen Nancy enter the room, but waited for her to approach, a gentle way of reconnecting with an old friend.

"Good afternoon William. I thought I might be late."

Nancy extended a graceful hand which the man took with warmth.

"No matter how often I come here, Blake always inspires me. Something profound about human despair, and hope, maybe."

Nancy turned towards the piece she knew well and smiled.

"He is still one of my favourites although you may balk at what interests me these days."

"Do not tell me you have gone contemporary," William said.

"I'm afraid I have."

"Well, we must debate this although perhaps later. I gather we have a more serious matter to discuss."

"Indeed, shall we find a corner?" Nancy asked.

"The members' room is usually quiet at this time."

They found a couple of comfortable armchairs and settled there, waiting for their orders to be delivered.

"I am advising Henry Crowne in the Anthony Albert murder case."

Nancy had decided that there was no point in fishing for information. William was far too astute to play games and he was also a friend.

"Are you fed up with retirement? Selfishly, of course, I would very much enjoy seeing you again at the Bar."

Nancy accepted the compliment but shook her head.

"The profession is no longer for me. Let me simply say that I am helping a friend."

Her contact raised an inquisitive eyebrow but said nothing more.

"I am convinced that there are many moving parts still in this affair. Call it intuition if you will. I know I can mention this to you," said Nancy, touching her friend's arm with warmth. "And you won't think I am a female lunatic reading the runes."

"I am all ears, Nancy but you will have to give a little more. Your intuition is right as always, however. I can't comment as openly as I once could. Seniority is a burden to bear."

The sentence had been spoken with no vanity, a pure statement of fact. He was indeed a very senior man at Whitehall.

"Let me therefore elucidate. I believe that the crux of this particular matter is rooted in the intense rivalry between Crowne and Albert."

Nancy paused to observe her contact and allow the waitress to serve their tea. The slight tension in his jaw and bat of his eyelid encouraged her to go on.

"It is an unusual form of rivalry, something visceral, rooted in the deepest of hatred."

"Although I do not know these people personally, let's be clear. I know enough of them through their work to be in utter agreement."

"In the battle for pre-eminence during the takeover, I wonder who would have been designated to head up the combined team. As I suspect there would have been a merger between Albert's team and that of Crowne."

Her contact took another sip of his tea and considered his answer.

"Albert," he said, a statement of fact, no speculation.

"And this is not a last-minute change?"

"It is a very good question. I was assured it is not."

"So even before Henry's fall, Albert's name was going to be put forward as head of the combined team."

"Are you in doubt?"

"On the face of respective aptitude very much so. Which begs the question. What did Albert know to warrant this good fortune?" said Nancy, still incredulous at the outcome. "Was Albert aware?"

"You mean, would he have been told informally?"

"Or seen the signs and for that matter what about Henry?"

"They might have suspected, but then again these very large deals make rational people behave in the most unpredictable of fashions."

"Was McCarthy being blackmailed?"

"I could not possibly comment," William replied with a faint smile.

Nancy paused. She drank a little of her tea. William had chosen well.

"Is GL's financial position seriously affected by the current subprime crisis? I mean, beyond the fact that all banks are affected? I remember reading they are big in the CDO business."

"I do not see the relevance."

"I am trying to establish whether there would be any particular reason to frame Henry or to sacrifice Henry?"

"I don't think Henry would have been *framed*, as you put it. Sacrificed, well – it's a takeover."

208

"Are you protecting someone, William?"

Nancy's contact shook his head in deep approval.

"This is your strongest quality, Nancy, and whether I reply one way or the other, you will make something of it."

"How very kind of you to say so. But you have not answered my question."

"Not someone, my dear, something."

Nancy looked at her contact with a frown, slightly taken aback. After a short moment her questioning look was replaced with astonishment.

"Do you mean …?"

"Yes, the UK financial system. I leave the rest of the world to the Americans."

"And I thought this affair was complex."

Nancy's contact shrugged his shoulders. He would not be fazed by the enormity of the task or indulge in the absurd idea that he could defeat the monster he was facing.

Their exchange was nearly over. Nancy decided to enjoy a few moments with her friend and moved the conversation onto other interests they shared. They soon parted and Nancy decided to hail a cab. She raised her hand and a black Mercedes S-Class slowly pulled alongside the pavement where she had stopped. The window came down with a mechanical purr.

"Good afternoon Ms Wu. Would you care for a lift? My current commission is taking me to the City. I could make a small detour?"

Nancy recognised Charlie's voice.

"Most kind of you Charlie. But I would not want to impose."

"It would be my absolute pleasure."

"In that case, to Islington."

Chapter Twenty-Two

The black cab screeched to a halt but Henry did not notice. Nor did he, as he stepped out into the road, remark upon the cabbie opening his window, shouting insults and gesturing in an unequivocal fashion. Henry was going back to the bank. No traffic lights, men in suits or uniforms would stand in his way.

His mouth was dry, the blood pumped in his ears, his security card had not left his wallet. It had probably been deactivated by now but he knew most of the security guards by name. He might find a way. No, he *would* find a way.

Henry was rehearsing what he would say, if the card didn't work. He saw himself going up the flights of escalators and launching into Ted's office. The concern for his team had vanished with the news they were no longer his. They could have put up a fight for him and they had not. Still a pang of pain hit him and he clenched his fist. It was Ted he now wanted to see. The little shit had taken his job away, he who called himself a friend. Yes, he would see Ted. Henry could already savour the pleasure of savaging him, this nobody, this coward – Henry would grind him to nothingness, a worm beneath the sole of his shoe, less.

The side of his office building was now visible, an eighteenth-century edifice only the facade of which had been preserved. Henry fetched his wallet and checked his hand. It was no longer bleeding. He took his security card out, the face in the photograph was smug and slightly heavier. He had had the good idea of wearing a suit to visit Pritchard QC and was carrying a small black satchel for paperwork. He looked at his watch, 16.42. He could have been coming back from a meeting. The timing was good, the early morning security team would be eagerly waiting for the next shift to come in. They started work at 6am.

Despite all his mental calculation since he had left the cafe, Henry felt nervous as he strode along the large bay windows of GL's front atrium. He was annoyed by this lack of control. He replaced the security pass in his wallet and stuck his wallet in his back pocket. He started composing himself, trying to look casual yet absorbed by the task at hand. GL's entrance hall was large and imposing but the walk to the escalators leading to the trading floors didn't take long.

As predicted, most of the security guards had retreated to the far end of the atrium leaving only one young man in charge of the turnstiles. Henry recognised him instantly. He had started his job only a couple of months ago. He was keen but impressionable. Henry pushed the revolving doors with confidence, his coat unbuttoned. He stuck his mobile phone to his ear and walked with what he judged a measured but assured pace towards the escalators, taking his wallet from his back pocket in an irritated fashion. The phone got stuck between ear and shoulder, as Henry tried to get his pass out of the wallet, pushing, shoving as if the card was stuck and with a sudden move the card sprang out, flying over the turnstiles to land on the other side. Henry looked annoyed, muttering his apologies, now curtailing the non-existent conversation on his mobile to give his full attention to the young guard.

"So sorry, John. Could you please?" said Henry gesturing at the gates.

The young fellow jerked upright and stuck his own pass over the electronic eye.

"Certainly Mr ..." he had forgotten Henry's name.

"Much appreciated," replied Henry with one of his best grins, picking up his security ID and starting his speedy climb to the third floor.

He was in.

He had to be fast, his next goal, Ted's office. He carried on climbing the stairs two at a time as he always did and within seconds found himself on the Equity Trading floor. He inhaled deeply, the atmosphere was intense. Out of habit Henry cast one eye over the screens that were hanging at regular intervals across the immense open-plan room. Five hundred traders were packed together and the herd smelt fear. All major indices had dropped by over ten per cent since the opening. Henry made a quick calculation – $900 billion had just been wiped off the market since the opening in Tokyo. Henry kept going. He had slowed his pace but was still crossing the floor in haste. Ted's office was at the far end. He saw from the corner of his eyes the incredulous look of Morag his PA. He quickly moved his finger to his lips. Silence. She closed her eyes in acknowledgement and with this, anger burning, Henry found himself in front of Ted's office. The door was shut. He spread his hands on the glass wall and took a few seconds before entering.

The expression of terror on Ted's face was exquisite. Ted was reaching for the phone in slow motion, his hands weighing a ton. Henry moved swiftly. He opened the door, crossed the office in one stride and tore the headset from Ted's hand. Without a word he turned back, closed the door he had left open and closed the blinds, ensuring privacy. Ted had picked up his mobile but fumbling with it, did not manage to place the call before Henry threw the first punch. He caught Ted in the stomach, the young man's eyes opened wide, his mouth agape in a silent scream. Henry grabbed the mobile and crushed it underfoot. His attention turned now to Ted, who was still leaning against his desk but had not yet recovered his breath. Henry pulled a petrified Ted to his chair. The little bastard had never thrown a punch in his life, he reflected, with a smile on his face. It was one thing to play hardball at the bank, another on the streets.

"You and I are going to see the old man," said Henry calmly.

He was sitting on Ted's desk, his hands ready to throw the next blow.

"You're mad," stammered Ted, his face growing redder.

He had grabbed the armrests of his chair, his eyes still wide open, bracing himself.

"You try to prevent me from reaching McCarthy and I will break your neck before anyone can rescue you, understood? Understood?" repeated Henry, slamming his hand on the desk.

Ted nodded and stood up, grimacing in pain. Henry gestured for Ted to move and open the door. Henry ignored the havoc of the trading floor. He stood uncomfortably close to Ted who was already in front of the lifts.

"I forgot my pass," said Ted lamely.

"*Voila*," replied Henry, with a sarcastic grin on his face as he produced the much-needed item between his index and middle finger. "Thank God one of us has got brains."

Henry pressed the ninth floor button and shoved the card in the security slot. Ted eyes grew dim, there would be no escape.

The elevator pinged open. Henry pushed Ted out.

"Not one sound or you are dead."

Ted simply nodded and started moving. At the far end of the large open space was Cindy. She was typing and Henry knew Cindy would not be diverted from her task. She was not expecting anyone but must have heard the lift. She would probably be preparing one of her spectacular rebuffs. Henry smiled at the thought.

As predicted she finished her typing before looking up. She would not be distracted by unacceptable behaviour. She had no time to utter one of her scolding remarks. Henry and Ted had crossed the hallway, Henry shoving Ted abruptly forward, Ted's panic etched across his face.

Cindy had barely stood up when Henry pushed her back into her chair with a rapid harsh movement. She nearly screamed.

"Don't," commanded Henry with a menacing finger.

He looked around. There was no way he could silence these two for long enough to do what he had decided to do. Cindy sensed the hesitation and made a small gesture towards the panic button. Henry stopped her with a sharp move of his hand. He had to act ruthlessly right now or give up. He pulled the telephone cord from the wall in a firm and precise move, a sharp pang and the wire sprang up. Henry caught it with the same hand, he had not left Ted for a second.

"Tie her up," he ordered Ted, rummaging in Cindy's desk.

"I can't," stuttered Ted.

Henry's fist tightened and Ted took the wire with a feeble hand. Cindy made a second attempt at screaming but a large piece of gaffer tape covered her mouth in an instant. It was way too late despite Ted executing Henry's order at the slowest of paces.

"Tighter," ordered Henry.

Ted pulled the wire and Cindy winced. Ted proceeded, he was not doing a bad job thought Henry. Little Ted had succumbed to fear. Like Cindy, little Ted never saw the fist coming down on him for the second time. Henry caught the side of his head, below the eardrum. Ted fell to his knees. The other blow sent him into the middle of the room, unconscious, the deep and luxurious carpets muffling the sound of his falling body. Henry used the rest of the gaffer tape to tie him up.

McCarthy was alone in his office, no interruption. Henry turned towards the old man's office. He was only a few feet away but suddenly he felt he had a gulf to cross. If he crossed that gulf, Henry knew the consequences would be devastating, not only for him but also GL and so he slowed down. Cindy had followed him with a sceptical eye. Would he dare? Henry's hesitation gave her hope. He saw the fever in her eyes and stopped. He marvelled at that hope, anchored in the belief that there could be at this very moment restraint or consideration. The slow motion gave him an immense sense of power that he savoured silently.

"The time has come," said Henry and with one single push fuelled by the fire burning in his gut he opened McCarthy's door wide.

McCarthy was facing the large bay window. He was standing in his favourite corner of the room, a place that overlooked the City. He enjoyed that position in which he felt he held dominion over the world below. McCarthy was making a call on his private mobile, with headphones on. He certainly did not want his call to the Global Head of Risk to be recorded in any way, shape or form. The door opening with force did not startle him, Cindy entered his office in such a fashion at least once a day, when she felt matters required his full attention. No other member of staff would have dared cross the threshold without his say so. It was only the much heavier footsteps moving behind him and a tall shape profiled in the window that caused him to interrupt his call abruptly, and turn. As he did so he found himself face to face with Henry.

Henry saw the unmasked shock in the CEO's eyes and enjoyed it. A mixture of fear and astonishment was swiftly replaced by anger. Henry sat on the corner of DMac's desk, his leg squarely masking the panic button. Henry and DMac had locked eyes when they faced each other and their gaze had not shifted. Henry leaned backwards, running his fingers along a small shelf on McCarthy's antiques desk. He pressed the secret button twice and a small drawer no bigger than a matchbox opened. Henry reached inside for a key. McCarthy shouted,

"Don't you dare you little shit."

He lunged forwards, instantly meeting Henry's fist. The punch to his face made him retreat but it had not managed to bring him down. He fought back, finding his footing and lunging again. His last move had given Henry enough time to turn the key of the top lefthand drawer, pulling a loaded gun out of it.

Henry sat down calmly in his boss's chair, a triumphant grin now on his lips.

"Good afternoon Douglas."

McCarthy did not reply, he needed the gun back. His eyes darted from Henry's face to his hand, assessing the determination of the other man to shoot.

"Don't try Douglas, I didn't come here to kill you." Henry's voice was a strange blend of excitement and anticipation.

McCarthy changed tack. Confrontation was not an option, neither was reasoning. He had to anticipate Henry's next move if he had any chance of surviving.

"How?" asked McCarthy, no longer hiding his amazement at Henry's knowledge of the secret drawer.

"You hired me because of the accuracy of my observations, Douglas and so I observed. The undisclosed documents, the hidden cache. I know all your dirty secrets Doug."

McCarthy was about to try another tack when Henry interrupted him.

"I know what you are trying to do Douglas and time is of the essence."

"That's the name of the game, I guess," shrugged McCarthy.

A touch of admiration for the old man ran through Henry, under threat and still unfazed.

"Open the top drawer nearest to you," asked Henry.

McCarthy did not flinch.

"No."

"Suit yourself," replied Henry.

The gun discharge deafened them, resounding against the windows, shattering the wood in a burst of violence Henry had not experienced for decades.

Fear and shock showed for the second time in McCarthy's eyes, both men facing each other, on their guard. McCarthy moved first, desperation and rage overtook him, the thought of his impotence in front of Henry unbearable. Henry avoided the charge and McCarthy came crashing down on the side of his desk, displacing it. He was about to turn back and resume his attack when Henry gave a single kick, hitting McCarthy in the face. The blow threw the old man flying across the room. He landed on his back with a harsh muffled thud.

The drawer was pulled open frantically and Henry grabbed the file that McCarthy had concealed there only a few hours ago.

"What are you going to do with it?" mumbled McCarthy, incapable of getting up.

"What you should have done, Douglas, had you had a shred of honesty," replied Henry.

McCarthy lifted himself on one elbow so that he could see Henry but rolled on his back again. Through a mouthful of blood, he started laughing, stopping and starting in pain.

"You are not going to give me a lesson in ethics, are you Henry? Not you."

Henry did not reply. He took his new BlackBerry out of his pocket to find a number and punched the digits on McCarthy's phone.

"The office of David Cooper-James, HXBK," replied a male voice.

"Is he there? This is extremely urgent. My name is Henry Crowne."

"Mr Cooper-James is in a meeting."

"I have vital information concerning the takeover of GL,"

interrupted Henry. "This information will change the value of the bid. What fax number can I use?"

McCarthy took a few seconds to realise what was about to happen. He summoned his last ounce of strength and lunged forward one last time. He met Henry's foot again, this time in the stomach. It left him crying in agony. Henry had pressed the mute button just in time. McCarthy's body curled up in the middle of the room, in a heap, motionless.

"David Cooper-James," announced a very nasal voice on the loudspeaker.

Henry depressed the mute button.

"You wish to give me core information," carried on the voice.

"I do indeed, sir. It concerns the exposure of GL to the subprime market – several billions worth of it."

"How can I be sure?"

Henry did not have time to justify himself, instead he read a string of figures to HXBK's CEO. The phone stayed ominously silent. Henry thought he heard some noise in the reception area. He needed to act now.

"Are you still on the line?" asked Henry.

"I am," said the other man in a strangled voice.

"The fax is on its way to you."

Henry dashed to the fax machine. It swallowed the document, a familiar strident noise started.

From the corner of his eye Henry detected movement.

* * *

Inspector Pole had finally received the transcript of Liam's interview. He had read the document in one breath, after each page assessing the impact of its content, increasingly aware that this case was about to escape him.

The document had landed on Pole's desk with a soft feathery sound, so little noise for such heavy content. Pole had to locate Henry fast, before the Counterterrorist Squad took over. Something about the interview worried Pole. He wasn't satisfied, a sense of unfinished business began to set in. Pole opened the door of his office and called Nurani who had just arrived back from Belfast. She turned, the phone pressed to her ear and indicated she had nearly finished. Pole then called Andy. The young man pushed his heavy glasses up from the tip of his nose where they had slid and rushed into Pole's office.

"I need to find Crowne as soon as possible. Call his lawyer to check whether he is there. I have tried the mobile. No response."

Andy nodded and disappeared. Nurani made her own entry, knowing that the transcript had just arrived.

"Bloody good job, no?" she said with pride.

"It is pretty compelling. Not in Henry's favour as you can imagine."

Pole found himself annoyed at this admission. Nurani sensed this but not knowing how to respond, remained silent. Pole handed over the report and closed the door of his office. Nurani started reading. She remained standing throughout and moved, as she was finishing, towards the chair in front of Pole's desk. She cautiously pushed it with her foot and sat down slowly before handing the document back to him. She was looking at Pole with a broad smile on her face. For the first time since he had started working with Ms Shah, Pole resented her sense of victory. He liked, and cultivated, restraint in shows of success.

"So, Mr Crowne, the darling of the structured product world in the City, is contributing to an undisclosed Swiss account, which turns out to be run by his good friend Liam O'Connor, who in turn uses it as a slush fund for his IRA pals. Mmmmmm, naughty!"

"Used to," Pole corrected her. "The IRA is now officially decommissioned."

Nurani waved her hand in the air; that was but a small technicality. Of course, she was right. Henry Crowne had been contributing to an undisclosed fund for years and it was only a matter of days before the link with that fund and the IRA would emerge. These donations stretched as far back as his first big City bonus, Liam had said with a hint of admiration for his friend. Pole had no intention of sharing his new line of thoughts with his young colleague. What other terrorist organisations were linked with this fund and why had Liam been heading to North Africa when he was caught?

"I've asked Andy to locate Henry," said Pole changing the subject. "I want to get to him before the other guys do."

"They can't take the case over, can they?" said Nurani.

"You know the rules as well as I do – yes they can and they will without hesitation. Careful what you wish for my dear," said Pole, satisfied his DS was about to learn a valuable lesson.

"Don't tell me you are going to roll over just like that Jon!"

"No, it's not my style. We may still have a chance to salvage the situation if we can prove the case is not related to a terrorist act," continued Pole.

"But you need to speak to Henry to get him to confess to us first." Nurani sounded sceptical.

Pole did not have time to reply before Andy burst into the office.

"There has been a disturbance at GL's offices. The security guards think Henry has entered the building without authorisation. They don't know where he is."

"Let's go," shouted Pole, "Andy you're on."

Pole's car screeched down Waterloo Bridge, turning onto Aldwych and then Fleet Street. The flashing light was making it easier to move but Pole still cursed the traffic.

"Shit, we've hit rush hour."

"We should have taken the tube," replied Andy.

Nurani looked at Andy with an expression reserved for the demented and Pole flashed a black look at the young man in the mirror.

A voice came on the radio and they all focused on what was being said. The Counterterrorist Squad was on its way. Pole doubled his efforts to avoid the traffic, using the horn, winding the window down and waving madly at the cars that would not move. His car finally burst into King Edward Street and came nose to nose with another police vehicle. Pole rushed out without closing his door.

"Who is the ranking officer?"

"On his way," answered a tall middle-aged man as Pole presented his ID card, "The traffic's holding him back."

"I am Inspector Pole, I am going in to assess the situation."

"You should discuss with Commander Jeffries," replied the other man aggressively.

"Not if we are in a critical situation that involves my case and your commander is miles away. He should have taken the tube!" replied Pole with a grin.

The other officer grabbed his radio and made contact with Commander Jeffries. Pole, Andy and Nurani did not wait to hear the conclusion of the conversation. The three moved swiftly towards the entrance of GL's offices and barely noticed the shouts calling them in the distance.

Chapter Twenty-Three

The bay window exploded into Henry's back. He had dived onto the floor seconds before rolling onto his side to avoid the shower of glass. The dark silhouettes of the Counterterrorist Squad moved into the room but Henry was running. He ran towards the lift deaf to the shouts and noise behind him. He shoved Ted's ID card into the slot, turned the switch back on to reactivate the elevator, pressed the fourth floor button all in one. A hand poked in as the doors were shutting but it was too late and the lift started moving. Henry's tall body collapsed against the wall, sending reverberations into the side of the elevator. He was shaking uncontrollably.

Henry had not given any thought as to what he would do next. The fourth floor was Mergers & Acquisitions. He noticed he had blood on his jacket. He removed it, slung it casually over his shoulder and composed himself. When the doors opened, Henry had regained some control and opted to go in the direction he knew best. He veered swiftly to his left, meeting rooms on both side of the long corridor. Each room that was occupied had an engaged sign below the name of the room. He dashed into the first free room he found. He closed the door and sat on the floor. He did not want to think about the last hour. He simply wanted to enjoy a few more moments of freedom, a few more minutes of respite.

Loud voices startled him, they were coming down the corridor, he held his breath as they walked pass. He stood up. As he retraced his steps back to the lift, he noticed the door of one of the rooms was open, papers spread over the meeting table, laptops showing figures and diagrams, jackets on the back of the chairs. Henry looked into the room – no one there, how careless! Henry managed a smile and picked up one of the jackets that looked large enough to fit him, in exchange for his blood-stained one. He slung it over his shoulder again. Henry started walking in the opposite direction, the elevator might not be such a good idea. He remembered that there was a set of stairs between the fourth and third floors. This enabled the M&A people and their analysts to communicate without having to share lifts with other parts of the bank. He still had Ted's ID, it should be good enough. He accelerated his pace, grabbing a pile of documents that were being photocopied as he walked past. He looked over at the far side of the large open-plan office and stopped in his tracks. A figure he thought he recognised was walking towards him.

* * *

Pole had flashed his inspector's ID at the security guard, demanding to be led immediately to the control room. The security team was on high alert. One of the men at the entrance door accompanied Pole to a room behind the reception desk, a couple of people were scrutinising the CCTVs, all other staff dispatched throughout the entire building to search for Henry. Information was being exchanged but nothing concrete had yet emerged, the hunt for Henry was picking up pace.

"Have you seen him?" asked Pole with minimal introduction.

"We think he is on the fourth floor, but not sure yet. Some of your team have just stormed the CEO's office where Crowne previously was. The lift on the ninth floor dropped someone on the fourth a couple of minutes ago."

Pole clenched his fist. He did not have time to question why the rapid intervention team of the Counterterrorist Squad had been put in position without his being informed. That would come later.

"The fourth floor you said, which lift side?"

"The right-side Inspector," replied the older man in charge, without looking at Pole.

Pole turned around and started running towards the lifts. Nurani was at the entrance surveying the arrival of the Counterterrorism Squad commander. Pole called her on the mobile and she turned around.

"Nu, don't follow me but go back to the car and get into the MD's garage with Andy."

He did not wait for a reply as the elevator had arrived. A few people walked out unaware of the drama unfolding a few floors above.

The doors opened onto the fourth floor. Pole walked out and quickly tried to get his orientation. He decided to turn left away from the meeting rooms, he would get a much better view of the entire floor from the other side of the open-plan office, a 50/50 chance of getting it right.

Pole recognised Henry before Henry saw him. He stopped. Why should Henry trust him? Why wouldn't he try for a final escape? Pole decided to stay still, waiting for the other man to see him, signalling his willingness to talk, to give Henry the option of a less violent outcome. He waited, knowing that in a few seconds he would be noticed. The silhouette that Henry had seen in the distance was now staring at him, no movement, an immobility that was waiting for acknowledgement and Henry understood. It was Pole, giving him the time to take a decision, expecting him to make the first move. The two men faced each other for a moment. Henry slowly moved towards the internal staircase, his eyes riveted on Pole. Pole could catch him if he moved fast but he remained still. Henry stopped, Pole immobile, both men aware of the other's proximity. Henry started moving fast, he accelerated as he reached Pole's side.

"There is an internal staircase to the third floor," said Henry before Pole could say anything.

"Can we get to the garage from there?" replied Pole as he started walking swiftly with Henry.

"We can do better, we can get to the CEO's parking bay." Henry managed a smile as he took Ted's security pass from his pocket.

"Do I even want to know how you got that?"

They reached the staircase. Henry flashed Ted's ID again in front of the electronic eye. The door released silently and they ran down the narrow passage.

Pole called Nurani on his mobile. "Nu, find a way to wait for me at McCarthy's parking bay."

He terminated the conversation abruptly and shut down his mobile altogether, not wanting to get his mobile tapped into. He gestured to Henry to switch off his BlackBerry too.

"Left mine behind and borrowed McCarthy's – don't want to be traced either."

"For someone with no criminal record, you are doing pretty well."

"I am a man of many talents."

Henry was trying to sound amused but a cloud passed over his eyes as he spoke. Pole remembered Henry's IRA links. They reached the third floor and entered the executive lift in silence. Ted's card was put to use again and the elevator glided to its destination. When the door opened, Pole's car was waiting with Nurani in the driving seat. Henry and Pole got in the back, she accelerated, barely stopping as she flashed her ID card at the security guard who had let her in. The car radio picked up a message. The CT Squad were not getting their way and they did not like it.

A couple of calls came through for Inspector Pole whilst Nurani was driving them back to the Yard. Inspector Murphy told him that Bobby had been caught without a struggle once Liam was involved. Pole would not elaborate with Henry in the car. Pat had managed to extract a statement from Bobby, the transcript of which was on its way to London. Pat sounded amazed at the content but gathered that his friend was in no position to talk. Then again Bobby had the reputation of being a crackhead. Pat surely knew that and it was unlike him to overdo the evidence. Pole went back to his passenger. Now that the chase was over, Henry's face had sagged into that of a much older man.

"What happened in McCarthy's office?" asked Pole, not expecting an answer.

"I settled a few scores," replied Henry.

"You did not—" said Pole.

"No, Inspector Pole I did not," cut in Henry.

He turned and Pole noticed his clear blue eyes.

"Although I had a moment of hesitation."

"Hesitation is good," said Pole nodding.

"I also sent some documents to HXBK. Compromising documents, of course. I will be surprised if this takeover is one of the reverse types, to quote my former boss," said Henry through gritted teeth. "In fact, I will be very surprised if this takeover happens the way McCarthy and his team had envisaged."

"What do you mean exactly?"

Like most people, Pole had been following the market meltdown closely but he had also assumed, as everyone did, that GL was above the mess that the less worthy banks had succumbed to.

"GL is up to its eyeballs in the subprime business." Henry said.

Pole raised an eyebrow, surprised.

"I know," continued Henry. "Who'd have thought? Such a respectable firm! McCarthy thought I did not know. What a stupid man, too wrapped up in his superiority. The only way we can survive the next big drop in the market and there will be one, mark my words, is to merge with HXBK. Of course, the guys at HXBK don't know that or rather did not know that until this afternoon that is."

"But surely, they have looked at your books," said Pole unconvinced.

"And so what?" said Henry. "Do you really think that the complex derivatives structure we have on the books can be understood and valued easily? Neither the FSA nor the accountants fully understand the ramifications of what has been bought. They rely on the rating agencies having done their work. The best credit is AAA, for example a country like the UK is AAA. GL created the famous Collateralised Credit Obligations, these are full of US subprime loans. These CDOS are tranched, like a cake. The best part of the cake, the one with icing and a cherry on top is AAA rated. But if you start eating at the cake from the inside both the icing and the cherry will collapse. This is what's going to happen – today, tomorrow, very soon. I just don't know how big the bubble is going to be."

"Are you telling me, Henry, that even you don't know what the hell is going on?" said Pole, incredulous.

"Yep, I don't know what it means for the financial markets, let alone the economy. It will all depend on how much leverage, I mean borrowing, has been created around these structures."

Pole absorbed the information but refrained from asking his next question, keeping it for later, when it would be properly recorded as he suspected the answer would be Anthony Albert. Instead he came back to the documents that had been sent out.

"So, what was it exactly that you sent HXBK?"

"The summary, with simulations, of our exposure to subprime, unadulterated. It does not make good reading – at the moment at least $30 billion."

"Should you … " Pole stopped, this was a stupid question.

Henry smiled.

"I came to an abrupt but very clear realisation that no matter what, I will never work in the City again."

"Is this justice?" said Pole.

"Revenge," Henry didn't hesitate. "We are all wired very simply in investment banking despite appearances. The most we can do is think about justice in a biblical sense, an eye for an eye."

Pole remained silent, he would no doubt read the results of Henry's fax in the press tomorrow. It was indeed an unforgiving world.

A new mail flashed on his BlackBerry, it was Dolores. She was chasing Albert's solicitor and was promised a call as soon as his will had been read.

* * *

Nancy was standing in one of Scotland Yard's waiting rooms looking through one of the windows. Her mind had drifted towards art. She had been neglecting her role of patron and mentor, aware of the several missed calls she had not yet replied to. *The Raft of the Medusa* emerged from the depths of her mind the way it must have emerged on the horizon of the ship that rescued it. Its power, reinforced by the events of the last few hours, struck her. The despair and violence it described could be read at two levels: society and individual, such was the power of the *Raft*. She knew something extreme had happened when the BBC reported the CT Squad intervention at GL Headquarters. She was on her way to the Yard already when her mobile rang. Henry and she exchanged very little. Nancy's patience was about to be tested to the full. For a fleeting moment she wondered why she had ever got involved. A last remnant of ego, a moment of intellectual vanity? Yes, there was the mistake she had made with the airline tickets, but she had owned up to it, she could have moved away with a suitably clear conscience. Whatever it was that had pushed her, she also had a sense of duty. She would see this case through just the way she had all those years ago in France.

She had been mesmerised by Jacques. He was a powerful intellect and a true showman in court. The law was a means, a tool he used to take on the most controversial of cases. She had dived into the world of criminal law head first, moved by her own background, a Chinese father, an English mother and a childhood between Mao's China and France; Jacques Vergès shared a similar background, a French father and Vietnamese mother together with an association with communism. Was it what she shared with Henry? The impact of a cross-cultural upbringing in a world hardly ready for it? The anguish of not knowing where to belong?

Nurani interrupted her thoughts by calling her name. Nancy composed herself before facing the young inspector. She gave an affable smile and followed without a word. When she entered the meeting room, she sat in front of Henry and listened. He did not omit any details this time, including the impact of Liam's confession. Nancy still listened when he finally spoke about the regular payments into the Swiss bank account.

"You knew it would support some IRA operations, even though Ireland is trying to move on." Nancy did not intend this as a question.

"I never asked," replied Henry.

"You knew it would support the IRA," repeated Nancy. She would not be put off by some non-answer. The Irish cause could be fought through other means but Henry gave a small shrug.

"Why? Henry why?"

"You and I are very different, Nancy," said Henry.

"That is rubbish and you know it," replied Nancy.

"You think there is always some goodness to salvage in someone but I don't. I was born with anger and violence around me and that has become part of me, forever."

"That is not a good enough reason, I understand anger more than you can imagine—"

"Do you know what my first childhood memory is?" interrupted Henry. Nancy would not have the last word.

"A wall full of hatred, murals and slogans that spoke of death and retribution. Did I ever want peace? No, I wanted revenge and then I compromised; money makes you complacent. I wanted to grind those stupid bastards underneath my foot and I became one of them. So, somewhere I still had to have some truth in me, not to forget 500 years of abuse and exploitation. OK I am a manipulative arrogant bastard of a banker but at least …"

Henry paused as if considering the veracity of his statement.

"I have remained true to my only friends."

A total and yet childish admission, a boy who had never grown up was speaking. Nancy extended a hand as if to reach Henry's.

"Did you have to go that far? You had escaped."

"You never escape Nancy. I can still hear it all: the bombs, the sirens, the gunshots, the insults and the cries of those who had lost someone they loved. It will never go away."

"It will never go away if you keep fuelling it. Did you kill Anthony Albert?"

The question startled them both.

"NO."

"Are we having a discussion about semantics?"

"NO."

"Bobby is giving evidence as we speak."

"Bobby is a crackhead; he will do anything."

"Anything for you?"

"What do you mean?"

Henry paused, as the unthinkable began unfolding in his mind. Unwanted thoughts, now unleashed, rushed around his head. The door opened and Pole appeared, alone.

"It won't be long before the Counterterrorist Squad arrives."

"On the strength of Liam's deposition?" asked Henry.

"No, on the strength of Bobby's."

230

Chapter Twenty-Four

The will itself was particularly short. An up-to-date statement of assets had been appended to the document. This attracted Pole's attention as it was only a couple of months old. The entirety of Anthony Albert's wealth was meticulously accounted for. The appendix was longer than the will itself but the decision unequivocal. All of Albert's assets were settled in trust for his children. The forceful Adeila received nothing.

Pole read the document again, motivated by professional habit rather than a need to check the content. Pole dialled Dolores' extension. There was no reply. He looked at the clock, the reading of the will had been over for less than an hour. Would Albert's widow contest it?

"She will have to. What a mess."

The phone rang, he picked up without checking the number. The voice was unfamiliar, but Albert's solicitor introduced himself.

"Have you received the document?" enquired the voice.

"Yes, certainly. I have read it too. May I ask what the reaction at the reading of the will was?"

"You mean Mrs Albert?"

"Were there other relevant parties attending?"

"Yes, the appointed trustees but to come back to your question, well …". The voice on the line was searching for a proper way to qualify the scene, "we thought she might be surprised, but there was not a moment of astonishment or even anger."

Pole took note. That was out of character.

"In fact, I am almost certain she knew the contents of the will. I find this amazing because Mr Albert was very particular about keeping the new will from his wife. In any case she was prepared. She immediately declared she would contest the will."

"When did Mr Albert decide on the changes?" asked Pole.

"Less than two months ago."

Pole exchanged a few more words with the solicitor then the conversation was over. He had picked up the phone again to call Dolores when the humour of the situation hit him. There had never been any real discussion between Adeila and Brett about Anthony Albert. All must have happened through innuendoes and half-spoken words. Brett thought he was wooing a woman who might become rich, she was hedging her own bets trying to attract a man whom she thought was wealthy. If Adeila knew about the will, which now seemed likely, she certainly did not want her husband's death. Allner-Smith did not know but it was now unthinkable he would have planned the murder on his own. All this amounted to a laughable game of deceit, smoke and mirrors. Adeila was, Pole had to admit, pretty good at it. He looked at his watch; time to reconvene with Henry.

* * *

"We don't have much time, Henry," pressed Pole. "This is Bobby's deposition, take a look."

Henry lifted an eyebrow and took the piece of paper with a lack of interest. He could imagine Bobby's disjointed mind coming up with some insane storyline. A convenient tale the police would pursue but easily torn to shreds by his lawyer.

Both Nancy and Henry started reading. They read all ten pages in absolute silence. Henry put the document down before Nancy did. She was surprised. Henry could still, under exceptional strain, retain a distinct capacity for absorbing and interpreting information.

"Bobby is insane," said Henry softly but it did not sound like a reproach to his friend rather a realisation that was long overdue or perhaps a reproach to himself.

"What do you mean," said Pole perceiving the unexpected change in the tone of Henry's voice.

"I need to think, Inspector," carried on Henry, "… alone please."

Pole was about to mention again that time was running short but thought better of it. Something was happening. He ruffled his goatee and signalled to Nancy that they should leave the room for a few minutes.

The scales of justice were now starting to move imperceptibly, a momentous decision was about to take place. She knew. She had witnessed it before. The turning point in a life that had suddenly veered off course.

Pole arrived with coffee, which they drank in silence. When they had finished, he gave a small sign that it was time.

"Give him a few more minutes, please," said Nancy.

"We are cutting it very fine."

Nancy nodded but did not reply.

"Since we have a few minutes Ms Wu, may I ask what happened to Jacques Vergès? You worked with him once upon a time."

If Nancy Wu was prepared to dig into his past, he surely was in a position to do the same with hers.

"Who?" asked Nancy in earnest.

"Jacques Vergès," said Pole.

Nancy's look of surprise gave way to a short laugh.

"Well Inspector. Serves me right for digging around people's past."

"You still have not answered my question."

"It is a long story Inspector and you said it yourself, we don't have that much time."

Pole was about to protest when she continued.

"Those were dark days in which I learned a lot about being a barrister, about myself too. I worked with Jacques once, when he defended a war criminal called Klaus Barbie. I was a very young lawyer then."

"An affair in Bordeaux, in the late eighties," said Pole.

Nancy looked at her watch.

"You're right, let's go."

"How about a contact with Vergès in late 2008?"

Nancy was already walking down the corridor.

When they had reached the room Pole opened the door, gallantly pulling back to let Nancy enter first. She acknowledged him with a small movement of the head.

"I had introduced Bobby to Anthony Albert," said Henry as both Nancy and Pole sat down.

"It was a completely fortuitous meeting," he carried on in a knotted voice. "We were celebrating a closing in Dublin, we found ourselves all in the same pub. Albert was there and I could not care less anyway. I had just closed the biggest god damn deal ever!"

Henry stopped, it now sounded so meaningless.

"Bobby caught onto us I vaguely remember, although by that stage we were all pretty drunk."

Henry's eyes stayed focused on his friend's written confession.

"Albert had invited himself to the party, we were closing the transaction with HXBK. Hardly anything to do with him but it was a high profile deal. This little shit had to pretend. We went for drinks after the closing dinner. Liam has a job now in Dublin, turns out he was at the same pub as we were with Bobby. Still we hardly spoke. He does not feel comfortable outside Belfast and does not like me in my work clothes."

Henry could not help a sad smile.

"You mean Bobby and you hardly spoke?"

"Mmmm, he just wanted to know who the guy who was left on the side was. I gave him his name. I probably told him he was a waste of space," continued Henry.

"Did Bobby speak to Albert?"

"I don't know Inspector. As I said, Bobby does not feel comfortable outside Belfast. I certainly can't remember him leaving, I don't even think I said goodbye."

Henry sat back for a minute. His hands had not left his friend's confession. He kept looking at it.

"I think I might have ..."

Henry stopped and Nancy stood up.

"Henry, we need to discuss this," said Nancy. She must control the next few minutes.

"Bobby seems to dislike Albert a great deal, there is an entire page on why it was a good idea to do what he did."

234

Pole was ignoring Nancy. He knew Henry was wavering, almost ready to talk.

"Bobby has never had a clear view as to why he hates. It is a rant, a long-lasting condition, he simply hates, with passion and without reason. I am surprised he could be so precise," answered Henry.

"Henry, I need to speak to you in private," said Nancy, in a final attempt.

"He said he spoke to you a few times and got instructions through voice messages. He could have dreamt it but then again it takes a lot to circumvent the security of any bank, let alone of an airport. Henry?" Pole was pushing on.

"Inspector that is enough!" interrupted Nancy.

"Nancy, this is OK," said Henry.

"I need to know, Inspector. It could only have taken a few hints."

"What do you mean?"

Pole looked at his watch, they had five minutes at the most. If Pole was to extract Henry from the clutches of the Counterterrorist Squad, Henry had to admit to the unthinkable. Nancy knew Pole was right, she had no time left to coach Henry. She changed tack.

"Henry, speak to us if this is truly your choice, we don't have much time," urged Nancy.

Pole turned towards her, amazed.

"Is that the QC's advice?" said Henry.

"And your friend – you do NOT want the Squad to take over."

Henry nodded

"We had a plan, it was such a long time ago. At university," Henry hesitated. "It now sounds ridiculous, arrogant or simply crazy, but during the Troubles, in Belfast it was so – normal."

"You mean the bombings?" asked Pole, pushing Henry back to darker times.

"Politicians used to fly a lot from small airports. Getting a bomb through was not all that difficult."

Henry paused and a sense of clarity took hold. He knew what Bobby had done, and he now knew what it meant to him.

"I was a student at Trinity College. I took it as a challenge, a way to see whether I could outsmart them all. I don't even remember whether

I believed they would actually do it – I didn't care."

Henry stood up unexpectedly.

He was deliberating, his thoughts nearly palpable. For so many years he had skirted around the issue. Was he in, was he out? Could he truly have done what Liam and Bobby had done? The time had come to find out. He wanted it, at this very moment and in this room, with a passion he thought had deserted him when he left Ireland.

"Is the Squad on its way?"

Pole nodded.

"You can still save yourself, Henry."

"No. Not any more. Bring them on." Henry's eyes blazed with hatred.

Pole faced Henry. Henry held Pole's gaze – the desire for a fight in the air. Henry wanted to feel the sweet taste of blood, just once more, the crush of bones beneath his fists. What respect could he have for a man who wanted to compromise, a man he realised was trying to save him?

Pole understood immediately, it took a few more seconds for Nancy to see it. He opened his mobile and dialled Nurani's number, a few words were exchanged. He would not reason with Henry any longer. Pole felt strangely disengaged.

Henry was at the gates of Hell and wanted a taste of it – so be it.

It took all but the best part of a minute for the Counterterrorist Squad commander to arrive with four more men. Henry was handcuffed roughly but did not wince.

Nancy and Pole left the room and shook hands without exchanging a word, there was nothing else to add. Pole walked back to his office. His view of the situation had been proportional. Yet a moment ago he had stopped caring. Now an infinitesimal feeling of regret, an imperceptible sense that the job was not altogether finished started troubling him. Pole hesitated and changed direction, time for a quick catch up with Dolores.

Chapter Twenty-Five

Henry was sitting in the police van that was taking him to Paddington Green station for interrogation. He was preparing himself, anger pumping through his veins, the rage of years long past rising once more. *Had he been so careless?* he wondered. Everything had worked so well: the financial arrangement, the multi-tier structure, the tax havens, the numbered accounts in Switzerland. Did he truly want this fight? A fight with Pole was not worth it but the Counterterrorist Squad was. Excitement replaced anger. How far could he go? He looked at the three officers sitting in the van with him. They knew violence and death all right. He carried on inspecting them. A strange form of combat had already begun. He had been pushed to the far end of the van, the three men were gathered near the door. Henry tried to remember Belfast, the Troubles, the sounds of the bombs and the blasé remarks of those who had escaped.

"It's near College Square."

"Na, it's Victoria Street, they have done the Europa again."

And so it would carry on for a while until the news confirmed the location.

Henry moved position to discover that the back of his shirt was wet with sweat.

Not that tough anymore, Henry. A small ironic smile curled his lips, a good thing he had learned from the English – the power of self-deprecation.

He moved again. The three guards looked at him and decided he wouldn't be trouble. The cuffs were pretty tight, very small but so effective a tool. The van was taking an eternity to cross the red light, this time Henry shuffled his feet. Were they stuck in a traffic jam, surely they could sound their siren and get through?

It all happened in an instant, a surge of energy never experienced before. An uncontrollable force threw Henry against the walls, the floor, the ceiling of the van, his ears incapable of taking in the noise. Space had been torn open and consciousness ripped from him.

Yells of agony and anguish brought him back. With all his might Henry willed himself awake, reaching new depths he had never suspected existed inside him. He drew deep to stay alive.

For an instant it all sounded quiet again as if nothing had happened. The cries started again, a siren in the distance, then a second one. Amid the suffocating smell of burning flesh, Henry wanted to open his eyes, he wanted …

A hand shook his shoulder and someone was shouting.

"I need to move you, mate, can you hear me?"

Henry mumbled, he could see a vague shadow over him, an awkward shape, a heavy weight was pinning him down as he was trying to move.

"Can't," he tried to articulate, his eyes still out of focus.

"You must, mate, the van is on fire, it's about to explode. Come on, you can do this," the voice was pressing.

Two hands grabbed his shoulders and started to drag his body. Henry moaned, and summoning all the energy he could, pushed something away from him. He opened his eyes, finally able to focus, to look at what was preventing him from moving. The severed body of one of the guards lay on its side, the explosion had ripped open the door, tearing apart his torso. Henry's mouth opened, his eyes bulged. He was looking into the eyes of the guard, empty and glazed. A scream that never came suffocated Henry. He crawled forward ignoring the helping hands that were trying to move him out. The van rocked heavily on its side. Two arms pinned him down to stop the van toppling over altogether. Someone else dragged him onto the road. One of the other guards, who had been fiercely searching for his keys, released Henry from his handcuffs.

"The driver is still trapped in the front," urged the man, "help me."

A small woman, a passer-by, ran towards the scene. Henry did not move, she followed the guard to drag the driver out. The smell of burning petrol was overwhelming.

For all his years in Belfast Henry had never been close to a bomb blast as it happened. He had heard them, seen the aftermath, read about them. He had imagined all the gory details. He had become blasé about them to the point where his only concern was to pinpoint with precision the site of the explosion from the sound it made. He had always been prepared – the mangled bodies, the smell of burning flesh, the yelling of the wounded. But reality had now dug its claws into his belly, twisting and turning like a hook. He fell to the ground, limp. People were running around him, strangers helping strangers. Henry thought he should be there too, his eyes turned towards the van, he bent forward and threw up. It was not easy to kill a man. Henry tore his jacket away from his body and wiped the blood and vomit from his face. He stood up, looking but seeing nothing. Henry started walking, his mind filled with images he needed to escape.

He walked past the screaming ambulances, the howling police vans. He walked, blinded by emotions. Faster and faster he went, chased by the furies of destruction. Henry was running, escaping what had always been a part of his life. He was running when a cold sensation hit his face. He could not understand it to start with, a thousand needles attacking his skin. The rain fell harder; he welcomed it, its vicious bite bringing him back to life, his chest burning. The torrent drenched him, blinded him, pushed him to run faster. Where was he? He did not care.

Henry turned into Marylebone. He was running. His clothes clung to his wet body. But suddenly the rain stopped, subsiding like an ocean wave, its violence gone and with it the promise of relief. Henry's pace slowed. His hand found the cold strength of an iron gate, he was spent. He clung to the metal frame with a ferocious grip, gasping for air. He was wrecked, just as those men must have been who clung to the Medusa's raft. There was no hope left.

A black Mercedes stopped beside him. The driver's door opened and a gloved hand grabbed Henry, pulling him into the car. Henry collapsed on the back seat.

"Mr Crowne, I think you need a lift," said a familiar voice, a voice that came from a past not so distant and yet that belonged to another life.

Charlie started the car again and drove off. He looked with kindness at the heap collapsed on the back seat of his car, the man he had so often driven to one airport or another. Henry knew he was safe, he did not know why. Finally, he sat up, articulating with great difficulty.

"Charlie, you should not …"

"Nonsense," replied Charlie. "I would be a poor limousine driver if I could not offer a much-needed ride to my best client."

"You don't understand," protested Henry, each word requiring a crushing effort.

"What don't I understand – that you are a wanted man?" Charlie kept his eyes on the road ahead. "It takes one to know one. I was once in a very bad place too, as you well know."

"You don't owe me, Charlie," said Henry.

"It is all about respect, Mr Crowne, that which you give and that which you receive."

A comfortable silence fell in the car.

"There are some fresh clothes in the boot of the car and I won't take no for an answer," said Charlie still looking ahead. "Where are you going to go Mr Crowne?"

"Charlie, I think you can drop the Mr."

"As you wish … Henry."

"I don't know is the answer. I just don't know."

The comfort he had felt vanished. He thought about Nancy but the police would know. He had no money, no ID. He was stripped bare.

"I have finished my day. We could go for a drink."

Charlie spoke slowly in a manner that seemed hesitant. Not knowing whether it came from discomfort or anxiety, Henry was about to decline the offer. He met Charlie's eyes in the rear view mirror. There was genuine sympathy.

"You know that the cops are after me?"

Charlie smiled at Henry, a generous smile that said it all. He became serious.

"As I said earlier, Henry, very few bankers were prepared to give an ex-con much of a chance."

"You don't have to repay me. You have always done your job well. In fact, more than well."

"Have you done time?"

"Not exactly."

"But you know what that means ..."

"I am probably about to find out sooner than I would have wanted to."

Henry closed his eyes and inhaled. Could he ever give up being an arrogant ass?

"If you need to get out of this country, you have very little time." Charlie's tone had changed. It had a palpable urgency.

"What do you mean?" Henry looked up suddenly, his heart jolted with a pang of hope.

"I know people."

"I need to think," said Henry, nodding slowly.

He froze as a police car screamed past them. Charlie kept his composure.

"Let's have that drink. I know a good place in Hackney. You will be fine there, for a while."

Henry remained silent, the siren still echoing in his ears. He recalled the earlier vision of *The Apocalypse* by John Martin. He clenched his fists so hard his fingernails cut into the palms of his hands. He thought about the mangled bodies, he saw Liam and Bobby's faces, he saw *The Raft of the Medusa* waiting for him in his apartment.

"Don't do this to yourself. It won't solve anything."

Charlie's voice saved him from the abyss. Henry sat back, surrendering to the moment. He looked at the streets around him. He had lost track of where he was.

* * *

The distant noise startled Nancy. It was unfamiliar and yet not unknown. She looked at the large clock hanging on the wall of her conservatory. It indicated half past six exactly, evening rush hour at its peak and she knew a bomb had gone off.

She threw away her gardening gloves in an angry gesture and ran across the length of the room. She climbed down the stairs, nearly tripped, grabbed the banister. She swore as she found her balance again and rushed to the nearest phone.

Nancy dialled Inspector's Pole number from memory.

"Pole," he answered.

"Inspector Pole, where are you?"

"Good afternoon Ms Wu," replied Pole in an amused tone. "I thought I was the one who—"

"No time, Inspector," interrupted Nancy. "I think a bomb has just gone off in Central London. I can't quite be sure but if I can hazard a guess. I'd say west of me, possibly Hyde Park, Marble Arch – that sort of way."

"Do not hang up, my other phone is ringing."

Pole voice lost some of its clarity but Nancy could still hear his side of the conversation.

"Where exactly? I see. I am on my way."

Nancy could hear him fumbling with both phones.

"The bomb exploded at Paddington." Pole hesitated. "It caught the van in which Henry was being transported. It's chaos over there."

"Is he dead?" asked Nancy.

"I don't know. I am going, right now," replied Pole.

"I'll meet you at Paddington," she would not be told otherwise.

"Fine, ask for me."

Nancy sat down. The news nearly overwhelmed her. She thought of Pole and drew some comfort knowing he would be there. She had to find Henry. Nancy stood up, grabbed her coat, checked again that she had put her mobile in her bag and left the safety of her flat without hesitation.

Chapter Twenty-Six

Tube and buses had stopped. Nancy managed to convince a cabbie to take her as close as he could to Paddington. She could hear the distant howling of ambulances. Her left hand started to shake uncontrollably and she grabbed it with her right to make it stop. An image was slowly forming in her mind, people running and screaming, the smell of tear gas, but the cabbie's voice dispelled it.

"It's as far as I can go, love."

Nancy gave the driver a £20 note and rushed out without asking for change. The acrid smell of smoke and melted plastic assaulted her. People were walking in all directions, some still fleeing the scene, others frantically moving towards it. She could make out a number of police vans in the middle of the road. She saw officers stopping people. She needed to find Pole. Nancy grabbed her mobile and, still walking, pressed the redial button. The number was busy. The engaged tone played with her nerves. She gritted her teeth and tried again. She was about to terminate the call when Pole's name appeared on the screen. She switched line.

"Where are you," asked Pole.

"At the corner of Paddington and Westbourne Grove."

"I am coming for you."

Nancy stood still in a sea of people – injured, helpers, relatives in search of their loved ones. A strong grip on her arm made her turn around. Pole was standing in front of her. His pale face stood out against the darkness of night. He had seen the bomb site. She did not know how to ask the question.

"Henry is alive," Pole managed.

Nancy simply shook her head. Words meant very little and she could not find the right ones. They faced each other speechless. Pole was still holding Nancy's arm, the way a drowning man may cling to his rescuer. He realised it and reluctantly let go. She managed a quick smile.

"Is it very bad?"

"Atrocious," replied Pole, his eyes now avoiding hers. "I need to go back – and you need to find Henry."

Pole did not move and Nancy knew he would not until she did. She shook her head and put her hand on Pole's square shoulder, pressing it gently. She was finding it hard to move away too but a yell of despair in the distance jolted her into action.

She took a step back, still facing Pole and finally turned around. She moved faster and faster, her chest pounding. She felt nauseous. She stopped abruptly but the moment passed.

She must indeed find Henry.

* * *

The Vortex Jazz Club was a busy place, an intimate setting for the jazz aficionados who came to listen. Henry followed Charlie into the club and noticed his driver giving a quick gang style handshake to the bouncer at the door. They found a free table at the back of the room. The redheaded woman on stage had just started her first song.

"She is Irish," said Charlie, "the best Jazz fusion in town at the moment. Beer?"

"Guinness."

Charlie simply nodded and disappeared.

Her song had the broken, intellectual rhythm of original jazz yet peppered with some melodious, melancholic undertones. Henry drifted into the music. Jazz had never been his favourite but somehow he felt carried by the tune or maybe the words. It was familiar. Henry realised she was singing in Gaelic, the wheel of time spinning in reverse.

He was seated at a similar table in Belfast. Bobby had brought a wad of papers to the pub and Liam had gone mad at him for it. It was a partisan pub, but still. It had been agreed that they should not discuss their latest plan in public. Bobby had disappeared into the crowd and not reappeared until the following evening. Henry could see the papers but the pages were blank. He did not want to look at them, to turn those pages and remember.

"Good stuff!"

Charlie's voice startled Henry. His Guinness was sitting in front of him. Charlie raised his own pint of lager and Henry raised his drink, clinking Charlie's glass softly. He took a sip. He liked the gentle sensation of the froth hitting his lips before the bitter taste engulfed his tongue. He took another sip. The wad of papers reappeared in front of his eyes.

Liam was talking to him about the airport. He had gathered good quality intelligence. The airport was small and therefore ideal. A lot of high ranking civil servants and even royalty flew from it. The perfect target.

The song ended and Henry noticed that his glass was nearly empty. He was about to offer to pay for a round but remembered he had no money. A sensation of helplessness he had never known choked him. A plump waitress dressed in black and wearing the requisite piercings brought some chips. Charlie signalled for another two drinks. He had said nothing, content to be listening to his favourite music. Henry finished his pint and regained some composure.

"We can talk if you'd like," said Charlie looking at the stage, "but it may not be what you want, that's fine by me. No pressure."

Henry nodded. He knew he had to make the effort soon, but maybe not just yet. He let himself drift into the redhead's next song.

* * *

Nancy walked all the way home. She felt she was losing valuable time but there was no other option. She wondered how she could find Henry – no BlackBerry, penniless. Who would he turn to? She did not know his friends although she suspected his City pals would never be his first port of call. Who?

Henry had been betrayed but was it not of his own doing? A harsh situation, thought Nancy, but one she knew only too well. The core of Henry's belief was unravelling. He was at a crossroads but would he recognise it? Nancy remembered the events that had tested her in much the same way. Pole had been right when he had asked about early 2008. Jacques Vergès had offered to defend Tariq Aziz, Saddam Hussein's close adviser, and after all these years contacted Nancy. She knew full well why. Vergès was getting old without losing his appetite for controversy. Nancy had just won a spectacular case against the extradition of a world-renowned hacker. Her name had been in the papers for days and coming out of the Old Bailey, she had addressed the journalists with the mixture of tact, humour and defiance that so characterised her. She knew Vergès' decision was a media stunt, she saw straight through it and yet the temptation was too great.

She had arranged to meet him in Paris. A good shopping trip along the Rive Gauche would not go amiss if she decided not to work with Jacques. She was about to board the Eurostar when an old friend spotted her. They had both studied at The Sorbonne and corresponded for a long time until Nancy's professional life took over, consuming all hours of day and night. They were sitting in the same carriage, a strange turn of fate which Nancy would reluctantly interpret as destiny. They sat together and talked the way old friends can sometimes do, with candour. Nancy heard her own voice describing what she did and it sounded alien, false. She was not lying of course when she was recounting her successes at the bar. But doubt was slowly creeping in. Her friend nodded and smiled. Nancy could see on her face a mixture of admiration and regret. When the train arrived at the Gare du Nord, Nancy's friend embraced her warmly with only a few parting words: *"I am glad you enjoy this all-consuming job so much, take a little time for what else matters will you?"* There was some sorrow in her voice, which did not betray envy but gentle disappointment. Nancy took the cab that was waiting for her but never saw Vergès. She instead walked the streets of Paris the way she had done so many years ago. She took time again to look at life unfolding around her. At the pinnacle of her career Nancy had started the process of self-transformation. She knew now why but it would take her time to see clearly the root of it all.

The rain surprised her with its intensity. She shivered. She yearned for the tranquillity of her home. She wanted to get rid of the acrid smell of smoke and death. Her mind would not settle until she had reached her destination. She accelerated her pace. She would be there very soon. Then the answer would present itself.

* * *

The music had banished his anxieties for a while. Jazz had been the perfect music and he thanked Charlie for it. The first part of the show had finished, a young saxophonist was now filling the room with a doleful solo.

"Have you ever been betrayed, badly?"

Henry's question came as a surprise, its frankness almost unbearable.

"Don't you mean to say, have I ever grassed on someone, in a way that is unforgivable ever for best friends?"

Charlie's rephrasing of the question felt brutal. His voice had lost its manicured tone but not its precision. Charlie looked at Henry as he replied. In the darkness of the club, Henry felt his eyes on him.

"I have paid my dues. I decided it was enough, my slate is clean. It's hard to acknowledge who you are."

"Was it worth it?"

"You already know the answer to that."

"I am not so sure anymore. It's easy to think about it when all is good but today ..." Henry's voice trailed off.

Charlie's phone buzzed. He looked at it with distant interest. He looked at Henry again and decided it was time to leave.

"I've got to go. You can stay here for the rest of the night. Marco at the door will help and ... I'll be back here before the club closes. I will make some enquiries. If you want to leave the UK, I'll come back with a contact."

"Why?" said Henry almost childish.

"If you truly want to make a choice, you need to have a choice."

Charlie stood up, so did Henry. He extended his arm and shook his driver's hand. Something he had never done before.

* * *

The redhead was back on stage. Charlie had vanished. Memories of Ireland stormed back into Henry's mind. The papers were now scattered before Liam and him. They shared the same house and had gathered in Henry's small room. Bobby had not been invited. He would be told when the plan had been fully hatched. Bobby's impatience had become far worse since they had moved out of Belfast, his restlessness a constant concern.

The papers had finally come to life, a shorthand written description of how to wire a detonator, the list of items required for the construction of a bomb. Henry had been amazed at the simplicity of its ingredients. He saw the map of the small airport with yellow highlights in a couple of places, the points at which security was at its weakest. A page with columns and ticks with their three names flashed in front of Henry's eyes, airport staff schedules, unscheduled flights. He could hear the sound of his own voice declaring sanctimoniously, "It works. We can do this anytime."

Henry raised his pint to his lips, he had nearly finished his drink. He looked at the small amount of dark liquid at the bottom of his glass. Who had decided not to go ahead and why? Had it been an intellectual exercise, a way to prove to himself and his friends how clever he was? A way to belong?

The pain of realisation savaged him. He had wanted to look after his friends as if they were family. He wanted to be part of them, just the way he was when kids had taunted him at school *"English boy, Mummy's boy, little shit we'll get your toys."* Liam had grabbed the kid who spat at Henry by the throat and Bobby had sworn he would kill anyone who touched him. No one messed with the O'Connor clan. And Henry was one of them. But Henry Crowne would never be a killer. The well-rehearsed plan was a mock exercise. He could not bring himself to act upon it but Bobby had. To Bobby it was no mere intellectual conjecture, it was a call to arms. The seed had been sown no matter how long it would take to mature.

Henry sat back in his chair. The Vortex Club reappeared. The agony of self-doubt assaulted him. He was a nobody.

248

"No," said Henry aloud.

No, he would not accept this. He stood up quickly and knocked the table. A few heads turned but the music covered the noise for the rest of the room. The waitress had approached the table more concerned by an unpaid bill than a drunken man. Charlie had left a £50 note in the tray. Henry pocketed the change, uneasily. He looked at the room around him. There was nothing left for him here.

He walked out of the club and stepped onto the pavement. It was damp and cold. He zipped up the fleece that Charlie had lent him and started walking through the crowded streets of Hackney.

* * *

Nancy had taken the time to have a shower. She had checked her mobile several times. Pole had not called and she knew better than to call herself. She was confident he would let her know as soon as he had news.

The TV was on and she flicked channels. Identical pictures and comments were being repeated without giving her much to go on. She found the reporting distasteful.

Nancy pressed the TV mute button and closed her eyes. She knew there was a connection somewhere that she was missing. A way to reach Henry she had not yet thought about. She decided to go through her case notes. She opened the file that had been abandoned on her sofa and started reading through them, methodically.

* * *

Despite the plummeting temperature, Hackney Central was bristling with activity, young people moving from club to club, huddled together and speaking at the tops of their voices, cars cruising with open windows, blasting rap or techno. Henry was walking slowly, observing the sea of faces. He had been so remote from this crowd only a few hours ago and now here he was, immersed in it with so little in his pocket that he understood once more the vulnerability of the destitute. A brightly lit shop attracted his attention. He crossed the road and stood in front of an electrical goods shop where three ultra large TV screens were relaying different news programmes. The bomb blast dominated all channels.

Henry recognised the police van that had carried him a few hours ago. He couldn't move. A passer-by bumped into him. The man was drunk, mumbling some insult. He moved on, preferring another pint to a fight. The sound of a police siren caused Henry to jerk round to see the police car rush past him. The scenes at Paddington remained so vivid, he started walking again. The noise of the street mingled with the screams surrounding the bomb site, he turned left into another street then right and found himself in a small alleyway. The activity had subsided to give way to a seediness he had not witnessed for years. Henry spotted a wine bar at the far end of the street. He walked in and sat at the bar. He fingered the £20 note he had in his pocket and ordered a large glass of red, any red would do; he had stopped being fussy. The barman stuck a menu in front of him with a choice of tapas, an indication that Henry was expected to do more than just drink. He wasn't hungry but he placed an order, anyway.

The place looked unexpectedly welcoming in contrast to its neighbourhood. On the stool next to him a man shuffled. He pulled a crumpled handkerchief from his back pocket and wiped his eyes. His friend had just come back to his seat and, extending a large hand, grabbed the other man's shoulder. Both stayed silent for a while.

"Have you heard anything?"

"I have not checked again. They said they would call as soon as they had found him."

"Yes, well. Do you trust them?"

The man next to Henry shrugged his shoulders.

"I tried to get close but there are coppers everywhere."

His friend nodded.

"I supposed they have to get to the people injured and to the …"

The friend's voice trailed. He could not bring himself to speak about death.

"The hospitals near Paddington are not responding either. Frankie always calls me after an interview. He was so proud. He thought he might get the job."

"He is a good son, your lad."

The man next to Henry took his handkerchief out of his pocket again. His mobile rang and he froze. He hesitated for a few seconds. Did he really want to know? He grabbed the phone and listened. The voice on the other side was clearly familiar as his entire body slumped.

"I don't know yet. No, Frankie hasn't come back. Look, I need to keep the line clear."

He ended the call and placed the mobile slowly on the counter torn between the respite of hope and the despair of not knowing.

Henry's food had arrived but remained untouched, his glass still full. There would be no escape. He closed his eyes in an effort to still himself. He could stand and go, but where to – another bar, another club, another country? None of these would bring him peace. He felt the agony of the man sitting next to him. No cause was good enough to inflict so much pain.

How far and why had he been involved in this madness? He wanted to know, the money, the planning? A few hours ago, Bobby's statement had read like a jumble of incoherence. Bobby, always the weakest link of the three and yet prepared to die for his cause and his friends.

The two men next to Henry had left. As they did, the barman refused their money. He just wanted to have news of Frankie when it came.

Henry looked at his food. He had toyed with it, moving a piece of omelette round his plate. He put it in his mouth and chewed it a little. But the taste of food no longer interested him.

Henry's attention returned to Bobby. His friend's confession had been madness and yet Bobby was convinced. Albert was a threat, the takeover a rigged exercise – and they had their old plan. Bobby was losing his mind. He had never discussed the impact of the peace process on his friends. Liam and he spoke less frequently than they used to. He had not mentioned Bobby in months. Henry paid his money into the fund structure he had created. He felt he was doing his bit, a convenient illusion. Bobby had lied. Did he want to know why? The imaginary calls with Henry, the revival of the old plan, the briefcase. Henry rubbed his hands over his tired face. He looked at his watch. It was 4am and the little bar was still half full. Charlie would be waiting for him until the club shut. With both his friends in jail, would he flee again, the way he had when he fled to London, the way he had a few hours ago from Paddington? He looked at his watch again in a mechanical fashion. He still had a few hours before the sun rose.

Chapter Twenty-Seven

The weather had changed so dramatically that Henry wondered whether he had walked into a brand new country. The canal path was peaceful, a few people walking their dogs or riding their bikes. The cab had dropped Henry on Upper Street Islington. Henry Crowne was now strolling along the footpath. He knew where he was going. It had come to him gradually – the answer had always been there waiting for him to acknowledge. He would soon reach his destination and in a few hours it would be over. He was glad of it.

* * *

Nancy woke with a jolt. Her phone was ringing. She answered with an unsteady hello and recognised Pole's voice.

"Have I woken you up?" Pole sounded exhausted.

"Do not worry, Inspector. At least I have had some sleep which sounds more than can be said for you," replied Nancy, grateful for his call.

"Henry has been spotted in Hackney but we seem to have lost him."

"I should try to find him before the Squad does," said Nancy. The idea had come to her yesterday as she'd been searching for clues amongst Henry's account of his past.

"Well, if you do find him before we do then please make sure he does not do anything stupid."

Despite the dire situation, Nancy could detect the smile in Pole's voice.

"Inspector, this is precisely why I intend to find him before you do," replied Nancy with determination. "I will let you know, and Inspector," Nancy changed her tone of voice for what she needed to say should be said only among friends. "I could not have had a better partner on the case than you."

She did not wait for Pole's reply. Yes, she knew where to find Henry.

* * *

The bench was in full sun. Henry had reached his final destination. He had been sitting there for a while now, resting against the back of the bench, his legs folded underneath him, hands stretched over his thighs. His mind had wandered down strange avenues since he had left Paddington. He must soon look, consider, measure the extent of the devastation but for now he was content to bask in the sun. For a few seconds more, he wanted to enjoy the simplicity of life.

He felt her presence before she laid her long-fingered hand on his back.

"Am I that predictable?" asked Henry, without looking round at her.

"No, we spoke about your first few months in London when you arrived from Ireland. You said you had escaped as far away as you could from Kilburn and decided on London Fields," replied Nancy calmly.

"Mmmmm," nodded Henry.

Nancy sat beside him, she was looking in the same direction.

"The cops will be here soon," said Henry in a low voice.

"We have a bit of time."

Henry nodded again.

"How bad?"

"You mean the—?"

"Yes," he did not want her to speak the word.

"Last count forty-seven dead, over sixty wounded."

254

Henry grabbed his thighs and squeezed hard, digging into his flesh but pain was no release. A question was burning him alive and yet how could he formulate it?

"Probably an Al-Qaeda splinter group, videos were posted on YouTube and sent to the press shortly before the explosion," said Nancy.

Henry inhaled deeply and forced himself to utter the words.

"Any IRA connections?"

Nancy hesitated for a fraction of a second too long before giving her answer.

"Nothing concrete."

"Which means, they supplied some of the logistics," Henry concluded without hesitation.

He looked at her for the first time since she had arrived. The intensity and pain of his look startled her.

"But we are not sure yet," she replied.

"You don't need to be sure Nancy. I know."

He shivered, the sun was still shining on his bench but the deepest cold had settled in his chest. It was time. He had been looking for words that could describe the turmoil within. And it had come to him in the dark alley in Hackney, in the little cafe he had never visited before amongst people he did not know.

He was too tired to be angry, too tired to nurture the will to destroy, a desire so intense that it negated life itself.

"I am scared, I expect you know that," said Henry.

"It is not easy to look at truth in the face, Henry."

"I am scared, I am going to pretend again I can fight this."

Nancy did not reply.

"It is time to be honest and I am not sure I know how anymore," carried on Henry.

"I could try to give you more advice or say that it takes time but that would be bullshit."

Henry managed a smile; he loved it when she swore.

"Can I ask you for something that sounds crazy? A sort of final wish before they send me to prison and throw away the key," said Henry.

Nancy nodded.

"Buy the painting, *The Raft of the Medusa*."

"Now? Why?" replied Nancy.

"Because I never want to forget. I understand what you said a few days ago about *The Raft*. It is the first piece of art that means a lot to me, no, I think it is me."

"Is it?"

"Yes, and I am tired. Tired of hating so much, tired of succumbing to the impulse that destroys."

He no longer wanted to inflict pain, a pain that could never be soothed. The word atonement had come to him with sudden and unexpected clarity.

Henry's attention switched to some movement in the far distance. The forms moving towards them had not escaped Nancy either.

"Shall we do this?"

"If you are ready, I am ready too," replied Nancy.

She had stood up.

"Remember I am not only your brief," said Nancy with kind determination, "I am your friend. I am with you all the way."

Henry stood up too.

"Even after all this?"

"Even after all this."

They moved together towards the south side of the park. Men in uniforms were approaching them.

* * *

"Did he sign a confession?" asked Nancy.

Pole started walking the corridor with her.

"Did the Counterterrorist guys not let you see him at all after his arrest?" asked Pole, half surprised.

"Henry is not exactly thinking straight at the moment. I had to be the one informing Pritchard, his defence lawyer."

Nancy stopped to face Pole. "I don't think he cares much about what he has actually done but what he thinks he has done."

"What do you want me to do? The case is no longer in my jurisdiction," replied Pole calmly.

"Do you think it stacks up altogether? I don't, but I can't exactly tell you why," replied Nancy hoping she would catch Pole's attention.

"You're his legal counsel. It's your job to get your theory checked out," retorted Pole.

"Come on Jonathan!"

"You've got your instinct, I've got mine, Ms Wu," said Pole smiling at the elegant woman in front of him. "You don't think I am going to roll over so easily do you?"

"*Bien sûr que non.*"

Nancy smiled in return, she could indulge him. Pole blushed slightly but changed the tone.

"You never finished your story about Jacques Vergès," said Pole.

Nancy slowed the pace and took her time to gauge Pole's intentions.

"Vergès is one of the reasons I stopped practising. He contacted me when Tariq Aziz, Saddam Hussein's minister, included him in his defence team. I nearly said yes."

"What stopped you?" asked Pole amazed at the revelation.

"It was one step too far. I was so tempted by the challenge. I tried to reconcile this with my belief that all deserve legal representation but it was pure ego and nothing else I feared."

They had arrived at Pole's office. Nurani stood up to join them but Pole shut the door after Nancy. He would have this discussion on his own.

"Ms Wu, the facts are overwhelming."

"Call me Nancy," she said.

"OK, Nancy," replied Pole emphasising her name. "Let's recap on the evidence. Henry has for many years contributed to a 'charity' which we know is in reality a slush fund for the IRA. Fact. Furthermore, we know that he is the mastermind behind the legal structure, also fact."

Nancy nodded in acknowledgement.

"He has admitted concocting a plan, albeit many years ago, to bring down an executive aircraft with his pals Liam and Bobby. Fact."

"Agreed."

"We also know that his two friends are members of the new faction IRA and, contrary to expectation, they have not 'retired'. Liam and Henry have stayed in contact since they were children. OK, the contact with Bobby is less strong but he is always in the background.

And we also know that Liam and Henry saw each other only a few days before Albert's plane came down."

Pole was about to continue but Nancy interrupted.

"Just so we are clear, I am not contesting this. Henry should not have contributed to this slush fund, it was stupid, in fact more than stupid. It was disgraceful altogether, but—"

"We have Bobby's confession."

"Which I find extremely tenuous," finished Nancy.

"In what way?

"As far as I can tell, they never spoke face to face about it."

"You mean always through text or phone call."

"Precisely."

"That may be a very good technique to distance oneself from Bobby. He is an unpredictable guy to say the least."

"Yes, maybe," replied Nancy unconvinced. "But it still leaves evidence behind and Henry can perfectly well justify at least one other trip to Ireland without arousing suspicions."

Pole did not reply. She could feel a shift.

"Someone else could have made those calls," she ventured.

"You would have to be able to fool Bobby very well." But Pole did not reject the idea as preposterous.

"Well, Henry has taken elocution lessons to get rid of his Irish accent. This would shape his voice in a particular way. I am a barrister. I can tell the impact these lessons have on someone's voice."

"OK, let's assume that we have one element of illogical and inconsistent behaviour. It is still unbelievably slim but what else?" replied Pole, this time more encouragingly.

"Jonathan, you are going to have to help me a bit there. Please?"

"All right," Pole replied. "The one element I find not completely conclusive, which is key to this entire story, is the delivery of the bomb."

Nancy was all ears.

"Forensic tells us that the bomb was small but powerful enough to be contained in a small space. Anthony Albert took away a briefcase from Henry's flat, more precisely from Henry's block of flats. We can't confirm that he actually entered Henry's flat."

"Bobby says in his statement that he left the briefcase in Henry's garage but never saw him take it. It is a hell of a risk to leave a live bomb unattended," said Nancy.

Pole nodded and extricated a heavy file from the piles of documents laying on his desk. He enjoyed working methodically with Nancy through the evidence.

"Henry could have, again, calculated that he did not want to be seen with Bobby but I agree it is a huge risk to take. Even for a short period of time, who would want to leave an unattended bomb in the basement? Henry now remembers meeting with Albert to give him the case but can't tell us exactly what happened. Yet Henry has an excellent memory."

Nancy stood up and walked to the window. She was looking at the Thames, letting herself gather her thoughts. She turned around to face Pole.

"And yet he has confessed."

"And yet he has confessed," repeated Pole, "and the Counterterrorist Squad need to score quickly. The latest carnage in Paddington, right on their doorstep, does not give them much of an option."

They remained silent.

"No other credible leads by the way," confirmed Pole, anticipating Nancy's next question.

Pole suddenly stopped in his tracks. Nancy read the change on his face.

"Is this worth mentioning?" she hesitated, not wanting to interrupt what could be a vital train of thought. Pole did not answer but grabbed the phone.

"Dolores, what did Adeila exactly say about the will? Yes, sorry. Hi."

Pole grimaced, indicating a major lapse in common courtesy.

"OK."

Pole took some notes on a pad that was perched on a pile of documents.

"Could I please have Adeila's number?" finished Pole, after listening to what Dolores had to say.

Pole put the phone down and immediately dialled another number.

"Good afternoon, may I speak to Mrs Albert please?" Pole switched on the loudspeaker.

"It is she," replied Adeila's polished voice.

"Inspector Pole here, I am sorry to disturb you but would you have a moment?"

Pole half expected Adeila to put the phone down but she volunteered a short go ahead. Pole decided there was little merit in spinning out his question and went straight to the point.

"You mentioned to my colleague Dolores Patten that you expected your husband to leave you very little in his will when he died. It might be a little too literal in which case I apologise profusely, but was there any reason why you thought he might die soon?"

"No need to apologise, Inspector," replied Adeila. "I used the term because I knew Anthony was dying. He had a terminal illness which he tried to conceal from everyone." Adeila continued unprompted. "You may ask how I knew. Well, I am sure you have done your job thoroughly, Inspector, and you must know that Anthony had an affair a little while ago. I decided to check regularly his conversation after this and had a private agency firm install a recording device in his office at home. A very boring conversation in the main, Anthony really lacked imagination. However, I learned about his illness that way together with the content of his will."

Pole and Nancy were taking in the information, already envisaging all the possibilities it contained.

"Are you still there, Inspector?" asked Adeila, somewhat amused.

"So sorry, yes of course."

"I am glad to hear I have silenced you for once. Anthony was treated in Switzerland."

"It would be incredibly helpful if you could–"

"… give you the address of the clinic?" interrupted Adeila. "Give me a few moments."

Pole could hear movements at the end of the phone. Adeila gave him the details he needed and hung up with little more than a surprising good luck.

"How can this help?" asked Nancy.

"I don't know yet, it may be nothing, but I need to understand what happened in Switzerland."

He stopped, and Nancy realised that her time with him was over.

She stood up.

"You will let me know?"

"Of course, I'll keep you posted," replied Pole with a reassuring smile.

She put her hand on the door handle and turned back before opening.

"Why do we believe in Henry's innocence? *Oui, pourquoi?*"

"*Ma chere Nancy, je crois que nous avons la même réponse,*" said Pole, in his impeccable French.

Pole dialled the number of the clinic in Switzerland that had been treating Anthony Albert for the past few months.

* * *

Henry walked through the doors and the warden removed his handcuffs. Nancy felt a shock when she saw him wearing the standard prison track suit. His hair had turned silver overnight but his face looked calm, maybe resigned, she was not yet sure.

She stood up to greet him. He waved a quick hello and sat across the table but said nothing more.

"I saw Pole this morning. We learned something new," she hesitated.

Nothing of what she could say was going to change the path he had decided to embark on. As Henry remained silent Nancy decided to continue.

"Anthony Albert was terminally ill."

"So, are you trying to tell me that terminating his life a tad early was a form of mercy killing?" said Henry springing back to life. "How about the pilot of the plane, was he also terminally ill?"

This is more like it, thought Nancy, ignoring Henry's aggressive tone.

"No, I am simply giving you the facts."

"Nothing you can say, Nancy, will change the fact that I have killed these guys."

Nancy was about to reply but Henry cut her short.

"I don't care whether this is directly, indirectly, whether Bobby was a sicko who heard voices. I have known that all my life, I kept meeting them, I kept giving money. I also knew the reason, so what does that make me? A guy who thinks he still has principles because he sticks to his old school friends, a guy who believes in a cause? That's a lot of bullshit, a feel good factor as long as things don't go wrong or I don't know the bloody details. I did what I did."

"No one is contesting that, Henry, but pay for what you did, not for what you think you did," replied Nancy, her tone matching Henry's.

"You have never seen a man die in–" started Henry, through gritted teeth and could not complete his sentence, the lump in his throat too large for him to continue.

"Yes, I have, bodies torn apart, the smell of blood. Do not assume you are the only one who knows about savage killings," Nancy retorted with more vehemence than he had ever heard before.

The anger and anxiety in her voice shocked Henry. They both remained silent, facing each other and not able to say any more.

"Then you know," concluded Henry.

She said nothing. He needed to find his truth. She knew the validity of the search. She would for her part keep doubting. Her intuition told her that Henry's story had not been fully unravelled yet.

* * *

Pole was standing in front of the fax machine. Documents were pouring in from Switzerland. His police contact had managed to convince the doctors in Geneva to lift the doctor-patient confidentiality. The word terrorism had done the trick again. Everything he had received so far confirmed Anthony Albert's condition. He had indeed reached the terminal phase of his illness with possibly less than six months to live. Albert had been diagnosed two years earlier and was going to Switzerland regularly for treatment. His job had brought him regularly to Geneva so no one ever suspected. Pole thought about the sheer willpower the man must have had to endure treatment and carry on his job. Rumours, of course, had circulated in the City that a lot of what he had structured was linked to the subprime market. Then again, he probably would not have cared a damn. Pole looked at the documents churning out and gave an irritated grunt. They were hardly legible. He walked back into his office, shut the door and dialled Nancy's number.

Pole had dialled from his hands-free set. He would pick up if she answered. The phone rang four times and a small click indicated that the answer phone would kick in any second:

"Oh dear! You've just missed me but fear not I will call you back as soon as I can, *et pour les Anglophiles non Anglophones*," chimed Nancy's voice.

The message carried on in French, a story about Anglophiles not being Anglophones followed, bringing a smile on Pole's face. He needed a trip back to his roots in Aquitaine. Pole disliked having to leave concise messages on voicemails and was preparing to deliver a witty response.

"*Chère Madame Wu, mes hommages*. I am devastated I have just missed you but if you could—"

Nancy's elegant voice took over.

"*Mon cher* Jonathan, I thought we agreed you would call me Nancy."

Pole let out a short laugh.

"*Trés bien, avec plaisir*, Nancy, I am sorry to disturb you but I think I need a little help."

"I am all ears, Jonathan."

"It is proving rather difficult to obtain the documents we need from the Swiss Clinic. Using my natural charm does not seem to work, and my French has become a little rusty."

"And you would like me to add a certain *je ne sais quoi* to your natural charm," said Nancy.

"*Voila*," exclaimed Pole

"The number please, I will call you as soon as I have results."

* * *

Nancy was navigating a number of options to find the right correspondent. A young voice finally answered. She introduced herself to her *interlocutrice*, now using her perfect French. She was one of the lawyers on the Crowne-Albert Case, she explained, and was asking for a copy of all documentation that had been sent to the police. This was a matter of urgency. It was imperative that she should have access to all relevant material.

"I am very sorry," replied the voice, "but these documents are patient notes, some of them handwritten and subject to doctor-patient confidentiality."

"Of course, I can see your dilemma but you must remember that I am also subject to the same rules as you are. Lawyers always are. You could check my registration with chambers," carried on Nancy in an affable but determined voice. "It is essential for the case that we understand the extent of Mr Albert's illness."

"Well, if I could check your registration, I could courier a copy to you, this might work better," yielded the young voice.

"Very kind of you," replied Nancy as she gave Pritchard QC's number.

She would make a call and Pritchard would back her up. Nancy was calmly giving her old friend's chambers details when she felt she could press on with more questions.

"I need to complete my findings as soon as possible. It is a rather unusual case," she ventured.

"I read the story in the news. It is unbelievable that one of our patients could be involved in such a terrible thing. At least, Mr Albert was at peace with himself."

"I am so glad to hear this," replied Nancy.

Perhaps she could encourage the young woman to say more.

"It is an unusual thing to see coming from someone like Mr Albert," said Nancy tentatively.

"I did not know him so well you see," replied the voice in earnest, "but I go to the chapel very often with patients. It is a lovely place in our gardens, always full of flowers and so peaceful."

"*Et bien Mademoiselle*, you used to care for Anthony Albert?"

"Mr Albert was a very private man, but last time I looked after him he was spending a lot of time there. It was unusual because I'd never seen him there before. He looked … relieved. People come to terms differently with the end of life." She stopped abruptly, afraid she might be embarrassing the other woman with her remarks.

"I can see Mr Albert was in good hands. This is very comforting. Although he spoke little it must have been important to have a confidant."

"Well, he only spoke much about his children. When he did he was always transformed. I think he was at the end at peace with what would happen when ..." again her voice trailed.

"I am taking much of your time, *encore un grand merci*," concluded Nancy.

What had Albert done next? He was not a religious man. Why such need for deep thoughts, the will? But that had been changed a few months prior.

She thanked the young woman profusely and dialled Pole's number. Pole needed to trace Albert's movements in the last few weeks before his death. Pole took the call and grabbed his mac, walking out to his unscheduled meeting in a hurry.

* * *

BIG BOSS BANGED UP

The tabloid press knew how to compose a headline. A pile of newspapers lay on the sofa. She was in a comfortable spot, in her favourite little coffee shop on Chancery Lane. Pole entered the place holding more papers under his arm. He had hardly had time to greet her when he saw a tantalising cup of coffee and an apricot Danish placed in front of an empty chair.

"I could have been late," he said feigning reproach.

"*Mon cher* Jonathan," replied Nancy in her best barrister voice. "You are not the type, and in any case apricot Danish turns out to be my favourite too."

Pole changed the subject, fearing he would make some corny remark.

"I presume you have read all there is to read about McCarthy's arrest?"

"Extremely precise reporting, for once the papers have done a good job of investigatory journalism. The explanations of what has happened are well researched. I suspect they had a lot of help from Whitehall."

"You mean about the large subprime business GL was running?"

"More to the point, the ridiculously large losses GL were trying

265

to hide, at least until the merger was completed – $51 billion all told, unthinkable."

"Henry never touched that stuff, though."

"True but he knew something was up. The minute McCarthy brought the CDO team from Credit Suisse First Boston, he had doubts. McCarthy should have played his cards even closer to his chest."

"CDO?" questioned Pole.

"Collateralised Debt Obligation – product packaged with subprime loans," Nancy replied confidently.

"Extremely dodgy stuff I take it. Henry mentioned them I now remember, and before you ask, yes, we will have a chat with McCarthy about Anthony Albert and his CDOs business, although my feeling is that it won't yield anything."

"Much to my disappointment, I think you are right."

"Nancy – you mentioned Whitehall?" said Pole enjoying the use of her name.

"Ah yes, Whitehall. They know the party is coming to an end. A few economists disagreed with the government, in particular one of Tony Blair's advisers. Whitehall understand how out of touch politicians can be with real economic data. One way to monitor the real state of the economy is to let some of the City bosses court them in return for, let's say, a few favours."

"How do you know that?" said Pole in disbelief.

"The judiciary is always close to the civil service." She raised her cup of coffee with a grin.

"I am surprised that none of the papers mention Henry."

"Well, the Counterterrorist Squad is keeping a keen eye on what is being published I assume. I am also sure they do not want to advertise that they lost Henry when he was wreaking havoc at GL."

"You have a point."

"I do, very much so," said Nancy and this time Pole raised his cup of coffee.

"Enough about Whitehall. How about Switzerland?" said Nancy, ready for a much-needed update.

"Albert seemed to have behaved oddly shortly before the crash," replied Pole.

He took another sip of coffee and gave Nancy a full account.

"When will you have the results from the tapes?"

"The Swiss have a reputation for being slow but thorough, however they understand the urgency."

"Jonathan, that is not an answer," Nancy frowned.

"When is Henry's preliminary hearing?"

"Two weeks."

"That soon."

"He has confessed, remember?" said Nancy.

"I will see what I can do."

Pole took a sip of his coffee.

"Remember this is Geneva, jewellery shops everywhere so ... there is a hell of a lot to go through."

Nancy nodded. The next few days would be uncomfortably quiet.

* * *

To Nancy's surprise, Pam Anderson's PA had managed to find a slot in Pam's overflowing diary, Nancy had braced herself for an exacting conversation. Pam had returned Nancy's call within a few hours simply giving her the choice of a couple of dates. Pam Anderson wanted to speak, Nancy concluded.

The lobby of Chase and Case was predictably large and possibly a little old fashioned. Nancy had decided to sit in one of the armchairs that enabled her to watch the toing and froing of Chase and Case's clientele. She was observing with interest a small podgy man who had taken over the cluster of sofas next to her. He had arrived, ordered a coffee from the staff at reception and extricated from his briefcase two BlackBerrys, a small laptop and a number of financial newspapers. He was happily conducting his business in the middle of the lobby, his voice carrying right across the space. He did not seem to care.

Nancy saw her from afar. She instantly knew it was Pam and smiled. She saw herself as she was all those years ago as a young and ambitious lawyer. She could also see that Henry would have enjoyed being with her. There was something harmonious about her presence, the slightly less severe suit and the unexpected details of a colourful brooch pinned to her jacket.

Pam extended a slight but decisive hand. She shook Nancy's and both women walked out of the lobby.

"Let's go to the Barbican's cafe," suggested Nancy.

"Agreed, it will be quiet at this time of day."

Pam had been thinking about the meeting with Nancy and had something to say that mattered or at least mattered to her..

The cafe was empty. They chose a couple of armchairs in a secluded corner.

"Thank you for seeing me so quickly," started Nancy.

"The least I can do. How is he?", she said, finding it hard to speak Henry's name.

"Well, I would be lying to you if I said he is fine." Nancy could not pretend.

"You know about the QC," interrupted Pam.

"You mean Wooster QC's sabbatical? Yes, I do."

"I am so sorry," continued Pam in a shaky voice. "I have kept thinking about it again and again."

Nancy was taken aback by her tone of voice. She extended a hand and gently reached for Pam's arm.

"Pritchard QC is a friend and a very competent man."

"I know, but Henry was a friend too. I should have done more."

She turned her head away.

"A friend …"

It was unkind to be exploiting this sudden rush of honesty but she needed to know more.

"Any details, anything you can tell me that might help Henry."

Pam nodded. She inhaled and sat back a little.

"That is why I wanted to speak to you." Pam's voice had recovered some composure. "I will say this to you in confidence."

Pam stopped and Nancy took over.

"I understand, Henry won't know."

"Well, it was at the closing in Dublin. Has Henry ever told you about his best success?"

"He has, worth several billion dollars. You were there as his lawyer and so was Anthony Albert, if I remember correctly."

Pam blushed and glanced away.

"We had an affair." She was still looking away.

"You and Henry?"

"No." Pam was now facing Nancy with wide open eyes. "... Anthony."

Nancy was speechless. She let the information sink in and suddenly a million questions rushed into her mind, jealousy, passion, revenge.

"Did Henry find out?"

"No."

"Are you certain?"

"Nothing changed between us after the closing and Henry would never have tolerated ..."

Pam could not say any more and Nancy recognised the suffering that unspoken love can cause. She could not reconcile why Pam would have an affair with Albert when it was clear that she loved Henry.

"Before you ask about me and Henry ... there has never been anything."

"Because he was your biggest client."

Pam nodded.

"And because you've just been made a partner."

Pam was surprised by the forwardness of the question but she knew there was no point denying it.

"It's inconceivable but that night, in Dublin, maybe." Pam said.

Nancy bent forward a little, encouraging Pam to confide.

"Why then?"

"I thought ... it was Henry. You see they have the same voice. I mean Henry and Anthony had the same voice."

"The same voice," said Nancy, trying to hide her surprise.

Nancy extended her hand and rested it onto Pam's clenched fist. She could no longer speak, the memory of her ugly affair burning in her mind. Nancy asked gently,

"Why do you think it is so material?"

"Because Anthony Albert hated Henry with such determination, I think you should know."

Nancy nodded. Pam looked at the other woman with pleading eyes but asked nothing. She slowly stood up.

"I have to go now."

Nancy stood up too and squeezed Pam's hand reassuringly.

"Thank you for your honesty."

"Just look after him."

Pam did not wait for an answer and left the Barbican café without turning back.

Chapter Twenty-Eight

"I still have not decided whether we have been unbelievably lucky or whether it would have somehow surfaced," said Nancy as Inspector Pole and she were walking rapidly along the corridors of Scotland Yard.

"I could reply that this was without doubt an excellent piece of police work," retorted Pole with a grin, "but I agree with you," he added, this time thoughtfully. "I might not have pursued it if you had not spoken to the young lady at the clinic."

They stopped in front of one of the interrogation rooms. They both knew Henry was waiting, unaware though of the content of the document he was about to read.

"What has he been told?" asked Nancy.

"Very little, apart from the fact that a letter has been recovered from Albert's lawyer in Geneva destined for him."

"And the date?"

"You mean that it was destined for him in twenty years' time rather than today."

"Yes."

"He knows."

Pole opened the door. With few formalities he placed a handwritten note in front of Henry.

It read:

I nearly started this letter with Dear Henry. How conditioned can one be, even in one's last hours? You are anything to me Henry but dear, of course, but you know that and you don't care.

By the time you open this letter a good twenty years should have lapsed, a long, long time to reflect on the human condition. It has taken a lot less than that for me to come to terms with mine.

You see, Henry, I have little time to live, six months at most says the Doc. I was told I could do so much in six months. What a joke! He does not understand men like us, he does not feel power and ambition the way we do. He does not see that a man who has lost everything he once valued, who has been stripped bare, has nothing left to him but his burning ambition. My wife thinks that I am uncouth, unsophisticated, the son of an immigrant that has never evolved to be the upper class man she wishes for, a lowlife that can barely keep her in style. My children hardly speak to me, although I suspect it is their mother's doing. You will never understand this, Henry, as your ego precludes you from loving anyone. But I would die for them, no, I am dying for them. They won't see me in my final hours, a body hooked to a machine, stripped of all dignity. In the meantime, I have become the stranger who signs the cheques and sleeps in the spare room.

So what's left? The job, but even that is no longer enough. I want what you have Henry, all of it! Why? Because I can. For all your intelligence, your immense ambition and the violence underneath, you are not a killer, Henry, but me … I am.

Did you know that I did a deal with McCarthy? Actually, by the time you read this you might have figured it out. He was so easy to convince, so wrapped up in his desire to have more, to be more, to hide all the shitty deals we did together and still be the hero of the day. I would never have lived long enough to enjoy it, the merged teams under MY NAME, so I did what I had to do.

You probably are starting to have a hint, aren't you? Can you feel on the back of your neck your hairs bristle, the slight churn in your stomach? Yes … I know you can.

So, let me tell you how it all started.

You must remember the famous closing dinner in Dublin. Everyone wondered why I was there, celebrating with you. I know, I had little to do with this god damned incredibly 'oh so clever' deal of yours and boy you did not let me forget that for one minute.

I don't think you spoke to me once but you sure spoke enough about me. By the time we all rolled to the pub you were so fucking drunk (champagne and glory are a very lethal mix) that you had finally forgotten I was there. And then it happened, your two pals, Bobby and Liam. You might have been more cautious another day but on that day of splendour you did not care.

So you poured Guinness down their throats, introduced them around. I listened, I observed, I saw an opportunity. Which one I did not know yet. I can still play the foreigner role when it suits me, I forget this altogether in the City, as you have done yourself, but there in Dublin I felt Italian again.

Liam was cautious, but somehow the gate opened up. I played the oppressed Catholic and he got friendly with me, me – your worst enemy. Bobby was getting stoned in the corner of the bar and he blabbed about the IRA. He must have scored on some good stuff and he was on a high at seeing his friend (you, Henry). He, Bobby, knew the real Henry, the City was only a cover up. What a treat this all was.

Then came the icing on the cake, if I may say. Did you know as an aside that you and I have the same voice? Partially the result of taking elocution lessons I presume, the other quirky twist of fate, at least according to the lovely Pam. I know you fancied her and I can tell you she sure did you, oh boy! But I am afraid … I got there first.

She tans in the nude by the way.

So now we have the ingredients. What am I going to do with them?

But you don't decide to do what I did suddenly, the idea slowly creeps into your mind. It does not emerge in one go, it tentatively surfaces, alternatives shock you, they come and go and you become daring. You are amazed that you can think the unthinkable and then The Plan hits you with its logical, implacable certainty. Its insanity leaves you speechless but it fascinates you. Will you dare? Will you pull it off? Will you see it through to the bitter end? If you are reading this letter then I guess I succeeded. I simply hope that in Hell where I belong I will be able to see your face when you read. But enough indulgence, back to The Plan.

I bought a top-up mobile phone, simple, untraceable and I dialled Bobby's number. For some ridiculous reason Bobby insisted on giving it to me before we left the pub, he was too smashed to care, I loved the deceit. Bobby told me he was depressed at the thought of the IRA decommissioning, a sell-out, a surrender. I stirred him up a bit, it was not difficult, so we nearly became pals. He told me a lot about you and your childhood in Belfast. I nearly felt sorry for you, not for long mind. I have no mercy, remember, neither have you.

So I called Bobby. When he replied I nearly hung up but lovely Pam had me convinced that our voices were the same and it worked. Your best pal, your childhood friend, could not tell the difference, what a coup! I had a good old rant at the fucking bastard who wanted my business and Bobby got onto it straight away. The Plan, Your Plan to bomb a small executive aircraft back in the day. I had agonised for hours, how was I going to convince him and it was there all ready to fly (excuse the pun, I am a dying man)?

So he reminded me of The Plan, in all its details committed to memory by Bobby, everything was there, impeccably thought through. I nearly got jealous, but then again, I should be graceful in victory.

The rest was easy, the money, the timing, the secrecy from Liam. For someone who looks so wasted, Bobby is pretty focused when it comes to killing. He followed my instructions to the letter, no question. I even got him to agree to leave the briefcase in your garage without us meeting – if only all my staff were as well trained.

It was easy to leave you the odd email and cryptic message that would confuse the coppers. The most difficult part will be transporting the briefcase. I have to bring a live bomb home. Adeila is wondering why I want the kids to board that week. She is a nosy bitch that one. I had a warm feeling at the idea of blowing up half of Belgravia but that would leave you off the hook – I could not do that, I'm afraid.

The airport will then be easy, I know the guys so well. The car will drop me just at the bottom of the aircraft stairs. I fly too often with them to be considered a security risk – how touching.

I will die a brutal and remarked death and you will be my unwilling murderer. In time you might even believe you did it Henry ... until you open this letter that is and then, well ...

Here we are, Henry, you alive but barely, and me dead, thankfully.

Don't be fooled by my earlier comment, I don't believe in Hell. I walked through its gates when I was born and will check out in a few days' time, oblivion awaits. Anthony A.

Henry closed his eyes, the letter dropped from his shaking hands.

A very small but painful tear rolled from his eye, traced the side of his nose in a slow but certain journey. It finished its course upon his lips, a sad, salty kiss.

Words swam: pain, freedom, hatred, peace, revenge ... and when he opened his eyes only one sentiment remained. Forgiveness.

* * *

BREAKING PO!NT

HENRY CROWNE PAYING THE PRICE BOOK 2

SAMPLE CHAPTER

The room erupted into applause. Nancy joined in as she crossed the stage, then she clasped Edwina's hand warmly. She grinned at her friend. Edwina had delivered a trailblazing speech that had provoked a robust Q&A session. She could soon be joining the most powerful women in the world, tipped to become the next Governor of the Bank of England. Edwina had discussed the offer with Nancy in confidence.

The Women In Enterprise conference had become the highlight in the calendar of professional women striving to make their marks, not only in international investment banking, but now in the whole of UK industry. The conference theme was the reworking of an old chestnut "How women can break the glass ceiling" But the developing financial crisis had given it a new twist … Would all this have happened had women been at the helm? To give the debate more bite, some high-profile men had also been invited. The panel was well constructed, a mix of captains of industry and bankers. Nancy, the newly appointed Chair of the WIE, had accepted the invitation to act as moderator. The atmosphere had been electric as senior ladies in the audience had taken a gloves-off approach and the gentlemen were having none of it.

"One final question … one."

A sea of hands shot up, waving, snapping, eager to attract Nancy's attention.

"The FT will have a last say tonight … Pauline, go ahead please."

"A question for Edwina. Christine Lagarde is the Managing Director of the International Monetary Fund. Janet Yellen is almost certainly going to be appointed by Obama as head of the FED. Is the Bank of England ready for a woman at the helm?"

Edwina stood up again, moving back to the lectern with slow deliberate pace.

"Any institution, private or public, must consider how to deliver the best outcome. Talent will be found in a pool of diverse people and the most forward-looking organisations will not shy away from it." A roar of approvals interrupted. "I know what you are asking me Pauline … indirectly. I have only this answer: may the best of us win."

How clever, Nancy thought. *An answer that will inspire the women, appease the men and say nothing about herself. Quite simply brilliant.*

Nancy had been a high-profile barrister practicing criminal law, then became the youngest ever appointed QC at just thirty-five. For a very long time she thought talent would prevail. But the latest report on the lack of progress had pushed her to advocate for set quotas for female employment at all level of the corporate structure.

Edwina had concluded the debate with a masterly final intervention. The voice of a woman who could inspire by her exemplary career. The standing ovation was still going on.

"Thank you," Nancy said. "Thank you for the extraordinary show of support." She was broadly smiling to them and turned to Edwina with a nod. "It has been an exceptional event. I must again thank the participants for the quality of their intervention, and for the quality of the audience input."

The room erupted once more.

"I know, I know," said Nancy whilst trying to appease the crowd with a gesture of both hands. "Please, you know it is not completely over. We still have drinks – much-needed – waiting for us next door.

You can strike up a conversation with our guests. Do be gentle with some of them!"

The room broke into laughter and the men in the audience took it in good humour. The protagonists were giving back their clip-microphones to the staff. Edwina approached Nancy.

"I think it's in the bag."

"It certainly is. Did Gabriel work with you on this? I detected a forceful yet compromising approach in your speech."

"Yes, Gabs helped me. But I was talking about the appointment. Osborne spoke to me."

Nancy grinned. "Oh, I see. We must catch up. I am excited for you."

"We must but agreed, not the place. Let's do lunch."

"Do let's. Utterly delighted for you Eddie."

Nancy moved away and started circulating amongst a crowd of women gathered on the roof terrace of One Poultry. She was mobbed by a group of enthusiastic young lawyers eager to speak about her experience as QC. She finally moved on and was about to join one of the panellists, CEO of a notorious airline, when someone grabbed her arm.

"Do you really believe in that bullshit of yours?" a voice slurred. The large man was standing too close for comfort. He swayed slightly, moved backward. His small beady eyes narrowed in a vengeful squint.

"And who do I have the pleasure of speaking to?" replied Nancy whilst slowly removing his hand from her arm.

"Gary Cook, former head of trading at GL. Courtesy of one of your females."

"I doubt any of these females are 'mine', as you put it," replied Nancy.

"Yeah right, but you … you and your little friends are not whiter than white. You lot are trying to say you are better than blokes on the trading floor. That's bullocks and I can prove it." Gary's heavy jaws had clenched so hard the muscle of his neck had leaped out. He had not finished yet.

"I say, how clever of you. Not 'whiter than white'. With my Chinese ancestry that is going to be rather certain."

"Gary Cook," exclaimed a voice that came from behind Nancy. "Great to see you again!"

Gary stopped in his tracks. The unexpected welcome confused him, then again the person who had greeted him was another man. The well-groomed young man interposed himself effortlessly between Gary and Nancy who slowly retreated. There was no point in making a scene. Gary was a loser who should not be humoured. Nancy could hear the smooth Gabriel holding the man's anger, absorbing it until it had subsided completely. Edwina had chosen well; Gabriel Duchamp was an impressive right-hand man. He manoeuvred Gary towards a more secluded part of the roof terrace, called for more drinks. Nancy was not sure Gary needed more champagne but no doubt Gabriel would move him gradually towards the exit and Gary would eventually take the hint. A small tremor of revulsion had run through Nancy's body. She had not recognised Gary's old, bitter face. She wiped her hand against her dress but felt she needed to do more than that to wash away the stickiness of Gary's feel.

She entered the Ladies' briskly, lathered her hands with sandalwood scented soap and ran cold water over them, watching the foam disappear down the plughole. An apt image of where Garry ought to end up one day. She retraced her steps but before she had time to turn into the corridor someone grabbed her shoulder. Edwina was standing close to her.

"Just had an email from George Osborne's PA. Final meeting in a couple of days' time." Edwina whispered. "Perhaps a little coaching may be warranted?"

"I somehow feel the student has surpassed the master," Nancy murmured, smiling. "But of course, I am here for you if you feel the need."

"Very much so." Edwina squeezed Nancy's shoulder gently, but let go on hearing the sound of voices coming their way.

Both women emerged from the corridor separately and as she reappeared Nancy found herself mobbed once more by a group of enthusiastic ladies. The banking industry had to change its ways. One of the young women mentioned the name Henry Crowne. She must have done her homework as to who Nancy was. Nancy returned the question with a frosty look. She would not be discussing Henry at this conference or anywhere else for that matter. Then a whirlpool of questions swept her away, away from Gary and Henry.

There was only a small group of people left by now, and Nancy was about to say her goodbyes when two uniformed officers walked through the left doors, alighting directly onto the terrace.

One of the officers bent his head towards his shoulder radio set.

"Yes, I'm on the roof now. There are a few people still up here."

Nancy thought she heard the instructions *keep them there*.

"Sorry ladies, I am PC Barrett and this is PC Leonard. We have a jumper."

The women looked at each other incredulous.

"I mean someone has jumped from the roof terrace. Dead, I'm afraid." PC Barrett asked to see the guestlist and the young security guard who had checked names at the door produced it in an instant. PC Barrett turned away from the crowd and towards his shoulder radio, sheltering his voice.

"Yep, got it there. Yep … Gary Cook."

Nancy had turned away, still all ears. She shuddered. *Gary … impossible.*

* * *

"One hundred and ninety-seven, ninety-eight, ninety-nine, two hundred. Shit!" puffed Henry as he rolled back onto the mat. He was nearly at the end of his routine in HMP Belmarsh gym. He needed to start stretching, but he lay there for another minute. A small luxury in a place devoid of the comfort he once knew. He closed his eyes and a face appeared out of nowhere. He sat up slowly, eyes still closed. Was Liam also exercising in the prison in which he was incarcerated? Northern Ireland's Maghaberry was a tough place, a tough place for a tough boy. Liam would survive it, but what of Bobby? Anger gripped Henry again. He stood up abruptly and started stretching.

"Let go. Just let go," he said softly, applying pressure to release the pain. His muscles screamed. He eased off the stretch a little.

The question had haunted Henry for months. Could Liam have

done anything differently? Could he have chosen Henry rather than his brother Bobby? The police in Belfast would never have spared the life of Bobby, a faction IRA operative, a man for whom decommissioning had no meaning. There had to be a deal and Henry was that deal. And what a deal he was, a financial super star, a City banker organising and contributing to the IRA finances. Henry's stellar financial career masking his terrorist's activities, how clever and daring. But how wrong.

"No ... no choice," Henry murmured, wiping his face with a towel. He ran it over his hair. The standard prison cut had left very little of what had been a dense mane.

Yet, Henry had wanted to be chosen, always wanted to be the one. And this yearning had cost him everything. Beyond the sacrifice of his own career and hopes, he had also sacrificed lives, many lives, and for that he would pay.

Henry threw the towel over his shoulder, got into the changing rooms, stripped down and started showering. He had been apprehensive to start with. Would he find a fate in prison only reserved for the bastard of a banker he was? Would he be molested, beaten up and humiliated? But the fear had not materialised and eventually it had faded away. He had learned to become unnoticeable amongst the Category A prisoners of Belmarsh. Henry was high-risk and on Nancy's advice he had played that card fully. He had been moved to a block in which cons shared the same Cat A profile except ... no bankers. Or at least not yet.

"Hey, good set of press ups, man."

"Thanks, Big K. I plan to get really fit over the next twenty-five years."

"Man, you got good muscle tone there. Respect."

Henry nodded, grabbed his towel and got dressed quickly. He still did not like to linger in the changing rooms. Another inmate had moved out of the showers too. Henry felt he was being observed, but when he looked up the man was facing the other way, going about his business. Henry noticed a face tattooed on his back. Big K had already left but he would know who this was. Big K had been allocated the cell next to Henry's and he had shown interest in him straightaway.

Drugs were his domain, and the words 'money laundering' had caught his undivided attention. Big K was someone who knew what it meant to survive prison life, so it was worth swapping a few snippets of info with him.

Henry rang the buzzer. The security guard opened the door and informed the next guard that Henry was on his way to his cell, running the gauntlet of the seven doors he had to cross.

"Thanks John," Henry said. The guard nodded and let Henry into cell 140–A. The door shut with the usual heavy clunk and Henry sat on his bed. He looked at his watch: 9:47am. Only thirteen minutes to mail time. He hoped for a letter from Nancy. Once the post had been delivered, he would take down a heavy art book sitting sideways on his small bookshelf. From its thick spine he retrieved his pride and joy – a small netsuke in the shape of a dog with pups. It had become a comforting ritual, to read a letter from the outside world whilst fingering this small object, a piece of art that did not belong to prison life. Henry had allowed himself this luxury. He was ever such a good boy otherwise.

Acknowledgements

It takes many people to write and publish a book ... for their generosity and support I want to say thank you.

Cressida Downing, my editor, for her no-nonsense approach and relentless enthusiasm for books – mine in particular. Lucy Llewellyn for her expertise in design and for producing a super book cover. Helena Halme, an author in her own rights, for getting me through the finish line.

To the friends who have patiently read, reread and advised: Kate Burton, Bernard McGuigan, Nicola Rabson, Alison Thorne, Susan Rosenberg, Elisabeth Gaunt, Anthea Tinker, Helen Janecek, Prashila Narsing-Chauhan, Adrian Lurie, Geraldine Kelly, Malcolm Fortune, Tim Watts.

Finally, a special thanks to two marvellous art professionals Josephine Breese and Henry Little, and last but not least the artist Tom de Freston for producing the most inspiring rework of the *The Raft of The Medusa*.

Dear Reader,

If you would like to find out more about the genesis of COLLAPSE, or receive information about the next two books in the series, please join Freddie's book club. Go to www.freddieppeters.com, where you can also find the Glossary of terms and abbreviations. Looking forward to connecting with you …

Freddie

Made in the USA
Middletown, DE
16 February 2021